Tainted Snow

Gwen Andrews Mystery #6

by Debi Graham-Leard

Riverhaven

Books

Tainted Snow is a work of fiction.
Any similarity regarding names, characters,
or incidents is entirely coincidental.

Published in the United States by Riverhaven Books,
Massachusetts.

Paperback ISBN: 978-1-951854-48-5

Printed in the United States of America

Back cover author photo: Ria MacKenzie

Edited and cover design by Riverhaven Books
Whitman, MA

Previous Novels

The Uninvited Guest
Introducing Gwen Andrews
2015

Where There's Smoke, There's Trouble
Gwen Andrews Mystery #2
2017

Bed, Breakfast, & Blackmail
Gwen Andrews Mystery #3
2019

Wedding Interrupted
Gwen Andrews Mystery #4
2020

The Life She Left Behind
a contemporary novel
2021

Regrets Only
Gwen Andrews Mystery #5
2023

Acknowledgements

I want to thank the following people for sharing their expertise during the development of *Tainted Snow.*

Pamela Loewy… treasured reviewer.

Jerri Graham Burket… my sister who provides a writing prompt each and every morning.

and

Vinnie Leard… my sweetheart of a husband, who never discourages my time spent writing.

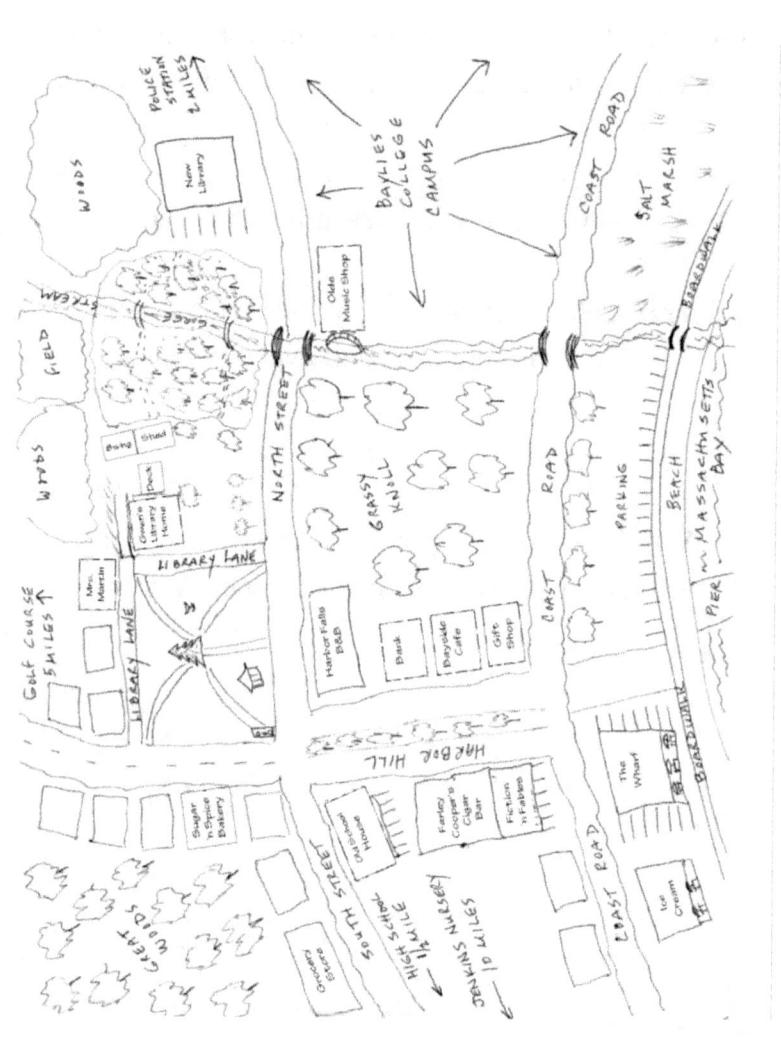

A Friend's Family Crisis May Soon Become Your Own

Chapter One

… pre-dawn Sunday morning, mid-January

The bland headlines of the *Harbor Falls Gazette* didn't surprise early riser Gwen Andrews. Now that the merriment of Christmas and New Year's had come and gone, nothing much was happening in her sleepy college town.

Gwen folded the newspaper and slipped off the kitchen island stool.

Despite the remainder of cedar and sage scents wafting from her wax warmer, the aromatherapy failed to bolster her spirits. January doldrums settled upon her shoulders like a ponderous winter cloak.

She stepped to the sliding glass door and swiped her fingers though the condensation to view her winter-weary back yard. In the pale predawn light, the brown lawn and forlorn flower beds did little to lift her spirits.

When she unlocked and slid open the door, the gust of air that whooshed inside felt much cooler than the persistent warmer temperatures of the past few weeks. Even on Christmas Day, a brief dusting of white flakes had switched to rain and washed away the magic of snow.

The sound of muffled knuckles tapping on her front door

distracted Gwen from her weather disappointment. Closing the slider, she scurried past the central staircase and entered the foyer. As her fingers stretched toward the antique brass handle, she hesitated.

With no peephole in the thick oak door of her converted library home, she wasn't able to identify her early morning visitor. Rather than yell to ask who was there, she drew in a deep breath and swung the heavy door inward.

The glow of her security light bounced off the auburn hair of Annabelle Fairchild, cub reporter and photographer for the *Harbor Falls Gazette*.

The younger woman's warm breath mingled with the cooler air, creating delicate white puffs as she spoke. "Hi, Gwen. Sorry to disturb you at this ungodly hour. I saw your lights on, so…"

"You must have a good reason," Gwen countered, moving her focus across Library Lane and into the village green where the blades of dull grass beneath the skeleton trees were turning white.

Gwen stretched her hand beyond the door frame, smiling as lacey flakes landed on her palm. "Are we expecting a snowstorm?"

"Not that I heard. But as you know, they sometimes sneak up on us."

Gwen retracted her hand and waved Annabelle inside. "Come in out of the cold."

Before stepping across the threshold, Annabelle flicked tiny white flakes from her hair and shoulders. Inside, she removed her bulky winter mittens, then hung her coat and slipped her feet from her waterproof mukluks.

Gwen pointed at Annabelle's chubby snowmen socks and chuckled. "It appears you've been wishing for snow."

Annabelle glanced down. "White brightens brown, doesn't it?" She wiggled one foot. "Cute, aren't they?"

Gwen nodded and waved toward the living room, where flames sparkled in the double-sided fireplace. "Make yourself comfortable. I'll be right back with something to warm you. Then you can tell me the reason you knocked on my door so early this morning.

A few minutes later, settled on the sofa that faced the fireplace, Annabelle wrapped her hands around the heat of the hand-thrown mug. "This herbal tea is perfect."

Gwen eased herself onto the other end, turned sideways, and tucked one foot beneath her. "I haven't seen you since you recorded that last-minute séance a few years ago. I'm happy to see you again but what brings you by before the sun is up?"

Annabelle again sipped the tea. "Shirley asked me to fetch you to her aunt's house."

Not expecting to hear the name of Shirley Knapp, long-time *Gazette* reporter, Gwen didn't respond right away. After Shirley published an article about that same séance, she'd remained a busy journalist with little time to develop a friendship with Gwen.

"Why didn't she call me herself?"

Annabelle stared into the gentle flames. "She didn't say. Apparently, she thinks an impromptu visit from the two of us will ease the tension at her aunt's house."

Curiosity aroused, Gwen leaned closer. "What's going on at her aunt's house?"

Annabelle's shoulder lifted in a half-shrug. "I don't know all the details."

"Then tell me what you do know."

Placing her mug on a coaster, Annabelle shifted toward Gwen. "I'll use Shirley's 5 W's. First, the 'who.' Shirley's aunt called and asked her to stop over as soon as she was up and dressed."

"What's her aunt's name?"

"Filomena Tucker, but Shirley calls her Aunt Filly."

"An unusual name." Gwen racked her brain but couldn't recall a connection. "Don't think I know her. Sorry to interrupt. Please continue with the W's."

Annabelle touched forefinger to forefinger. "I'm a bit sketchy on the 'what.' The problem involves an estranged grandson."

"And the 'when'?" Gwen urged.

"Last evening during a family dinner. But again, Shirley didn't fully explain."

Without prompting, Annabelle progressed to where. "Aunt Filly's home is a few doors past the old schoolhouse on South Street. As for the 'why,' she thinks you and I can ease the family tensions." Annabelle retrieved her mug and took another sip.

"Why me?"

"She claims that your calm nature will diffuse the situation before it gets out of hand."

"Very flattering, but I don't know how helpful I'll be for whatever trouble is brewing."

"Well, I guess we won't know until we get there."

Annabelle downed the last of her tea and stood up.

Gwen moved to the fireplace and separated the gently burning logs. As she watched the resulting embers float up the chimney, she considered that Shirley's family situation… whatever that might be… could help banish the January doldrums.

"Okay, Annabelle, let's go."

Chapter Two

… early morning, Sunday

After donning their winter coats, hats, and gloves, Gwen and Annabelle slid their feet into boots awaiting on the drip tray.

Gwen opened her front door to see that the winter grass on both sides of her walkway had nearly disappeared beneath the cover of white. Stretching out her hand like a child, she caught tiny snowflakes drifting from grey clouds.

Annabelle remarked, "I'm no weather forecaster, but this storm appears to be more than a passing flurry. Small flakes usually indicate that it won't be stopping anytime soon."

"Do you think this will become a nor'easter?"

Annabelle shrugged. "I admit I have no idea."

Ignoring weather concerns, Gwen noticed the empty curb at Library Lane. "You didn't drive?"

"I didn't," Annabelle confirmed. "No reason you would know this but last month I moved into the apartment above the Sugar 'n' Spice Bakery." She aimed one gloved hand toward the other side of village green, where golden rays beamed through the bakery's windows and cascaded across the accumulating snow.

"I've always been curious about that second floor."

"Then I'd love to show it to you on our way back. Aunt Filly's home is close enough to walk if you're agreeable."

Gwen indicated her compact car parked in the driveway, its windshield disappearing beneath the blanket of snow. If she'd been aware of the approaching storm, she would've parked inside her new garage the previous evening.

"There's no need to scrape the snow from my car for such a short distance. Let's walk." She pulled up her hood to block the snowflakes beginning to slant sideways.

The two women set off at a brisk pace, hurrying along the sidewalk that circumvented the village green, leaving behind footprints in the collecting flakes.

As they passed the Sugar 'n' Spice, the aroma of baked goods wafted to Gwen's nose, and she turned to Annabelle. "You're so slim. How do you resist those cinnamon buns?"

"Oh, I don't. But racing around snapping photos for the *Gazette* seems to offset the extra calories."

Reaching the end of Library Lane, they turned right onto South Street. As they passed the old schoolhouse, Annabelle pointed at a large house further along the street. "That's Aunt Filly's home."

They soon stopped in front of a grand Victorian that Gwen had admired many times. The fanciful features intrigued her. Now, a tired holiday wreath remained on the door with pots of drooping evergreens on the top step.

She'd never met the inhabitants nor been invited inside.

Her excitement mounted at the prospect of getting a peek.

Before climbing the concrete steps to the veranda that wrapped around the side of the Victorian, Gwen linked arms with Annabelle to avoid slipping on the accumulating snow. They safely managed the steps and walked across the covered porch.

Standing in front of the stained-glass door, Gwen pushed the highly polished brass button.

On the other side, a buzzer squawked.

A few seconds later, the lace curtain filling the sidelight parted and a pair of eyes peeked out at them. The doorknob rotated and the door began to open.

Gwen expected the squeak of rusty hinges associated with an old house, but the door swung silently inward.

Gazette reporter Shirley Knapp – her grey curls askew, her sweatpants and overshirt the polar opposite of her usual neat but outdated tweed business suit – offered a lop-sided grin. "Thanks, Annabelle, for bringing Gwen with you. And Gwen, I'm sorry I haven't reached out since your impromptu séance. That makes me doubly grateful that you were willing to come here with Annabelle."

Making a split-second decision, Gwen said, "Don't fret, Shirley. We can make up for it with a lunch when your activities for the *Gazette* give you a break."

"I'd like that." Shirley waved them inside.

Annabelle asked, "Where should we put our wet boots?"

Shirley pointed. "On that woven rug. My Aunt Filly is a nut about manners and cleanliness. Meticulous fits her."

Footwear removed, Gwen and Annabelle stepped onto the hardwood floor. The room was deep but narrow. Dimness – the result of dark paneling combined with low-light sconces – revealed only the outline of couches, chairs, and side tables here and there.

A grand staircase dominated the left side of the room. Beyond the slant of its steps, a dark hallway.

At the far end, an unmade and unoccupied hospital bed provided a glaring contrast to the antique surroundings.

To the right, a wide archway led into the adjacent room.

Shirley waved toward a door to her left, lowering her voice. "Let's talk in the front parlor. My aunt doesn't know that I asked you both to come over. Before I introduce you, I need to explain my family's current situation."

Following Shirley into a small room with tall front windows, Gwen and Annabelle settled on an uncomfortable settee while Shirley pushed the parlor door almost closed but not latched. Easing herself onto a stiff-looking side chair, her feet barely touching the floor, she squirmed as if seeking a softer spot.

She alternated her gaze between Gwen and Annabelle. "First, a little family history. Filomena Tucker, my Aunt Filly, was born and raised in this very house, built by her ancestors nearly two centuries ago. After she married my mother's brother, my Uncle Norman, Aunt Filly's parents created a master suite for the newlyweds, and they've lived on the first floor ever since. When her parents passed, Filly and Norman purchased this home from the estate. A few relatives who were staying here at the time arranged to continue living in their rooms. Others opted to move into their own homes. Aunt Filly has always been the glue that holds this family together."

Like a Jack-in-the-Box, Shirley hopped down from the too-tall chair and paced as she continued the family's backstory. "Filly and Norman recently returned from a month-long Mediterranean cruise. As they were getting off the ship, Norman slipped and broke his leg. You probably noticed his hospital bed at the far end of the living room. Until his cast comes off, he can't maneuver very easily."

As if by mutual agreement, Gwen and Annabelle didn't comment but simply waited for Shirley to continue.

"Last evening, Aunt Filly hosted her weekly Saturday dinner for the family. As we were finishing dessert, Hank Payne, Filly and Norman's grandson and my second cousin, burst through the kitchen door and scared us all."

Gwen raised one hand to ask a question, not only to seek details but also to give Shirley time to inhale a well-deserved breath of air.

Acknowledging the action, Shirley asked, "What is it?"

"Wasn't their grandson invited to the family dinner?"

Shirley eyed the side chair but didn't sit. "Hank is the black sheep of the Tucker family."

"What earned him that label?" Annabelle asked.

Shirley shuddered. "Hank was born a bully and his abusive nature continues to this day. Every member of the family has been his target at one time or another. As a baby, he yanked my hair hard enough to pull strands from my head and then laughed when tears streamed down my cheeks."

"Wow," Annabelle commented. "I imagine he only did that once before you stopped asking to hold him."

"That was my exact reaction," Shirley said. "When he grew to toddler stage, I cringed whenever his mother Thelma – my favorite first cousin – brought Hank to a family picnic. Hank would drop worms down our backs or chase us with a snake. When we jumped and screamed, little Hank only laughed."

As a firm believer in consequences for actions, Gwen asked, "Was he ever punished to break his mean streak?"

Shaking her head, Shirley answered, "Nope. His father always excused his son's behavior as harmless pranks, insisting Hank was just being a boy."

When Gwen and Annabelle said nothing, Shirley continued. "When Hank was a teenager, his father died in a work accident. At school, Hank got into fist fights and didn't keep up with his studies. Somehow, he managed to graduate from high school but at the bottom of his class."

Shirley straightened her rumpled clothes. "He continued to live with his mother, drifting from one menial job to the next, contributing little to the family expenses. My cousin Thelma gave into his demands to make up for his deceased father. I always suspected Hank abused her, though Thelma never admitted as much to me. "When Hank reached his twenties, Thelma was killed in a car crash. Hank couldn't afford their apartment, so he moved to a much cheaper one. He's never held jobs for long, so constantly evicted for not paying rent. Whenever he found himself homeless, he'd mooch off one of us until we asked him to leave."

Shirley glanced from Gwen to Annabelle. "Hank thinks the rest of us should take care of him. He's borrowed money from every one of us and has never paid back one penny. He long ago destroyed any compassion we felt for him."

"How old is Hank now?" Annabelle asked.

"Twenty years younger than me," Shirley replied, "so his mid-forties. One last bit to finish Hank's backstory. When I got home from the dinner last night, I did some research. Aunt Filly and Uncle Norman weren't aware that he'd just been released from jail for nearly killing another man in a bar fight and was about to show up on their doorstep."

Gwen and Annabelle gasped.

"When he barged through the kitchen door," Shirley continued, her voice rising, "we all stared. He looked like a mangy dog and I didn't even recognize him. He slurred his words and reeked of weed. When Hank mentioned he hadn't eaten, Uncle Norman instructed Aunt Filly to fix *'the boy'* a plate of leftovers. He told the rest of us we were free to leave. That they'd deal with Hank on their own."

With a quick intake of air, Shirley continued, "Early this morning, Aunt Filly called me to say Hank invited himself to stay. She'd objected, but Uncle Norman said he needed Hank's strong arm until his cast is removed."

Gwen glanced at the unlatched door. "He's here now?"

Shirley slumped. "I'm not sure if he's actually in the house. When I arrived a little while ago, Aunt Filly didn't know if he was upstairs in the guest room or had gone out. She's worried about a confrontation."

"With any Tucker in particular?" Gwen asked.

"Well, Aunt Filly herself for one. She's angry that he bamboozled his way into their home. And me for another. I've always suspected that Hank abused his mother, and I blame him for Cousin Thelma's death as well."

Hoping she wasn't getting too personal, Gwen asked, "Why do you blame him for the accident?"

"Something he mumbled at his mother's funeral made me suspect he'd been harassing her for money that day. She drove in a raging storm toward the nearest ATM, crashed into a pole, and died instantly."

"How tragic," Annabelle muttered.

Gwen had patiently listened to Shirley's retelling of

Hank's life to this point, still waiting to hear the reason Shirley had summoned her. But as Gwen was about to ask, the unlatched parlor door began to swing inward.

Chapter Three

... early morning, Sunday

Shirley jumped to her feet as the rubber tip of a carved wooden cane came into view. An elderly woman followed, her hair more silver than gray and pulled into a loose top knot. Tendrils curled around her aged but still-pretty face. Gwen guessed the woman to be in her mid-eighties.

Quite tall, this woman exuded command as she eyed the threesome sitting in the front parlor.

"Here you are, Shirley. We wondered where you'd gotten to."

Shirley stepped closer and hugged the stately octogenarian. "Aunt Filly, meet my friends Annabelle Fairchild and Gwen Andrews."

Rising to their feet in the now-crowded space, Gwen and Annabelle said together, "Nice to meet you, Mrs. Tucker."

"As Shirley's friends, please call me Filly."

Reaching over, she caressed Annabelle's auburn curls. "Lovely tresses. My hair used to be this color." She turned and tapped her way through the parlor door, beckoning them to follow. "Come to the kitchen. I've made hot chocolate."

Shirley looked at Gwen and Annabelle. "Let's go."

15

The three of them followed Filly across the living room, beneath an archway through a chandeliered dining room, then beneath a second archway into an oversized kitchen.

The chatter of the occupants halted immediately.

At the nearest end of the table, a man and woman turned around, murmuring hellos to the newcomers.

On the other end, an older man in need of a shave rested his cast-covered leg on an adjacent chair.

Despite his advanced age and broken leg, his steely grey eyes gave the impression of vigor as he glanced up at Filly. "I see you found Shirley plus two more." Switching his gaze to Gwen and then Annabelle, he tapped his thumb on his chest. "I'm Norman Tucker, Filly's husband."

He indicated the couple sitting quietly at the other end of the table. "They are our niece Doris and her husband Daryl Whitcomb. They live upstairs."

Daryl's chair scraped the floor as he rose to his feet, his hand swiping his receding hairline. "Nice to meet you."

With an almost imperceptible nod, Doris glanced at them, her curiosity obvious but she said nothing.

Shirley said, "This is Annabelle Fairchild, who works with me at the *Gazette*. Gwen Andrews lives in the converted library on the village green. I spotted them walking past and invited them in out of the cold."

Surprised by Shirley's fib about the reason she and Annabelle were standing in the kitchen, Gwen murmured,

"Hello," then volunteered nothing more, waiting to hear where Shirley planned to take this conversation.

Filly flitted her hand at Daryl. "Pull over some chairs, would you? I promised them hot chocolate."

Removing three mugs from a rack, Filly dipped her pinkie into a pot on the back burner, shook her head, and turned up the flame. Then she removed a thick-bladed knife from a wooden block and sliced what appeared to be banana bread, transferring servings onto individual plates before placing them in front of Gwen, Shirley, and Annabelle.

Shirley forked a bite into her mouth. "Delicious, thanks."

The steaming chocolate drink soon followed.

Before Gwen could express her appreciation, the kitchen door to the side yard opened. Cold air whooshed inside, along with a few snowflakes and a tall smiling man.

He stepped onto the worn linoleum floor. "Good morning, everyone." His eyes gleamed. "Nothing like a brisk morning walk in the snow to clear the cobwebs. The sidewalks haven't been cleared so be careful if you go out."

He turned to a younger woman entering behind him.

Equally tall, she squeezed the giggling baby in her right arm, a diaper bag slung over her left shoulder.

The man noticed Gwen and Annabelle. "Oh, hi. I'm Lawrence Tucker, Norman and Filly's youngest son. This is my daughter Jessica and my granddaughter Olivia." When he stroked the baby's reddened cheek, Olivia gurgled.

Shirley again introduced Gwen and Annabelle.

"Hello," Jessica said as she strolled toward Norman and kissed him on the cheek. "I need to take Olivia up to my room and change her diaper, so you'll have to wait for your hug, Grandpa."

As Jessica turned from Norman, Olivia stretched her tiny arms toward him, fussing when her mother kept walking.

Gwen concluded that this morning visit was a daily routine, wondering once again exactly why Shirley had requested she accompany Annabelle to this home.

The sound of heavy boots pounding down the back steps in the far corner of the kitchen halted all conversation.

A massive bruiser of a man paused on the bottom tread, filling the door frame. Multiple deep ruts scarred his face. His shaggy black hair and unkempt black beard gave the impression of a wild mountain man. The distinct smell of marijuana wafted into the kitchen.

Hank's hooded eyes attempted to focus on Filly, his gravelly voice slurring. "I see you've summoned some of the troops, Grandmother."

His gaze landed on Gwen, his lop-sided grin doing little to soften his imposing presence. "And two strangers have joined your little gathering."

Filly placed the hot chocolate pot into the kitchen sink and turned on the faucet. "Please don't embarrass yourself or your family in front of our guests."

18

"Embarrass?" Hank sputtered. "Haven't you heard I'm a reformed citizen?"

Still standing just inside the kitchen door, Lawrence looked Hank up and down. "Based on your appearance, Nephew, I find that hard to believe. I assumed you left last night after mooching a meal."

Hank glared at his uncle. "You call it mooching, I call it kindness when a guy is down on his luck."

"You're always down on your luck. You're in your forties, Hank. Your life should be settled. You should be supporting yourself."

"Yeah, well, I'm not. Gramps said I can stay here while I look for a job. I promised to move out as soon as I can."

Lawrence harumphed. "You've broken every promise you've ever made to everyone in the family."

Stepping off the last tread of the back steps, Hank's huge fists dropped to his sides, clenching and unclenching.

Doris stood up and stepped backwards through the archway to dining room, mincing her steps, a look of concern contorting her face.

Hank's eyes never left Lawrence's as he stomped to the table and reached around Norman, grabbing the last piece of bacon from his grandfather's plate.

As Hank chewed noisily with his mouth open, he switched his focus to Gwen. "Looks like I missed the early breakfast. When's round two for the lazybones upstairs?"

"Not everyone is an early riser," Filly snapped, her voice tight. "And they'll prepare their own breakfasts."

For the first time, Norman spoke up. "Your grandmother can cook another serving for you."

Filly's expression hardened as she stared at her husband. Hank held up his hand. "Nah. I've got a better idea."

The tension vibrated as they awaited his next words.

His hooded eyes bored into Gwen. "How 'bout you and the redhead treat me to breakfast at that harbor café?"

The hairs on the back of Gwen's neck quivered.

Shirley quickly stood behind Gwen and Annabelle, her protective hands grasping each of their shoulders. "You're high as a kite. My friends aren't going anywhere with you."

The scowl on his face revealed instant rage at the rebuff. "Forget it. I'm leaving."

He stomped across the kitchen, dried mud dropping from his heavy boots on what had been a spotless floor. Shoving Lawrence aside, Hank seized the knob of the side door and slammed it against the papered wall as he stormed out.

Antique stained glass rattled but didn't shatter.

Hank had left the building.

Regaining his balance, Lawrence muttered, "He's still a brute. I'm glad Jessica took Olivia upstairs."

The ear-piercing rumble of a departing motorcycle echoed off the kitchen walls.

Above the roar, Filly shouted, "Damn that boy. I hope

none of his biker friends show up while he's under our roof." She then focused on Gwen and Annabelle. "I apologize if our grandson's gruffness alarmed you."

Gwen took a moment to frame a non-judgmental response. "Family dynamics can be challenging."

"That's an understatement," the older woman snapped, glaring at Norman. "It's high time Hank stops bothering us."

"He's staying, wife," Norman shot back. "No sense in beating a dead horse."

Shirley strode over and touched her aunt's arm. "Has Hank made any demands besides a bed?"

"Not yet," Filly answered. "And he'd better not bully us for money. Just because Norman's stuck in that damned wheelchair..." Her voice trailed off, her own threat remaining undefined.

Shirley rinsed the dregs of hot chocolate down the sink. "I'm sorry to rush out but I need to check in at the *Gazette*. If Hank threatens you, call the police."

Gwen assumed Shirley was rushing off to avoid a second confrontation if Hank returned. *How had Shirley expected her to calm the members of this family?*

Jessica strolled in from the dining room, struggling with the wriggling Olivia. "I heard loud voices. Who was here?"

"Your cousin Hank," her father replied. "I'm glad you didn't come down until he left."

Olivia stretched her short arms toward Norman, who

held up both gnarled hands to receive her.

Shirley circled the table and kissed Filly's cheek. "Call my cell if you need me."

A feeling of relief washed over Gwen that she might be off the hook, so she pushed back her own chair. "I need to get home myself."

"Me, too," Annabelle echoed, rising.

Filly moved between Gwen and Annabelle, laying a conciliatory hand of each of their arms. "I'm so sorry you witnessed our grandson's bad manners. In the future, you'll likely think twice about escaping the winter chill for a mug of hot chocolate. Bundle up, ladies."

Gwen noticed a twinkle in the elderly woman's eyes as she gave them a gentle shove toward Shirley.

As the three slipped feet into boots, shoved arms into winter coats, and pulled on winter gloves, Daryl rushed past and held open the stained-glass front door. "Sorry about our family ruckus."

Chapter Four

… early morning, Sunday

Shirley, Gwen, and Annabelle had walked only a short distance when Shirley came to a halt in front of the old schoolhouse. "Hold up. My car's parked in the back lot."

She grasped one of Gwen's gloved hands, then reached for Annabelle's. "I apologize for disrupting your morning. I don't know why I thought your presence would soften Hank's attitude. My family will deal with him in time."

"Don't apologize, Shirley," Gwen began. "I was up and dressed, so you didn't disrupt my day. Did you leave your aunt's home because you were afraid Hank would return?"

Shirley shrugged one shoulder. "Partially. I hope he doesn't get physical with Filly or Norman when no one else is around. She's spry but old, and his cast isn't coming off for another week or so, but, right now, I do need to check in at the paper. Talk to you soon."

Annabelle blurted, "Wait. Do you have to clock-in at the paper right now?"

"Unfortunately, yes. Do you want a ride to the office?"

"Thanks but I promised Gwen a tour of my new apartment above the bakery. Want to join us?"

"Maybe another day. I've got to fine-tune an article before we go to press."

"Okay," Annabelle murmured, her disappointment clear.

They watched Shirley march down the paved lane toward her snow-covered car.

***

The snowflakes had hardened into sleet, so Gwen and Annabelle wrapped their scarves around their faces, saying little as they trekked along South Street. Crossing at the light onto Library Lane, they approached the Sugar 'n' Spice.

In contrast to the dark sky, a warm glow still escaped the bakery's front windows and sliced across the white sidewalk. When a customer exited, the scent of cinnamon buns again flavored the surrounding air.

Gwen tapped Annabelle's arm. "Can I treat you?"

"Thanks, but no. Do you want something?"

Gwen shook her head. "Not right now."

"Then follow me."

Annabelle rounded the far corner of the building and mounted the first step. "Hold the rail. The wood's slippery."

Reaching the upper landing without incident, Annabelle unlocked the door, entered, and flipped the wall switch. "Come on in."

Gwen glanced around the cozy apartment. "This is darling, Annabelle. You've only been here a few weeks?"

"More like five," the younger woman clarified.

Wandering the perimeter, Gwen spotted books with paranormal titles, reminding her of Annabelle's after-hours activity. "Are you still participating in outings with the ghost hunting group?"

"You remembered."

"Of course I did. After you borrowed their special equipment to record that re-located séance at my home, your investigations are not something I'm likely to forget."

Annabelle chuckled. "Parker;s spirit was quite mischievous that evening. Has he appeared since then?"

Gwen lowered herself into the nearest padded chair. "For the past few years, I've called his name when I wanted to talk with him and he materialized. But he hasn't responded to my voice since Halloween."

Settling on the couch, Annabelle reached over to take Gwen's hand. "So you haven't seen him for three months. Do you want to talk about it?"

"Maybe another time." Gwen's answer was a surprise even to herself. With so few residents of Harbor Falls aware of Parker's ghost, she should take advantage of Annabelle's kind-hearted offer.

Gwen stood. "Why don't you show me the rest?"

"Sure." Annabelle crossed her living room and opened one of two doors on the side wall, revealing a compact but functional bathroom. The shower curtain and matching window curtain boasted whimsical snowmen.

Glad for a distraction, Gwen asked, "Where did you find this matching set? They're perfect."

"Not a set, but two fabric shower curtains from Ocean State. I cut down the second one to fit the window."

Gwen's chuckle replaced her revived concern about Parker's no-shows. "Very clever. I'm guessing you'll change the motif as each season comes and goes?"

"And you'd be right," Annabelle replied, her grin wide.

Behind the second door, the bedroom boasted a patchwork quilt and matching drapes, providing a feminine mood without any seasonal connection.

Returning to the living room, Gwen decided to ask, "What's your take on Shirley's family?"

"Well," Annabelle began, seeming to consider her comments. "We didn't spend much time with them. Aunt Filly is definitely in charge but she's not happy that Uncle Norman forced her to let Hank stay."

"That's for sure. But those two have been married forever, so they've likely weathered disagreements before."

"You're probably right," Annabelle agreed. "Daryl was cordial but Doris didn't say two words."

"And I wasn't aware that Hank arrived on a motorcycle," Gwen said. "Can't say I blame Filly for worrying that Hank's biker friends might show up."

"Jessica and Olivia were a breath of fresh air."

"And Lawrence, too," Gwen added, warming at the

memory of the baby's giggles. "They were charming, weren't they? From their conversation, she and the baby live upstairs but I'm not sure about Lawrence. Hank mentioned other family members who live in that huge Victorian but hadn't joined the kitchen group yet."

Annabelle's cell phone dinged and she frowned as she read the message. "I hate to kick you out, Gwen, but I've been assigned to snap winter photos down at the harbor before anyone traipses through the pristine landscape."

Gwen buttoned her coat. "No problem. I'll watch for your pictures in the next edition."

***

Before heading home, Gwen ducked into the bakery to buy cinnamon buns plus quiche for her midday meal, resisting a Vanilla Chai that she rarely prepared at home.

Bag in hand, she shuffled along the snow-covered sidewalk, passing the Martin historic Colonial. The *For Sale* sign had appeared the previous month. The elderly neighbors now resided in an assisted living facility on the outskirts of Harbor Falls.

So far, no buyers. But how soon? And who? There was no way to predict.

The feeling that she was being watched prickled Gwen's neck. She stooped and pretended interest in a stick poking from the snow.

She snuck glances in all directions.

27

She peered through the leafless skeletons of the trees occupying the village green.

Only a lone dog-walker shuffled along a distant pathway. No one else came into view.

She blamed her unease on meeting Hank Payne. Life at the Tucker Victorian would not be pleasant during his invasion. Perhaps he'd honor his promise and find his own way for a change.

Chapter Five

...mid-morning, Sunday

As Gwen approached her front walkway, she paused to admire the brownstone and brick façade. Nearly a decade had passed since Parker converted the abandoned library into their unique residence.

Relieved to enter its presumed safety, she placed her goodies on the Parsons table, closed the heavy oak door, and slipped the lock into place.

Tucking her gloves in her coat pockets, she reached for the framed photo of Parker taken as they'd strolled Duxbury Beach only days before a freak bolt of lightning on the local golf course stole him from her.

As memories surged forward, she hugged his likeness.

For a long time, she'd been overwhelmed by grief until the miraculous day his spirit appeared and, to borrow a phrase, nearly scared her to death. His promise that they'd reunite in the afterlife had banished her melancholy, but she still missed his strong arms and physical affection – actions his ghostly self would never be able to provide.

Between Parker's initial appearance and now, she'd eagerly anticipated his occasional visits, whether she called his name or he appeared after sensing she was upset about something or in danger. But from the end of October until earlier that week, she'd repeatedly called his name to no avail. He hadn't shown himself since Halloween weekend. Not even during Christmas, their favorite winter holiday.

Gwen worried. Was their connection broken? Or had his allotment of earthly visits simply expired?

Well aware she'd never know the answers, she stretched his picture to arm's length and asked, "Where have you gone, Parker?"

She stood still for several long minutes as her keen sense of hearing listened for the slightest sign that his spirit had broken through from the afterlife.

Nothing.

Disappointed, she placed the photo of his smiling face on the foyer table, removed her coat, hung it on a peg, and kicked her boots toward the drip tray.

As she exited the foyer, a plaintive meow demanded her attention. She glanced up the split staircase to see Amber strolling down, the insistent cry a clear message. *'Where have you been? I want to eat.'*

Gwen plucked her pet from the bottom step and carried her to the kitchen. Stroking Amber's golden head, she lowered the squirming cat to the floor then topped off the food and water bowls.

Filling the tea kettle, she set it on the stove and turned on the burner, then wandered into the adjacent open space along the back wall and into her home music studio. She slid her fingers along the keys of the baby grand piano, a gift from Parker on the day they'd moved into this special home.

Several years ago, after uncounted semesters of teaching music at Baylies College, Gwen retired from her professorship for a variety of reasons. She now satisfied her love of music by passing her skills to budding musicians. But none of her young students would resume their private lessons until early February.

As her quiet surroundings brightened, Gwen glanced up and followed the winter sun as it snuck through rooftop skylights three stories above. She so admired Parker's architectural prowess.

Gwen's thoughts returned to her unexpected visit at the Tucker Victorian. The vision of happy baby Olivia made her smile. Shirley's family was expanding. Gwen's own relatives had dwindled with each passing year.

She and Parker had never been blessed with children, so there were no grandchildren for Gwen to spoil. Perhaps her childless status explained her fondness for her college-aged houseguest Jenna Jenkins, who Gwen considered to be her *sort-of granddaughter* – an inside joke between them.

Maybe Gwen should gather her own remaining relatives before any more were lost. Her sister Tess in the Berkshires, also widowed, also childless, plus several first and second cousins living in other parts of the country, were all out of touch except for the exchange of Christmas and birthday cards. A reunion in the spring or early summer would be perfect if Gwen could arrange it.

She realized that she may have stumbled upon a project to banish her January doldrums. The planning could fill many empty hours.

Tilting her head back, she spoke to the heavens in the same fashion as Clarence in *It's a Wonderful Life*, her favorite holiday movie. "What do you think of that idea, Parker?"

Not expecting an answer, she jumped when the tea kettle screeched and rushed to turn off the heat.

Then she glanced around the kitchen finding no sign of Amber. Her bratty pet was most likely cat napping in the second floor sitting room. The padded bench seat along the wide bank of rear windows provided the perfect perch for tail-swishing. When the winter birds fluttered into view, they teased the cat's inherent hunting instinct.

As a pot of tea steeped, Gwen looked out her kitchen's bay window at the barren landscape, so different from her kaleidoscope display of colorful summer flowers. Her backyard was a source of pride and joy, and often a location for garden club meetings and seasonal tours.

The new-fallen snow had improved the dullness of the landscape. Bright red cardinals perched on branches.

Goldfinches and snowbirds pecked beneath the bird feeders. Three squirrels chased each other around a tree trunk.

The sun sparkled off the white surface, marred only by the lightweight indentations of the birds and squirrels.

And then she spotted much larger gouges. Snatching her binoculars from the windowsill, she stepped to the sliding glass door and lifted them to her eyes.

The close-up focus revealed a trail of these curious imprints definitely made by human boots. Emerging from the patch of woods behind her potting shed, the imprints zigzagged between the raised flower beds, skirted the edge of the lower deck then disappeared from her line of sight.

Had the booted person continued through her side yard on his – or her – trek toward the sidewalk out front that rimmed the village green?

Gwen's insatiable curiosity grabbing hold, she carried the binoculars from one dining room window to the next but couldn't spot a continuation of the imprints. She deduced they might be too close to the foundation to spot from inside.

Reaching the foyer, she risked unlocking the heavy door and peeked through the narrow crack. Seeing no one, she gripped the door frame and stretched out to grasp the iron railing for a closer look. Straining as she might, she couldn't spot any more boot imprints. They'd disappeared as if the trekker had been plucked from the earth.

Returning to the kitchen's glass slider, she again focused

33

on the direction of the tracks. She couldn't determine if they'd proceeded around the corner or ended at the foundation door. The last time she'd been down in the basement laundry, had she checked if that door was locked?

If the imprint-maker had indeed entered her basement, wouldn't her keen hearing have picked up noises? Parker had always remarked that her ears missed little.

But she'd been with Shirley and Annabelle for at least the past hour, so maybe she hadn't been here during a possible break-in.

Gwen tilted her head sideways to listen. No sounds beneath her feet. No creaks. No groans as the old library continued to settle.

Did she dare march down the indoor flight of steps to check for a break-in?

NO. NO. NO. Bad idea. She'd watched enough horror movies to know that only the most stupid character made that mistake.

To err on the side of caution, she moved stealthily to the basement access door and slipped that lock into place, considering that she could be overreacting.

Harbor Falls residents could have crossed her backyard numerous times without her noticing. The woodland path near her potting shed led to a footbridge that crossed a stream, ending at the parking lot of the new library.

Without the morning snow, she wouldn't have seen the

evidence of someone walking thru her property.

Still, if retired detective Benjamin Snowcrest, her good friend and occasional sleuthing partner, hadn't been tending his ill father in New Mexico, she'd ask him to check not only the boot tracks but her basement as well.

Gwen decided against dialing 9-1-1, which would require her to wait in her home until an officer arrived. Jenna was spending the weekend with her college friend Samantha and wasn't expected back until late afternoon, so safely out of harm's way.

Instead, Gwen would drive to the Harbor Falls Police Station and request a wellness check. Surely Chief Brown could spare an officer to follow her home and inspect her basement for an intruder.

Though the station was located little more than a mile to her north, the winter weather discouraged Gwen from braving a second and even longer walk than the earlier one with Annabelle.

Bundled up once again, she scraped snow from her compact car, even as the light snowfall continued. She drove slowly to the police station, hoping an officer would ease her mind that the track maker had not breached her home.

Chapter Six

...mid-morning, Sunday

Gwen entered the police station through the visitors' door and made her way to the shadowed reception window.

A female voice asked, "How can we help you this morning?"

"I'd like to speak with Chief Brown, please."

"Sorry, he's out of the building. Is there anyone else?"

Gwen thought for a second. "Who's in charge of the detective squad now that Ben Snowcrest has retired?"

"That's Sgt. Ryan Rossini. I'll check if he's here."

As Gwen waited, she stepped to the bulletin board and perused the various flyers. Though she didn't possess a photographic memory, she could swear a few faces were the same as the last time she'd stood there. Were they repeat offenders or never caught?

For a split second, she hoped she wouldn't spot Hank's rough features among the mug shots. Shirley had said his most recent jail time was for a nearly fatal bar fight. Had he ever been involved in more serious crimes?

"Ma'am?" the female officer called.

Gwen recrossed the lobby to the window.

"I'm sorry, but Det. Sgt. Rossini is out of the building."

"Can I speak with one of the detectives in his squad?"

"Of course. Your name, ma'am?"

Gwen spelled her first and last names for the logbook.

"Please wait at the side door. Someone will be right down to speak with you."

Seconds later, the door swung inward and away from Gwen, revealing a young man. He stood in the opening, his boot propped against the door so it wouldn't close.

Gwen tried to neutralize her reaction. Accustomed to more mature officers like Ben and Chief Brown, this burly blonde youngster looked more like a high school football player than a detective. Gwen considered excusing herself and driving back home to explore those tracks herself.

But the young man spoke too quickly. "Good morning, Mrs. Andrews. My name is Cole Martin. I understand you've spoken to Det. Ben Snowcrest in the past?"

Too late to turn tail now. Seeing no reason to share that she and Ben had become good friends, Gwen said only, "That's right. Did you work with him?"

"Unfortunately, no. I was a new hire as he was retiring."

Gwen's face must have given away her disappointment, because the young officer quickly said, "I've heard nothing but praise for him from the older detectives."

The moment she thought their entire conversation was going to take place at the half-closed door, he pulled it open.

Moving aside, he said, "Let's go upstairs and you can explain the reason you stopped by this morning."

Grateful for his courtesy, she followed him into the elevator.

When the doors opened on the second floor, Officer Martin guided her along the zig-zagging hallways.

He led her past several occupied desks. Overtime on Sundays had always been a fact of life at the police department. As they passed, one detective glanced up and half-nodded before resuming his phone conversation.

Stopping at an empty desk that faced the window with a view of parking lot, Officer Martin indicated his guest chair.

Gwen sat, wondering how curious he'd be about her boot prints in the snow. She feared he'd label her a silly old woman and dismiss her with no further action.

He smiled as she settled. "What brings you in today?"

Taking a deep breath, Gwen explained the impressions, her inability to see where they led, and her concern that someone had accessed her basement. "I'm here to request a safety check."

Officer Martin studied her beneath blonde eyelashes. "That's a simple request. You could have called."

"I considered that but didn't think it wise to remain in my home by myself until an officer showed up."

He nodded as his brows lifted. "Good point. It's always best to be cautious. Before I commit to following you home,

I need to contact Lt. Rossini. Excuse me for a second, Mrs. Andrews." Typing on his cell phone, he wandered to the nearest detective and spoke in low tones.

The other officer glanced over and nodded. Though Gwen recognized his face from an introduction by Ben, the man's name now escaped her. She debated whether to join them so she could read his badge and greet him properly.

Before she could decide, Martin's cell dinged and he hurried back, reading the text message as he approached. "I'll handle your safety check. If you'll tell me your home address, I'll meet you there." He clicked into his map app.

After Gwen recited her location on Library Lane, Martin's eyes widened. "That's next door to the house where my grandparents used to live."

"The Martins?" Gwen questioned. "Of course. Your last name is Martin. I should have made the connection."

"Small world," he quipped.

"It certainly is. My home is the converted library next door to their Colonial. They were such sweet neighbors. I hope they're doing well in their new situation."

"They're adjusting. I'll pass along your good wishes."

The young officer jumped to his feet, his enthusiasm now off the charts. "Let's go. I've been curious about your unusual residence since the first time I visited my grandparents as a boy. Hope you don't mind if I invite myself for a tour after we check out your snow tracks."

Chapter Seven

…late morning, Sunday

Officer Martin suggested that Gwen remain inside her car while he inspected the backyard tracks.

When the snow flurries thinned, then ceased altogether, she decided that staying in her car was too frustrating and strolled to the back yard.

As she mounted her upper deck, she called, "Officer Martin, I'd like to observe your process."

The detective's head jerked up. "I'm not surprised, Mrs. Andrews. I've heard that you're quite independent. I'm fine with you watching my movements."

He leaned closer to the imprints, apparently inspecting the tread before snapping several pictures with his cell phone. When he turned toward the basement door, he disappeared from her line of sight, reappearing only seconds later. Looking up at her, he gave Gwen a thumbs up. As a tease of sunshine struggled to break through the clouds, he bounded onto the upper deck and stood beside her.

"What did you find?"

"The person who made the tracks did approach your basement entrance, then turned around and went back the way he or she came. You probably couldn't see that detail from inside the house, so I snapped some photos." He angled his cell so she could see the pictures from various angles.

After studying them, she said, "If I'd realized the tracks headed back out the way they came, I wouldn't have bothered you."

"It's never a bother to keep our citizens safe."

"Can you determine if it was a man or a woman?"

He shook his head. "Considering the bulkiness of winter boots, male or female is tough to determine. A guy with a small foot or a lady with a large one would make about the same size indentation."

He pulled up a different group of photos. "See the snow against your lower door? It's undisturbed. Has your basement ever been broken into?"

"Not that I'm aware of, but I only spend time in the laundry area. The rest of the space was my husband Parker's domain. Without the morning snow, I wouldn't have even known someone approached my basement door."

"Good point. Let's check your inside locks."

After she unlocked and opened the sliding glass door, he followed her into the kitchen, then echoed her removal of winter boots.

She led him to the inside basement door, flipped its lock, and proceeded down the steps, pausing at the lower door to the back yard.

Officer Martin peered closely. "This lock is old. You should replace it and add a dead bolt for added security."

Gwen nodded her agreement. "I'll contact a locksmith and have those installed right away."

Her thoughts flew to Parker. When he was alive, he would have taken care of this upgrade with no assistance. But as a widow, Gwen contracted assorted handymen when a repair was needed.

To Cole Martin, she said, "If you're still curious about my home, I'll give you the nickel tour."

His lips widened in a grin. "Sorry for inviting myself."

Gwen waved away his apology. Though she'd initially thought this officer was incompetent based only on his youth and good looks, she'd gained respect for him during the past half hour.

Beginning in her music studio, she was showing him the double-sided fireplace when she heard the front door open, something heavy hit the floor, and then the door slam shut.

Jenna Jenkins called out, "Gwen, I'm back from my weekend with Samantha. Where are you? And why is a police cruiser parked out front?"

"Back here, Jenna. In the music studio."

Within seconds, the young woman appeared, staring at Officer Martin before focusing on Gwen. "What happened?"

Stepping closer, Gwen said, "Everything's okay. I

noticed boot tracks in the backyard snow and was worried someone had broken into the basement. This is Officer Cole Martin. He determined that the person who made the tracks retreated without breaking in."

Jenna inhaled then released a lungful of air. "Oh, that's good news. Thank you, officer."

"Just doing my job, Miss …?" His voice trailed off as he waited for an introduction.

"Sorry, sorry," Gwen stuttered. "Where are my manners? This is Jenna Jenkins. She's my houseguest while she earns her music degree from Baylies College."

Jenna's determination to graduate couldn't have meant more to Gwen if she'd been the young woman's flesh and blood grandmother. But Officer Martin didn't need to know their faux-family connection.

He extended his hand. "Nice to meet you, Jenna."

She grasped his hand, quickly easing hers from his.

He indicated Gwen. "Mrs. Andrews was explaining the old library conversion into her marvelous home."

Jenna beamed. "I never tire of hearing how her husband transformed the abandoned building. I'll join you."

As Gwen led the way around the open floorplan of the first level, explaining Parker's architectural features, Officer Martin only tore his attention from Jenna for an occasional question or comment.

When they ascended to the second level, he asked about

the magnificent staircase that split halfway up to allow access to either the front or back of the original mezzanine.

His questions to Jenna were more personal. Did she have a favorite class or professor? What were her career plans? When she mentioned her grandfather living in Florida, he asked if she was going to move there after she graduated.

With Jenna's graduation only months away, Gwen had wondered the same thing, so waited to hear her answer.

Jenna paused. "Florida is one of many options but I haven't made any decisions yet. Harbor Falls is the only place I've ever called home."

Internally, Gwen jumped up and down that Jenna might stay in Harbor Falls and begin her teaching career at Baylies College as Gwen herself had done so many decades before. She certainly wouldn't object to Jenna sticking around.

Minutes later, the tour ended, and Gwen brought them to the foyer entrance. "Did I answer all your questions?"

Officer Martin responded with a deer-in-the-headlights expression. "You did, Mrs. Andrews. Quite interesting. Thank you."

Amused that he'd been more interested in Jenna, Gwen assumed he'd recall very few details if she quizzed him.

His focus strayed once more to Jenna. "Would you like to meet for a coffee one of these days?"

Gwen admired his boldness as she waited to hear how Jenna would react.

Grinning at him, Jenna said, "You seem to be a nice guy, Officer Martin, so I'll meet you for a cup one of these days."

"Please call me Cole."

Looking on, Gwen observed their similar blonde hair and blue eyes and decided they'd make a striking couple.

"All right, Cole," Jenna agreed, using his first name. "Classes resumed last week, so I could text you when I have a break. You can decide if the timing works for you."

Jenna pulled out her cell. "Let's exchange numbers."

That detail completed, Jenna checked the time.

"Sorry, Gwen. I only came home to drop off my suitcase. My entire class is meeting at the college library to work on a group project. Gotta go."

"I'll take your luggage upstairs," Gwen said.

Jenna kissed Gwen's cheek and picked up her book bag. "Thanks. I'll be home for supper."

"Nice to meet you, Cole. We'll talk soon."

For a long moment, he watched Jenna hurry away then turned his attention to the locks on Gwen's front door. "These are both reliable. After you replace that old lock in the basement and add a dead bolt, your home will be much more secure. I'd also suggest you add a security bar to the sliding door, especially since that back yard isn't visible from Library Lane."

"I'll add that to my list," Gwen said, then looked down at his stockinged feet. "I'll go get your boots."

A minute later, she handed him the heavy-duty police boots. He slipped his feet inside, tied the laces, and stood.

Gwen said, "Thanks again for inspecting those tracks out back. I'm relieved that my home wasn't breeched."

"You're welcome, Mrs. Andrews. And thanks for the tour. Hope to see you again under less worrisome circumstances."

Because of his interest in Jenna, Gwen had no doubt that she'd see this young officer again.

As she watched his cruiser pull away from the curb, she vowed not to quiz Jenna about their potential relationship. After all, Gwen had no right to poke her nose into Jenna's personal life, despite their fondness for each other.

But would she be overstepping if she googled Cole Martin's name to see what public information popped up? His grandparents had always been thoughtful neighbors, but just that morning Gwen had witnessed that being related to gentle people didn't guarantee their personalities had passed to a grandson. Case in point, Shirley's Aunt Filly and Uncle Norman compared to black sheep grandson Hank.

Gwen didn't need permission to follow her baser instincts. At the kitchen island, she retrieved her tablet and logged onto the internet.

First, she pulled up the Harbor Falls police department website for Cole Martin's full name. From there, google revealed he'd graduated from an out-of-state college with honors. Then the Massachusetts Police Academy. No negative press in the public domain. Gwen relaxed about Jenna's impending relationship.

Because Cole Martin had mentioned he'd been hired as Ben was retiring, Gwen wondered if Ben would be willing to check websites not available to a regular citizen. When he called that evening from Albuquerque, she'd ask him.

Hearing a meow, Gwen glanced over to see Amber strolling down the staircase like Norma Desmond in *Sunset Boulevard*. The cat had disappeared during Cole's house tour and was probably seeking a snack.

Despite Amber's resistance to close contact, Gwen scooped up her pet and hugged until the cat squirmed then wasted no time topping off the food and water bowls. Because as every cat owner knows a dish that isn't full is considered empty by most felines –

For lunch, Gwen savored the quiche she'd bought at the Sugar 'n' Spice, revisiting the idea of a family reunion to reconnect with her dwindling relatives.

She wandered upstairs to the elongated sitting room and pulled down the ladder from the third level loft. Climbing up and into the storage space, she retrieved boxes of old photo albums, worn address books, and a family tree prepared by a distant cousin many years before. She placed everything on the sitting room desk positioned against the mezzanine railing for further consideration.

Chapter Eight

...early evening, Sunday

Gwen's afternoon had disappeared while she flipped from one photo album to the next. Each picture revealed a grinning face at a long-ago family picnic or a frenzy of gift opening during the holidays. Each scribbled greeting in a card or letter brought the sender's personality into clear focus, whether living or now gone.

With the outdated family tree as her base, Gwen cross referenced old and new address books to create a list of invitees.

Would Jenna want to be included?

A different idea took hold. Would Jenna be open to merging her graduation party with Gwen's family reunion? Combining the polar opposite generations might be a crazy thought, but she'd let Jenna make the call.

The only family member she'd ever mentioned was her grandfather, Hal Jenkins. Gwen had considered him a friend until he demanded more from their relationship, insisting that she move to Florida with him. That was when they'd parted.

Switching her energies from the reunion to Jenna's graduation party, Gwen checked the Baylies website and located the notice for graduation ceremonies. A Saturday in mid-May. Months away. Lots of time to plan.

Gwen didn't doubt for a moment that Hal would attend his granddaughter's graduation ceremony. Whether he was Jenna's only living relative remained to be seen. Neither one had mentioned other family members.

Because Gwen's friendship with Hal had ended badly, she could only hope that while he was in town for Jenna's graduation, he wouldn't create any tension between them, especially with Ben in attendance. They should all be capable of acting like the mature adults they'd become.

Nonetheless, the chances of an awkward encounter with Hal was months away, so there was no need for Gwen to stress about a possible confrontation now.

***

That evening as Gwen and Jenna plated rotisserie chicken, baked potatoes, and roasted asparagus, Gwen debated whether to mention the family reunion idea. Then it dawned on her that she hadn't even approached Jenna about a backyard graduation party. What if another classmate had already invited her to a party?

Gwen was a bit premature to begin planning a combined event. Besides, asking people who didn't know Jenna to attend her party – if it happened at all – suddenly struck

Gwen as odd. Her relatives might feel obliged to bring a gift. There was a lot to consider before proceeding.

After supper, Gwen built a cozy fire and settled in Parker's recliner to read a mystery. The crackling of the logs was comforting, especially with Jenna on the leather sofa, balancing her tablet on elevated knees to edit a paper.

When Gwen's cell buzzed, she answered, "Hello, Ben."

"Hi. Is this a good time to talk?"

Hearing the roar of jet engines, Gwen suspected that Ben's hotel was located near the airport.

"Perfect timing," she replied as she got to her feet. "Jenna's here editing a paper, so I'm going to walk you upstairs so we don't disturb her. Hang on a second."

As Gwen hurried up the open staircase, she realized how much she missed Ben. She'd first met him as a crusty detective who ordered her to stay out of police business. Then he became a reluctant partner to solve an intricate crime that required Gwen's behind-the-scenes sleuthing. After that case was resolved, they drifted into a comfortable friendship.

Reaching the midway split, she glanced up the right-hand stairs toward the sitting room, deciding that their conversation would float over the balcony railing, spill into the living room below, and into Jenna's ears, and that would certainly be a distraction.

So Gwen scurried up the left-hand stairs, turning right toward her bedroom in the front gable. Closing the door, she sat on the corner chair and brought the cell to her ear. "I'm back. How's your father doing?"

Ben had never mentioned his father until the previous week when he'd called to say he was flying to Albuquerque to be with his rapidly fading father during his final days.

"Not well," Ben answered. "This morning he dropped into a coma. The doctor thinks he'll pass tonight."

Ben's tone revealed a mix of emotions. Gwen wanted more than anything to throw comforting arms around the man. Though their relationship remained platonic, they'd exchanged an embrace when circumstances required a physical connection. But with Ben more than halfway across the country, she couldn't hop in her car and go to him.

"I'm so sorry," she said now, at a loss for other words that might express her sadness on Ben's behalf.

"Thanks, Gwen. You must have been surprised to hear that my father is still alive, because I've never mentioned him. To be truthful, I've harbored a grudge since I was a teenager when my mother tossed him out because of his excessive drinking."

"Family dynamics can be challenging," Gwen said, repeating the words she'd offered to Filly and Norman Tucker after meeting their grandson Hank. Because her own parents and elder sister Tess had always been kind, Gwen hadn't been able to relate to a black sheep.

Ben commented, "Challenging is the right word to

describe my family back then. Before my father dropped into the coma, he apologized for failing as my dad."

"That must have softened your grudge a bit."

"Somewhat. He thanked me for making the trip and confided that he's made no final arrangements. No funds for a funeral and no burial plot. He's not a veteran so he asked me to cremate his body and toss his ashes somewhere."

"That's a heavy burden," Gwen said. "Would you like me to fly out and share the ceremony with you?"

"Thanks, but that won't be necessary. I'll be returning to Harbor Falls soon."

When he paused, she waited.

After a few long moments, Ben said, "Enough about me. What's happening back in Harbor Falls?"

"Several things," Gwen answered, then explained Shirley's early morning summons on Sunday and meeting the problematic Hank Payne. "He's a scary guy, Ben. He looks menacing with a scruffy beard and long straggly black hair. He had the nerve to suggest Annabelle and I treat him to breakfast at the Bayside Café. Shirley shared some of his backstory, so I now understand why the Tucker family considers him the black sheep."

"I hope you'll steer clear if you bump into him."

"That goes without saying. There was another odd situation when I got home this morning." She explained the boot prints in her backyard snow toward the basement door.

"Has that happened before?" Ben asked, worried.

"Hard to say. I was nervous about checking the basement myself, so I drove to the station and requested a safety check. A young officer followed me home to have a look. At first, I doubted his competency but was so impressed with his actions that I granted his request for a tour."

"That was brave of you, Gwen."

"Not so brave. Turns out, he's the grandson of the Martins, my next-door neighbors. They've put their home on the market and moved into an assisted living facility on the edge of town."

"Well, in that case, I'm not as concerned."

"This next bit will make you grin," Gwen suggested, hoping to offset Ben's mood. "When Jenna came home, the young officer was instantly drawn to her. Asked if she'd meet him for coffee."

Ben sighed. "Ah, to be young again."

"What?" she teased. "And give up all the wisdom we've gained over the years?"

He chuckled. "What's that young officer's name?"

"Cole Martin. He joined the squad around the time you were retiring last year."

"Cole Martin," Ben repeated. "The name rings a bell, but I had very little interaction with the newbies."

"Well, if he and Jenna become an item, your paths will probably cross one of these days."

"No doubt, but let's talk more about that Hank character. I'd think twice before getting any more involved with Shirley's family."

"I'm leaning that way myself."

"Good to hear. It's best that the Tuckers resolve their family issues without outside influence." Again, Ben paused. "Hey, how about I treat you to dinner at *The Wharf* when I get back?"

"I'd love that. An unexpected snowstorm surprised us this morning. The harbor will be a winter wonderland."

"After the Arizona desert heat, the coolness of a New England winter sounds refreshing." Ben's tone reflected a more upbeat attitude.

"Tell me your flight timing and I'll pick you up."

"No, no, Gwen. I wouldn't dream of stressing you with a drive into Logan. I'll grab the shuttle to my car in a day or two and call you after I've settled at my condo."

She echoed his farewell and disconnected. Rising from the chair, she stepped toward her bedroom window to view the village green. Each lamppost created a soft puddle of light on the surrounding snow-covered ground.

Anticipating Ben's return, she descended the staircase, settled into Parker's recliner, tucked a throw around her legs, and picked up her mystery.

Jenna glanced over. "Is everything all right with Ben?"

"Not really. His father will probably pass tonight. After

he deals with the cremation, he'll fly back to Boston."

For an untracked length of time, Gwen let herself be hypnotized by the flames as she recalled her heart-wrenching vigil beside Parker's hospital bed a lifetime ago. Ben was experiencing the same ordeal in Arizona. Though the relationships were entirely different, the ache from the loss of a family member was universal.

Chapter Nine

...before sun-up, Monday

In the muted light of pre-dawn, as Gwen steeped a cup of herbal tea, the shrillness of a passing siren silenced the warbling of winter birds outside her kitchen window.

Her cell buzzed, and Shirley's name appeared on the Caller ID. Remembering Ben's advice to think twice before involving herself in Shirley's family troubles, Gwen hesitated, then pushed the button. "Good morning, Shirley."

Not bothering with a greeting, Shirley spoke in rapid staccato. "Gwen, would you come to my Aunt's house?"

"Now?" Gwen asked. "I'm not even dressed."

"I wouldn't ask if I didn't need your moral support."

Gwen's caution battled her curiosity. "What happened?"

Shirley's words tumbled over each other. "When I stopped by Aunt Filly's a little while ago, I nearly tripped over Hank at the bottom of the front steps. He was face down in the snow with a knife sticking out of his back."

Gwen gasped. "How awful. Was he still alive?"

"He seemed to be breathing so I dialed 9-1-1. The EMTs are tending to him now. A policeman arrived and asked me a few basic questions."

Shouting voices and the rumble of a truck engine confirmed that Shirley was in the middle of frenetic activity.

"I'm afraid that policeman will arrest me for stabbing Hank," Shirley whined.

Before Gwen could ask why, Shirley said, "Hold on. The policeman is moving toward the front door. It appears to be open a crack. I'm going to follow him inside. Listen, Gwen, I don't know what else has happened here, but if you could come over, I'd be grateful to have a friend by my side."

Though Gwen didn't consider Shirley a close friend, she ignored Ben's warning – especially knowing that Hank was out of commission – and said, "I'll be right there."

***

Rushing upstairs, Gwen threw on jeans, a sweatshirt, and warm socks, minutes later adding her winter coat, hat, boots, and gloves before closing the heavy oak door behind her.

As she made her way around the village green, a second ambulance – siren wailing and lights blazing – whizzed past. Could it also be heading toward the Tucker Victorian?

As Gwen passed Sugar 'n' Spice, she glanced up at Annabelle's apartment to see dark windows. The girl was either still in bed or out on an early assignment.

Hurrying along the partially shoveled sidewalk, Gwen reached the intersection and turned onto South Street. A few houses down, lights of blue, white. and red rotated atop two ambulances, the color bouncing off the low-hanging clouds.

One of the ambulances backed out from the driveway and zoomed toward the emergency room to the north.

As Gwen neared the Victorian, a police officer – his face shadowed by his police parka hood – hurried toward her, his hand held up in the universal sign to stop. "Hold on there, Mrs. Andrews. Where do you think you're going?"

His familiarity bringing her up short, Gwen moved closer, hoping to see his face clearly.

Officer Cole Martin stared back, nodding a solemn greeting. His demeanor couldn't have been more different from the helpful rookie who'd inspected her snow tracks the previous day.

Raising his hand again for Gwen to wait, he turned to someone coming up behind her.

Gwen heard the footsteps and swiveled to see Annabelle, holding out her *Gazette* ID for him to read.

"Officer," Annabelle began, "I often step in as the police department photographer. Mrs. Andrews will be assisting me." She handed her duffle to Gwen, unzipped the flap, reached inside, and removed an oversized black camera.

Behind them, a different voice hollered, "Hold up."

Gwen turned and watched an imposing officer pushing his way through the dozen sidewalk gawkers, his business suit flapping beneath his unzipped police parka as he barreled toward them.

"What seems to be the problem, Officer Martin?"

"Not yet a problem, sir. This is Annabelle Fairchild, the *Gazette* photographer, and her assistant."

As the suit came closer, Gwen could read his badge. Det Sgt. Ryan Rossini, Ben's replacement on the squad.

The sergeant inspected Annabelle's ID, then waved her toward the Victorian. "The victim is being transported for medical attention, so snap close-ups of the area where he was discovered. I doubt there are any untrampled footprints but photograph whatever you find."

When Annabelle took a step, Gwen began to follow but was quickly jerked to a stop. She turned to see that Sgt. Rossini had grabbed the strap of Annabelle's duffle looping Gwen's arm.

"Not you, lady." His voice remained gruff. "I doubt this photographer needs an assistant, and you don't look like one." He hefted the duffle from Gwen's arm and extended it toward Annabelle.

Giving Gwen an apologetic shrug, Annabelle took it and hurried toward a bloody patch of snow.

Like a kid caught with her hand in the cookie jar, Gwen waited for whatever would happen next.

Sgt. Rossini turned to Cole Martin. "Write down this woman's answers to my questions."

Then Rossini swung his hard gaze down to the shorter Gwen. "Your name, address, phone number, and the reason you're so interested in this crime scene?"

Though Cole Martin knew Gwen's name from their boot impression investigation, she spelled her first and last name, added the other details, and answered Sgt. Rossini's question. "Shirley Knapp asked me to meet her here."

As though she'd heard her name, Shirley suddenly appeared beside them. Gwen considered herself short, but Shirley didn't even clear five feet. Still, she reached up and linked arms with Gwen.

Sgt. Rossini seemed to recognize Shirley. "Of course, our intrepid reporter from the *Gazette*. I understand you're the person who came upon the injured man and called 9-1-1. Is that true?"

"That's true," Shirley repeated.

Cole Martin jotted Rossini's questions plus the answers Shirley snapped in response:

"Why were you at this house so early this morning?"
"My Aunt Filly requested I stop by before work."

"What's your relationship to the stabbed man?"
"He's my second cousin."

"Did you plunge that knife into his back?"
"I did not! I found him in the snow when I arrived."

Sgt. Rossini's eyebrows shot up but he didn't comment

on her snarkiness as he returned his attention to Gwen. "And you – Mrs. Andrews, is it? Were you a witness to this reporter's discovery of her cousin in the bloodied snow?"

Feeling like a snitch, Gwen swallowed before answering. "No, sir. Shirley phoned minutes ago and asked me to meet her here."

Rossini delivered an artificial grin. "Thank you for clarifying. Officer Martin here has recorded your statement. If we need more details, we'll be in touch. But for now," he waved toward the small crowd gathered on the sidewalk, "either join those rubber-necking neighbors or go home."

A bit insulted by his dismissive attitude, but cautious when dealing with the police, Gwen backed away.

Sgt. Rossini signaled to Cole Martin, "Before they scatter, take statements from the others." He strolled toward the patch of bloody snow where Annabelle snapped photos.

Gwen remained on the front walk, knowing her keen sense of hearing could pick up their conversation.

First, Sgt. Rossini halted near Annabelle, who cradled her camera in both hands. "Any clear images?"

"A few boot impressions," Annabelle answered.

He leaned down for his own inspection. "This entire area was trampled by the EMTs. We'll eliminate their prints and focus on the ones that remain unidentified."

Moving to the side of the steps, he pointed at the bloody edge of the concrete tread. "We'll ask the ER doctors about other injuries but take a photo of this, Ms. Fairchild."

Annabelle aimed her camera and captured the blood.

Rossini shifted as Cole Martin approached. "Finished so soon, officer?"

"Yes, sir. There weren't that many onlookers, and they had no details to contribute."

"Understood. When we leave here, we'll drive to the urgent care facility and hope the injured man is conscious enough for questions." He pointed to the front door. "I understand there's a second injured man inside. Let's go."

Gwen's ears perked up. *A second injured man?* That was the reason for the second ambulance. She glanced around for Shirley but didn't see her.

When Rossini, Martin, and Annabelle disappeared through the Victorian's front door, Gwen could no longer hear their words but she wasn't ready to go home quite yet. She stepped to the edge of the remaining gawkers. Their seemingly innocent chit-chat revealed no helpful observations, and she didn't know any of them well enough to engage in conversation.

When the last neighbor hurried off in the opposite direction, a hand touched Gwen's sleeve. Shirley.

"Where did you go?" Gwen asked.

"To my car for gloves. I'm surprised you're still here."

"So am I. To Rossini, I'm no different from the average gawker. They've all gone, and I was about to leave myself."

Sgt. Rossini's voice boomed from the Victorian's front door, and they turned to see him waving at Shirley.

His shout carried across shallow front yard. "Go around to the side door and join us in the kitchen."

"Gotta go, Gwen. If you don't mind, I'll stop over later and catch you up with more details."

Not about to refuse, Gwen said, "Of course, Shirley. I'll simmer water for tea."

Shirley half-waved as she hurried along the sidewalk toward the vehicle-filled driveway on the far side of the Victorian, disappearing around the corner of the veranda.

Gwen's mind racing, she did an about face and strode along South Street toward home.

Chapter Ten

...early morning, Monday

Circling Library Lane, Gwen arrived at her front door and pushed in the thick oak panel. The high-pitched wail of her golden, short-haired feline fractured the silence. Neglecting to fill Amber's bowls before rushing out to meet Shirley was an oversight Gwen wouldn't repeat any time soon.

Luckily, neighbor Martins' house remained empty as it waited for its next owner. Would the elderly couple have wrongly thought a person was screaming next door rather than an unhappy cat?

As Gwen rushed to the bottom of the staircase to prevent further racket from waking Jenna, she glanced toward the living room, relieved that no pillows or cushions had been shredded by her pet's talon-like claws.

Glancing up the treads, she spotted queenly Amber on the mid-way split, the cat's mouth opening for another howl.

In her most threatening tone, Gwen warned, "Don't you do it," and pointed at the landing near her own feet. "Get down here."

The cat trained green eyes on Gwen, bounded down the remaining stairs, and soon waited near her empty bowls.

Food and water replenished, Amber gobbled nearly half of the morsels then lapped a bit of the water to wash it down. She flipped her tail and pranced up the staircase, her bloated belly slowing her usual speed.

Setting the tea kettle on the stove, Gwen headed for the upstairs sitting room to verify that the spoiled Amber had settled on a plush cushion at the bank of windows and was happily snipping at the backyard birds.

The feline crisis had been remedied.

***

Within a half hour, Shirley arrived, her expression grim as Gwen settled her on a stool at the kitchen island.

The frazzled reporter raised worried eyes. "Thanks for meeting me at my aunt's house earlier."

Gwen placed a mug of tea in front of Shirley. "You weren't arrested. Tell me why you thought you would be."

A moment passed before Shirley answered. "Over the years, I've reported on similar incidents. The person who called 9-1-1 was usually labeled as the prime suspect."

"Why?" Gwen wanted to know.

"Because the police assume the caller's trying to throw suspicion off himself – or herself. On occasion, the caller turned out to the be actual culprit."

"That's discouraging for good Samaritans."

"You're right about that. I can only hope that Hank got a good look at his attacker and will name that person when he

65

wakes up." Shirley looked directly into Gwen's eyes. "Because I didn't do it."

Gwen swallowed her thought that Hank might never wake up, luckily catching the words before they escaped. No need to stress Shirley any further.

Instead, Gwen tried a different tact. "While it's true you made the 9-1-1 call, who could possibly compare your petite self to Hank's massive body and think you could reach to the top of his back?"

Shirley blew on the steaming tea before shaking her head. "Ignore our size difference. If Hank had been squatting, the attacker could have snuck up from behind. Size wouldn't have mattered."

Gwen hadn't considered that scenario and said, "That didn't occur to me."

Shirley's eyes glazed with unshed tears. "I have to depend on the police to arrest the guilty person."

Unfortunately, Gwen was familiar with wrongful accusations. To Shirley, she offered what she hoped would be a comforting thought. "I don't know which family members were inside the Victorian before sunrise, or who else might have snuck in under cover of darkness, but there could certainly be more likely attackers than you."

While Shirley contemplated that idea, Gwen continued. "Tell me what happened after you followed the first officer through your aunt's front door."

Shirley wrapped her hands around the warm mug. "All right. Like I told you on the phone, the veranda door was partially open. The officer wasn't aware that I snuck in behind him. Inside, the light was dull, but I could make out that Uncle Norman's hospital bed had been moved sideways and his wheelchair was tipped over. He was splayed on the floor and Aunt Filly was cradling his head in her lap. As the policeman called for backup and a second ambulance, he turned and saw me. I thought he'd chase me out; instead he instructed me to watch for the second ambulance and wave the EMTs inside."

Gwen recalled the second ambulance siren wailing as it raced past her during her hurried pace toward the Victorian.

"Did your uncle wake up when the EMTs were working on him?"

"Not that I could tell. When they said they'd rush him to the emergency room, I offered to go to with Aunt Filly, but the policeman said I had to stay and speak with the lead detective who was on his way."

Shirley inhaled then kept talking. "And then you arrived, along with that Sgt. Rossini. I felt badly when he told you to go home." Shirley focused on Gwen. "Were you able to overhear their conversation from the sidewalk?"

Without mentioning her better-than-average hearing ability, Gwen answered, "If you're talking about Rossini and Annabelle, I heard every word."

"Good." Shirley squirmed. "Excuse me, Gwen. May I use your bathroom?"

Gwen replied, "Of course," and pointed.

When Shirley closed the half-bath door, Gwen hurried into her living room and lit a small fire to offset the chill that was raising goosebumps on her arms.

Within a few minutes, Shirley had grabbed her mug and joined Gwen on the sofa. She glanced around. "Very cozy, especially your magnificent fireplace. When I was here years ago to report on your séance, I didn't have a chance to admire your decor."

"That was quite an evening," Gwen commented, not wanting to get sidetracked. She wanted to hear what else had happened but said, "Even though these circumstances are not the best, Shirley, I'm glad we've reconnected."

"Me, too." Shirley reached over and squeezed Gwen's arm. "Okay, enough bonding. Here's what happened after Sergeant. Rossini ordered me to the kitchen's side door."

Gwen shifted her body to face Shirley straight-on.

"As I entered," Shirley began, "I heard Rossini tell Annabelle to print the clearest pictures that she'd taken. A few family members were sitting around the kitchen table."

"How many were there?" Gwen asked.

"At that point, only Aunt Minnie plus Daryl and Doris Whitcome, the couple you met yesterday morning."

"Not your Aunt Filly?"

"No. She'd gone in the ambulance with Uncle Norman. Rossini will have to interview her later. He asked who else lived in the house and sent the policeman upstairs to bring down the two other couples."

"Was the policeman Officer Cole Martin?"

"Yes, it was. Nice young man," Shirley commented. "He guided those additional relatives around Uncle Norman's hospital bed and into the kitchen. I guess they'd either slept through the commotion or were afraid to come down because all four were still wearing their pajamas."

Gwen decided not to comment, so she asked another question. "What happened next?"

"Rossini questioned each person in the dining room."

"Could you hear his questions and their answers?"

"Sorry, no."

"Did Rossini interview you again after his initial sidewalk questions?"

Shirley's head wagged side to side. "No, but he glared at me like he was already convinced I'd stabbed Hank. He's probably planning to grill me under hot lights at the station." She chuckled.

"This isn't funny, Shirley."

"I know, I know."

Gwen stepped to the fireplace and added a log, then leaned against the mantle to face Shirley head on. "Is there more?"

"Yes. After Rossini questioned the last resident, he stood at the end of the kitchen table and gave a speech."

To Gwen's amusement, Shirley deepened her voice. and quoted Rossini as her hands replicated his sweeping motion.

'Don't leave town until our investigation is finalized. The fact that you all live in this house automatically makes you suspects for both Hank Payne's stabbing and Norman Tucker's injury. Let's hope both men wake up and identify their attacker. Do any of you have additional details to contribute?'

"When they all remained silent," Shirley continued, "Rossini said, *'We'll be back if we need to question any of you again.'*

Shirley tilted her mug and swallowed the last of her tea. "That's all I can tell you, Gwen. Thanks for listening, but I need to get myself over to the *Gazette* offices. If I hear anything more, I'll let you know."

Gwen walked the reporter to the front door and wished her good luck, then headed upstairs. At the desk tucked against the mezzanine railing, she gathered the photo albums, the old address books, and her unfinished list of reunion invitees, and carried everything down to the coziness of the living room.

A short time later, Jenna appeared, wolfed down a piece of toast and headed off to class.

Chapter Eleven

...mid-morning, Monday

After the early hours of Monday passed with no repeated summons from Shirley, Gwen began to relax. The stress of the morning angst slowly seeped from her bones.

As the fireplace blaze offset the January chill, Gwen made herself comfortable on the leather sofa and continued her family union project. The list of family members grew as she added name, home address, landline, cell number, and email of family members from holiday cards or letters received over the years. Many lived out of state, so might not make the trip to Harbor Falls.

The doorbell chime reverberated, interrupting her focus and drawing her to the foyer. Expecting Shirley, Gwen didn't hesitate to open the door.

Not Shirley.

Instead, Sergeant Rossini stared at her. "Mrs. Andrews," he stated, his tone sounding more like a confirmation of her identity. His expression suggested a hint of superiority.

One step down, Officer Cole Martin exhaled a puff of cold air. Her concern about him and Jenna remained intact.

"May we come in?" Rossini suggested, one brow lifting.

Ever since his dismissive attitude toward her at the Tucker house, Rossini had rubbed her the wrong way. He must need more details about her presence there.

Gathering her wits, she calmly replied, "Of course," and swung the door inward, waving both policemen into the foyer. "Please place your wet footwear in the boot tray."

Sensing they weren't used to taking orders from a female, she waited patiently. "Would either of you like something to drink?" She was about to make a quip about Dunkin' Donuts but quickly decided against it.

Rossini shook his head. "Not necessary."

As she waved them into her living room, Rossini eyed her reunion paraphernalia and the fire burning brightly in her hearth but made no comment.

She stiffened when the gruff man sat in Parker's recliner, then convinced herself to let it go. After all, Parker's chair wasn't roped off like antique furniture during a historic house tour. Parker's absence from Gwen's life – both as her living husband and then his spirit – pricked her heart like a sliver from a rough log. She pressed herself to pay attention.

Rossini leaned his forearms stiffly on his knees, failing to impart a casual attitude. "Let me tell you why we stopped by unannounced." He paused to let his preamble settle.

"I am curious," Gwen admitted.

Rising to his feet, Rossini wandered about the room, pausing now and then to glance in Gwen's direction.

Officer Cole Martin didn't interrupt.

"When I updated the squad about the stabbing at the Tucker Victorian, your name was included on our list of sidewalk gawkers."

The haughty timbre of his voice reminded Gwen of the one-armed village commander in *Young Dr. Frankenstein.* In the movie, the actor had perfected the exasperating character. Pacing in Gwen's living room, Rossini was much more annoying.

She controlled her urge to object to his distasteful label, deciding that the quicker he finished his reason for interrupting her morning, the sooner he and Cole Martin would depart.

Oblivious about his insult, Rossini continued. "Two of the detectives in my squad spoke up to say you provided background details to Detective Benjamin Snowcrest during challenging cases."

Why was Rossini bringing up her efforts as Ben's confidential informant? Were those cases going to circle back and bite Gwen in the butt? When Ben retired, her C.I. status had been severed. Or so she'd thought.

Although saving a friend from false accusation by sleuthing unobtrusively had been rewarding, Gwen had too often come too close to bodily harm to seek out that activity any time soon. These days, she limited her mystery solving to a well-written novel. So much safer.

Unsure how to respond to Rossini's dismissive words, Gwen opted for meekness. "That's a piece of my life better left in the past."

As Gwen pondered if her partnering with Ben was the reason for this unexpected visit, Rossini's cell buzzed.

In a millisecond, he connected to the call, his face falling as he listened. Then he barked, "I'll be right there."

He motioned to Cole Martin. "Hank Payne died during surgery for his head wound."

Given Rossini's newly obtained knowledge of her past association with police investigations, Gwen didn't think she was out of line when she blurted, "Not from the knife wound in his back?"

Rossini re-pocketed his cell, stepping toward the foyer. "That would be a normal person's assumption, but no. After the man's head struck the concrete step, blood collected on his brain. The surgeons were attempting to relieve the pressure when the man's heart stopped beating."

In the foyer, as the two detectives pulled on their boots, Gwen waited without speaking.

After tying his laces, Rossini stretched to his superior height and gazed down his nose at her. "It won't surprise you that Hank Payne's assault case has now elevated to a murder investigation."

"But the head injury wasn't connected to the knife."

"True," he sneered, his tone remaining pompous, "but if

he hadn't been stabbed, he wouldn't have staggered out the Victorian's front door and fallen headfirst down those steps, making contact with the concrete."

When Gwen didn't comment, Rossini settled his cap on his close-cropped hair. "Thank you for your time."

Still in the dark about the reason behind Rossini and Martin's visit, she watched the two men climb into their unmarked sedan. Seconds later, the car sped around the village green, its rooftop light flashing.

***

For the rest of the day, as Gwen continued her reunion planning, she gave no more thought to Rossini but did wonder how Shirley's family was handling the news of Hank's death. If she had to guess, she'd assume they were all relieved. No more unease about his threatening presence.

Long after winter darkness had descended, Gwen heard the ping of an arriving text and reached for her cell phone.

'I'm going out to dinner with a classmate, then we'll return to the library and continue working on our group project. I don't expect I'll be home until late. Jenna.'

Trusting that the classmate label eliminated Cole Martin as Jenna's dinner companion, Gwen relaxed and texted back. *'Enjoy your dinner. See you later.'*

Before she had time to lower her phone, it rang.

Ben's familiar deep voice greeted her. "Hi, Gwen."

"Hi, yourself. How's your father doing?"

Ben's voice sobered. "He passed an hour ago."

"I'm so sorry."

"Thanks."

Ever since his call that he was flying to his dying father's bedside, Gwen had fretted about Ben bearing the burden of his father's death with no other family member to share the loss. She should have insisted on joining him. "What happens now?"

"When my father mentioned he had no will, I wrote his cremation request on a sheet of hospital letterhead. He signed it with his nurse as a witness. I've contracted a local crematorium to retrieve his body. I'm waiting for the death certificate and other required documents."

"Any idea how long that will take?"

"They'll let me know when his ashes are ready for pick up. I hope it's not longer than a day or two. I'm beyond ready to return to Harbor Falls."

"It'll be good to have you back in town."

"Sounds like you missed me."

"I missed your quick wit."

Gwen was also anxious to bring him up to date about Hank Payne's death and Rossini's curious visit. But she didn't want to distract Ben while he finalized his father's arrangements. Better to wait until his feet were solidly planted on Massachusetts' soil.

"When you get back," she ventured, "how about you and

I plan an outing to chase away my post-holiday doldrums and your misgivings about your father's passing?"

"I'm up for a road trip with you," Ben agreed. "I also promised you a dinner at *The Wharf.*"

In the background, a garbled announcement blared.

"I'm sorry," Ben said softly into her ear. "I'm being paged. I'll call when I have an update about my return."

Before Gwen could respond, Ben had hung up.

Chapter Twelve

…late afternoon, Tuesday

With Jenna out for the evening, Gwen opted to stroll down to the Bayside Café near the harbor for her supper.

Bundled up, and despite the chill of mid-January, she inhaled the clean scent of winter air as she traversed the snowy pathways through the village green. Crossing North Street, she finessed her steps down the slope of Harbor Hill to avoid a slip-and-fall.

Halfway along the row of stately Colonial brick buildings, the lighted sign for *Fiction & Fables Bookstop* swayed in the late afternoon breeze, its warm glow urging passersby to enter.

The bell above the door jangled as three laughing women spilled onto the sidewalk, their arms laden with multiple shopping bags.

Deciding she wanted company for supper, Gwen pushed the door open and spotted her friend Liz at the register.

A wide grin brightened the shop owners' face as she rushed over to pull Gwen into a welcoming hug. "I'm so glad you stopped in. Sorry I haven't been in touch since Tony and I returned from our cruise."

"You're forgiven," Gwen joked. No matter how much time passed, their decades-long friendship remained fresh.

Liz leaned sideways. "Ben's not with you?"

"Not this time. He's in New Mexico finalizing arrangements for his father's cremation."

"I'm sorry to hear that," Liz said. "Were they close?"

Gwen placed her handbag on the counter. "Not at all. They'd been estranged since Ben was a teenager. But when an Albuquerque rest home alerted him about his dad's condition, Ben flew out there before it was too late."

Liz laid her hand atop Gwen's. "Did they reconcile before his father died?"

"From what Ben said on the phone, they did."

"That must have been a relief for them both. How soon will Ben return to Harbor Falls?"

"He's hoping in the next day or two."

"Is he aware of this past Sunday's snowstorm?"

"I mentioned it when we spoke earlier."

"Then he won't be surprised that our quaint college town looks like a picture postcard."

"My exact words," Gwen agreed. "But listen. I'm having supper at the Bayside Café. Care to join me?"

Liz pushed back a strand of her pixie cut hair. "I would, but my clerk called in sick, so I'm on my own until closing. If you're not starving, can you stay for a while?"

"I'm in no particular hurry, so sure."

Liz waved toward the seating area surrounded on three sides by shelves displaying books of all genres. "Let's get comfortable while we catch up."

Gwen settled on the overstuffed couch before asking, "Have you heard what happened at the Tucker house?"

Liz squinted. "The large Victorian a few buildings south of the old schoolhouse?"

"That's the one," Gwen confirmed. "I wasn't aware that relatives of Shirley Knapp live there."

"The world gets smaller all the time," Liz commented. "In early December, Shirley and the *Gazette* photographer stopped by during my Santa Claus event. In fact, your Ben was my Santa."

"That's right," Gwen recalled. "His new white beard and longer hair were perfect for ol' St. Nick."

"But back to the Tuckers," Liz insisted. "I don't think any of them have ever come in here to browse or buy."

"The married women have different last names, so you might not connect them to the Tuckers."

"That's true," Liz conceded. "What happened?"

With the bookstore temporarily void of customers, Gwen summarized the recent events. Next, the introductions to a few members of the Tucker family, including their black sheep. Gwen ended with Shirley's discovery of Hank on Monday morning bleeding in the snow with a knife in his back.

"How distressing," Liz said. "Is he recovering?"

Gwen answered, "He died during surgery."

Though the bookstore remained shopper-free, Liz lowered her voice. "Do they know who stabbed him?"

Side-stepping the curious visit from Sgt. Rossini and Officer Martin, Gwen replied, "Not that I've heard."

The two friends fell into easy silence until Liz laid a hand on Gwen's sleeve. "When are you and Ben getting serious?"

Not surprised by Liz's change of topic – for Liz never tired of matchmaking – Gwen knew that a truthful answer would involve the baffling absence of Parker's ghost. Like many, Liz didn't believe in ghosts, even though she'd attended Gwen's séance a few years before.

That event had been planned to take place right here in Liz's bookstore until unforeseen circumstances had forced her to find an alternate venue. She'd cajoled Gwen to donate her library home, a perfect setting for a séance. Obligated to participate, Liz doubted the validity of the connections made with the attendees. Plus Liz hadn't seen Parker's spirit when he teased the other women by blowing on their hair and making the candles flicker.

Liz retained her skepticism about the spirit world, so Gwen never mentioned Parker's ghostly visitations.

Her disappointment that he hadn't appeared since Halloween weekend hadn't reduced Gwen's belief in his afterlife existence.

At least not yet.

She didn't doubt that her loyalty to Parker was the reason she resisted a more serious relationship with Ben.

"Gwen, did you hear me?" Liz reached across the space between them. "You seemed a million miles away."

Ponderings flew from Gwen's mind as she looked into Liz's concerned eyes. "I guess I was. Sorry."

Just then, the jingle of the shop's bell saved Gwen from responding to Liz's question about Ben. As Liz rose to greet the customers, Gwen waved goodbye and hurried across Harbor Hill to the Bayside Café.

After ordering a light supper, Gwen squirmed in the booth, undecided where to focus her attention. She'd always been more relaxed when enjoying a meal with someone else.

At the other tables were friends and couples, all engrossed in conversation. Gwen regretted that Liz couldn't join her to fill the void. To occupy her hands, she pulled out her cell and concentrated on her calendar until a pleasant server delivered her meal.

Gwen bit into the grilled cheese with cheddar, bacon, and a slice of tomato. She missed Ben sitting across from her exchanging clever banter. She'd be glad when he was back in Harbor Falls.

Her thoughts swirled to the afternoon he'd met Parker's spirit – a shock for sure. The confirmation that ghosts existed marked a distinct uptick in Ben's understanding of Gwen's loyalty to Parker in the afterlife, and the reason she'd resisted Ben's advances, agreeing to only a platonic but deep friendship.

Wiping the tomato juice from her chin, Gwen decided that a conversation with Betty Owens about the B&B's ghost might be helpful and planned her next stop at the Harbor Falls Bed & Breakfast at the top of the hill.

Chapter Thirteen

…early evening, Tuesday

When Gwen reached the upper section of Harbor Hill, she ascended the wide porch steps of the Harbor Falls B&B and approached its expansive burgundy door, no longer decorated with a lavish holiday wreath.

Lifting the antique bronze knocker, she released her grip and let it clang against the metal plate.

Footsteps echoed inside, and the door flew open.

Betty Owens' eyes lit up as her hand flew to her generous bosom. "Oh, it's you, Gwen. I thought you were our next guest. But I'm glad you stopped by. Come in, come in." Betty pulled Gwen into the pleasantly ornate entrance hall.

Gwen leaned down to remove her boots. "I'm on my way home and decided that a visit with you is long overdue."

As Betty led Gwen into the adjacent living room, where a vigorous fire filled the massive stone hearth, she asked, "When did we last get together?"

"Gosh, I can't be sure. I'm so sorry I haven't stopped by before now."

Indicating Gwen should sit in one of the wing-backed chairs angled toward the fire, Betty settled in the matching one and stretched her feet toward the warmth. "Don't fret. I haven't knocked on your door either. Our lives are busy, so we both have a good excuse for neglecting one another."

"I confess I have an ulterior motive for this visit."

Her expression curious, Betty asked, "And what is that?"

Gwen shifted her weight until she faced her friend. "I'm concerned about my connection with Parker. His ghost hasn't made an appearance since October."

She didn't worry that her words would spook Betty, for the B&B owner was no stranger to the spirit world. Betty and her husband Robert had purchased their historic B&B despite its ghost Theo wandering the halls for nearly a century. They considered Theo's spirit a noteworthy enticement for more adventurous guests.

Betty reached across the divide and squeezed Gwen's hand. "My, my, no visit from Parker is certainly cause for worry."

"Is your Theo still making herself known?" Gwen asked.

"Why, Theo appeared to me just the other day," Betty answered. "She smiled at me before drifting up the staircase."

Gwen absorbed the implication of Betty's revelation. "So there hasn't been a blockage of paranormal activity. That means there's some other reason for Parker's absence."

"It seems so, Gwen. What's happened in your life since the last time you saw him?"

Thinking back, Gwen answered, "Just before my sister Tess and I were about to ride the ferry to Nantucket for a Halloween party."

Betty scooted forward in her chair. "That must have been a fun weekend."

"It was at first," Gwen agreed. "Even more interesting when I bumped into the cousin of our hostess, the medium who led my séance a few years ago."

"Madame Eudora?" Betty asked, one eyebrow rising.

"The very one. The party invitees demanded a séance to end the Halloween party."

"And did Madame Eudora summon any spirits?"

"Unfortunately, no. The hostess wanted to communicate with the sea captain rumored to haunt her Nantucket home."

"And how about Parker?"

"We tried, but he didn't respond. Madame Eudora suggested that his spirit might be unable to cross the waters of Nantucket Sound."

"I don't know about that," Betty said, "but you must have been disappointed."

"I was."

"What else has happened since Halloween?"

Gwen hesitated, unsure whether to bring up Ben as a potential barrier to Parker's appearance. But if she couldn't discuss this topic with Betty, who else?

Cautiously, Gwen said, "There is one thing."

Betty's eyes twinkled. "Don't stop now."

Finding the right words as she spoke, Gwen said, "Do you remember Detective Benjamin Snowcrest who investigated the death on your back stairs at the garden club Christmas party?"

Betty nodded. "He was quite serious as I recall."

Nodding her agreement, Gwen said, "At first, he resented my amateur sleuthing on your behalf. Then Parker's ghost followed me here and located your Theo. She shared important details with Parker, which he passed to me, then I told Detective Snowcrest. Though he didn't believe my source, he encouraged my continued involvement and we captured the culprit. Since then, Ben and I have solved a case or two together."

Betty held up her hand. "Are you aware that our Theo appeared to your detective toward the end of that Christmas party investigation?"

Gwen sat back, suddenly understanding. "That explains why Ben didn't panic when I introduced him to Parker's ghost the following summer."

Her eyebrows lifting, Betty said, "If Ben is aware of Parker's ghost, then Parker is aware of Ben. Has your friendship with the detective deepened since the last time Parker visited you?"

Gwen was quick to clarify. "I wouldn't say that. We avoid a physically intimate relationship."

"Do you think your Parker could be jealous?"

The clang of the B&B's door knocker preempted Gwen's response as Betty struggled to her feet. "Sorry, Gwen, but that's probably our next guest. She needs to check in and get settled. Do you want to wait or get together another day?"

Matching Betty's rise, Gwen answered, "I'll let you tend your guest. Thanks for giving me food for thought."

After a quick hug, she followed Betty into the entrance hall and slipped her feet into her waiting boots.

When Betty swung open her front door, a smiling woman with wheeled luggage stepped back, and waved Gwen onto the porch.

Chapter Fourteen

...mid evening, Tuesday

After leaving the B&B, Gwen hurried the short distance along the snowy sidewalk to the North Street traffic light. Though there was little traffic, she pushed the button for the walk sign. Frigid evening air chilled her bones.

With the sparse number of cars and trucks passing through Harbor Falls, near silence surrounded her, making Gwen feel like the only person in the world.

And then boisterous laughter echoed off the stone buildings of Baylies College several blocks to her north.

A couple strolled in the opposite direction, their backs to Gwen. The streetlights shone down on the woman's red winter coat and matching hat. *Could that be Jenna?*

But who was her companion? Gwen had met only a few of Jenna's classmates over the years but couldn't identify the young man who was making Jenna laugh, especially from this distance.

When he half-turned, the evening breeze blew his parka hood from his head, revealing his profile and exposing his blonde hair. He was no college student. He was Officer Cole Martin.

Did Jenna purposely mislead Gwen that the dinner invitation was from a classmate?

Ignoring the now-flashing walk sign, Gwen's booted feet seemed glued to the sidewalk. She couldn't stop watching as the couple faded further away, thinking back to Jenna meeting Cole only a few days before.

Appearing instantly besotted with Jenna, Cole had asked all sorts of questions before inviting her to meet him for coffee one day soon. She'd agreed but they'd made no specific plans.

To Gwen, meeting for coffee was a less stressful event for a first date. Jenna would get to know Cole in a casual atmosphere before deciding whether to invest more time with him.

As an aging baby-boomer, Gwen wondered if her reaction was old-fashioned. She'd never thought so but her concerns about Cole befriending Jenna so quickly were a hint. Did today's young adults move toward relationships at a much quicker pace?

Inhaling the chilly air to calm herself, Gwen considered her role in Jenna's life. More than three years earlier, with the agreement of Jenna's grandfather, Gwen had offered her guestroom to Jenna while the girl pursued her music degree at Baylies College. As each semester passed, Jenna had matured. Now a senior, she'd bloomed into a thoughtful young woman with a mind of her own.

Gwen resolved to offer advice only if Jenna asked.

Forcing herself to turn away from the receding young couple, Gwen again pushed the button to stop a lone car. After the sign blinked its permission to cross, she hurried through the village green toward the comfort of her home.

***

With Amber purring beside her on the sofa, Gwen distracted herself from Jenna and Cole's budding friendship by watching a recording of *Columbo*, one of several favorite TV dramas from the 1970s and '80s. Opting not to begin another episode, she made sure all of the doors were locked and retired to her gable bedroom.

Propped against her pillows, she opened the mystery she'd been enjoying and flipped to where she'd left off.

As she absorbed the intriguing plot, the sound of the front door opening and closing, followed by the lock snicking into place, confirmed that Jenna had returned.

Resisting the urge to rush downstairs, Gwen turned to the next page.

She soon found herself reading the same paragraph over and over, so she slipped in a bookmark and switched off her bedside light.

But her mind refused to shut down, meandering from one topic to another.

First, spotting Jenna strolling and laughing with Cole Martin. Had she found him interesting enough to encourage a second date? Which situation bothered Gwen more? Jenna's misleading text message about dinner with a classmate or her connection with the rookie police officer?

Then Hank Payne demanded Gwen's attention. Hoping her involvement with the unfortunate Tucker family was over and done, Gwen mentally instructed her cell phone *not* to buzz with another urgent call from Shirley.

Snuggling into the warmth beneath her down comforter, Gwen's conversation with Betty Owens came to mind. Was the B&B owner right that Gwen's fondness for Ben could be the reason for Parker's no shows? Could a ghost be jealous? Gwen would try again to summon Parker, the only person who could put an end to her endless guessing game about their connection – now or in the future.

And lastly, Ben would soon return from his father's final days. Would he be mired in mourning for his father or relieved that they'd reconciled before it was too late?

Gwen tossed and turned as all these competing topics cycled in a never-ending loop. For hours on end, she bounced from one to the other then back again, unable to quiet her mind.

When four-thirty glared from the bedside clock, she gave up, threw a robe over her PJ's, and headed down to the kitchen.

Chapter Fifteen

...pre-dawn, Wednesday

In the ambient light, Gwen nearly stepped on Jenna lying on the kitchen floor stroking Amber's golden fur.

"Good morning, Jenna. Why are you up so early?"

Also in her PJ's, Jenna scrambled to her feet. "I couldn't sleep. Guess you couldn't either."

"Too many competing topics sparring for my attention," Gwen offered, stopping herself from mentioning the late hour of Jenna's return the previous evening.

Sliding onto an island stool, Jenna said, "My mind wouldn't stop editing my research paper, so I gave up on sleeping and came down to feed your ravenous cat." She leaned down to scratch Amber's ears, receiving a purr of satisfaction as a reward.

Despite her resolution not to interfere in Jenna's life, Gwen couldn't resist one innocent question. "Where did your classmate suggest you go for dinner?"

"Oh, you mean last night?" Without waiting for Gwen to confirm, Jenna continued her answer. "Samantha wanted a break from brainstorming our papers, so we found a quiet corner in the campus dining hall. You'll never guess who walked in as we were heading back to the library."

Again not waiting for Gwen to respond, Jenna filled in the blank. "That policeman from Sunday morning."

"Cole Martin?" Gwen supplied. "Was he hoping to bump into you?"

Jenna grinned. "He never really said. I teased him that he'd made a wrong turn on his way to Dunkin' Donuts. I don't think he appreciated the dig, but I agreed to a cup of coffee and a stroll around campus before he walked me back here. He made me laugh, but I'm too busy studying to be sidetracked by romance."

Relieved and at the same time impressed by Jenna's unwavering determination to earn her degree, Gwen was searching for wise words to share when her cell buzzed an incoming text. Hoping it wasn't Shirley, she checked caller ID to see Ben's name. She clicked it and read:

'Texting so I don't wake you. I hopped the red eye to Boston. I'm at a stopover and should be back in Harbor Falls in a few hours. I'll call you later about dinner tonight.'

Gwen typed, *'I'm up. How about breakfast with me and Jenna before you drive to your condo?'*

Within seconds, his answer arrived.

'Thanks for the invite. Home cooking will be a welcome change. See you both later.'

When Gwen placed the cell upside down on the island counter, Jenna asked, "Why are you grinning?"

"Am I?" Warmth tickled Gwen's neck. "That was Ben. I invited him for breakfast with us in a few hours."

Jenna's expression brightened. "Great idea. He'll be tired *and* hungry. What should we make for him?"

Envisioning her pantry contents, Gwen replied, "How about pineapple upside-down pancakes?"

"Those are delicious." Jenna remarked. "You haven't made them for a while. What can I do to help?"

"Nothing at the moment. We won't begin until Ben parks out front." Gwen glanced at the kitchen clock. "When is your first class this morning?"

"Not until nine," Jenna answered, then held up a finger. "Instead of going back to bed, let's go for a walk. Harbor Falls is still sleeping this early and I bet we don't cross paths with anyone. Maybe we can catch the sunrise over Massachusetts Bay."

"How can I refuse? I'll take a quick shower before I bundle up. Meet you down here in fifteen minutes."

***

The two of them circled the historic buildings of Baylies College, its security lights twinkling off the snow-covered hills and valleys.

Emerging on the far side of the campus, they waited for a milk delivery truck to trundle by before traversing Shore Drive. As the sun peeked above the horizon, they snapped photos across the bay with their cell cameras.

Trudging up Harbor Hill, they were passing through the village green when Gwen noticed Ben's red Corvette parked at the curb in front of her home.

Leaning back against his sports car, Ben raised his arm in a vigorous wave.

Gwen increased her pace. "Welcome back, Ben. I didn't expect you this early. Sorry Jenna and I weren't back from our walk to greet you."

His grey eyes gleamed. "I should have texted that the pilot found a tailwind and landed ahead of schedule."

As though on autopilot, Gwen reached up and stroked his beard. "I'm not yet used to your white whiskers."

"But you seem to like it."

"I more than like it. Also your hair is a little longer. You look more like a popular professor than a retired detective. Liz still raves about your Santa at her bookshop."

Under Ben's intense gaze, Gwen shivered, and not from the chilled January air. Flustered, she was grateful when Jenna pointed at the snow and mud spatters marring his bright red paint. "One of my professors doesn't drive his sports car when the roads are messy."

"I wouldn't either but a retired detective has lost access to a department vehicle, so my personal car is my ride."

"That's a shame," Jenna said, her expression sheepish.

Gwen stepped away from Ben and jangled her house keys. "Let's go in."

Unlocking the heavy door, she waved Jenna and Ben into the foyer. "Boots off, then take a seat in the living room, Ben. Long flights are tiring. Jenna and I will get to work on our breakfast."

Instead, he followed them into the kitchen. "I'll just settle on this stool and watch the two of you cook."

Though a bit self-conscious that he was observing her every move, Gwen asked, "Coffee?"

"I never refuse your coffee," Ben countered.

They all chuckled, and Gwen started the machine.

She then opened her pantry door and retrieved a can of pineapple rings plus a box of pancake mix.

Behind her, Jenna asked. "What can I do?"

"Wrestle the griddle from the cabinet and plug it in."

From the fridge, Gwen removed a carton of eggs and a jug of milk, soon mixing all the ingredients.

Fifteen minutes later, Ben laid down his fork. "Delicious. Thanks for breakfast on such short notice."

Gwen beamed. "Our pleasure."

Swallowing the last morsels on her own plate, Jenna gathered her dishes. "Sorry, but I have a class at nine."

Gwen reached over and hovered her hand above Jenna's. "I'll clean up. Off you go."

"Thanks." Jenna hopped down from her stool and kissed Ben's cheek. "Good to see you." Minutes later, the front door slammed shut.

As Ben helped Gwen load the dishwasher, she asked, "Is everything settled with your father?"

"Mostly," he replied without explanation.

She closed the dishwasher door and started the cycle. Her fondness for Ben grew with each new encounter, but she didn't think it fair to lead him on if she had no intention of allowing their relationship to progress beyond their precious friendship.

Chapter Sixteen

…early morning, Wednesday

As Gwen refilled their mugs, she asked over her shoulder, "Can you stay or would you rather return to your condo to unpack and get some sleep?"

Turning, she watched Ben as he weighed his options.

He finally said, "I'd like to stay but I need to make a pit stop." He stood and headed toward the half bath.

Gwen carried their two steaming mugs to the living room, then laid a fire.

As Ben came up beside her, she struck a match to the crinkled paper, then closed the Tree of Life fireplace screen.

He gazed into the ambitious flames. "I wish my condo had a real fireplace. The scent of a wood fire is comforting."

"I agree," she said, turning toward him. "I'm glad you can stay for a bit. The fire is my contribution toward your healing from your father's passing."

He sent her a sideways glance. "You've become a very caring friend, Gwen."

"And so have you."

He shuffled his feet but remained at the hearth. "Let me finish answering your earlier question. I decided not to spread my father's ashes out in Arizona but instead find an appropriate location here in New England."

Relieved that he hadn't shut her out completely, Gwen suggested, "How about the neighborhood where your family lived when you were a kid?" As she voiced her idea, she realized she didn't know where he'd grown up.

"That's one possibility," Ben remarked.

Picking up both mugs, he handed one to her and they settled on the sofa, focusing on the flames and sipping the coffee in companionable silence.

Then Gwen asked the question she'd been harboring since Ben flew to his father's bedside. "If I'm not being too personal, I'm curious about your father."

"As a caring friend, Gwen, you'll never be too personal. My father was an alcoholic, losing one job after another."

Getting to his feet, Ben leaned against the mantel and stared into the burning logs. "He wasn't a physically abusive drunk, so he never struck either me or my mother. He yelled insults and criticized non-stop, which was just as damaging. When I was in my teens, Mom had enough and tossed him out. Back in the '60s, most wives were homemakers, but my mother had to work to put food on the table and pay the rent. We never saw my father again."

"I'm so sorry, Ben. Flying out to see him on his deathbed must have been difficult."

After a long pause, Ben turned to face Gwen. "All these

years, I resented him for never reaching out to me. I thought he'd died years ago, long before my mother passed. That call from the rest home took me by surprise, but I knew I'd regret it if I didn't go."

"That was wise of you."

"I don't know if wise is the right word but it was the only way to close out that negative part of my life."

Returning to the sofa, Ben placed his arm along the back. "Enough about me. How about your early life?"

Gwen bit the inside of her cheek. Compared to Ben's sad childhood, how could she tell him that hers had been quite pleasant? Still, she felt obligated to share.

"My young years weren't nearly as dramatic. You're aware I grew up in the Berkshires with my sister Tess."

"Yes. The two of you seem close."

Gwen snorted. "As adults we are, but she teased me without mercy when we were youngsters."

"I wish I had a brother or sister," Ben mused and did a double-take. "Sorry to interrupt. What about your parents?"

Gwen sensed that her idyllic upbringing would somehow be soothing to Ben, so she continued.

"My mom and dad were supportive and encouraging but made sure Tess and I knew the difference between right and wrong. We received appropriate punishment when needed. Kinda like *Ozzie and Harriet* or the *Leave It To Beaver* show. Our dad died in his sleep many years ago. A few months later, Mom passed. The doctors said she died from a quiet heart attack. I think her heart broke from missing dad."

Ben let his hand drop onto Gwen's shoulder and squeezed. "We all face loss at some point."

Gwen laid her hand atop his and gave it a quick pat, "Unfortunately, death is part of life and eventually unavoidable." She pushed herself off the couch and added another log to the fire.

Putting down his empty mug, he joined her, stretching his hands toward the warmth of the flames. "Time for a change of subject. Did anything interesting happen since we spoke on the phone Sunday evening?"

Gwen appreciated his smooth transition. "As a matter of fact, I stopped at the B&B to chat with Betty about their ghost Theo."

Ben chuckled. "Did I ever tell you that I met Theo in the B&B's kitchen during our investigation? Seeing her in person changed my mind about an afterlife and prepared me for your introduction to Parker's spirit that summer."

"Which you handled admirably," Gwen reminded him.

"I shouldn't have been so shocked to come face to face with your husband's transparent self."

Before Gwen had a chance to continue, Ben spoke again. "Have you seen him recently?"

"That was the other reason I wanted to spend some time with Betty – the absence of Parker's ghost."

"His absence?"

"Parker hasn't appeared to me since Halloween weekend. I've called his name multiple times but he doesn't seem to hear me."

Ben's forehead furrowed. "More than two months ago."

Nerves jangling, Gwen turned to face him. "That's right. He hasn't materialized since the Nantucket fiasco."

Ben reached for her hand. "I'm so sorry, Gwen. I know you treasure your connection with Parker's spirit. Any idea why he's not showing up?"

"Only guesses. Maybe he's used up his allotment of earthly visits. Or maybe something has blocked his access. Or his spirit has moved on to the next level of the afterlife, whatever that is. It's not like he could text me an update." Her attempt at levity fell flat.

When her eyes filled with unexpected tears threatening to spill, she turned away.

Ben circled around her. "Gwen, you're crying."

Wiping at the drops, she tried to smile but failed. "I shouldn't burden you with my paranormal frustration."

In an instant, Ben wrapped his arms around her, easing her head against his sweater. "That's what friends are for."

Basking in his closeness until her tears subsided, Gwen slipped from his embrace and looked up. "Thanks."

"Any time, but I'm curious. What did Betty have to say about Parker's no-show?"

Feeling her face flush, Gwen considered her answer.

"She suggested that my fondness for you might be keeping Parker away."

Ben placed his finger beneath her chin and lifted her face, looking down into her eyes. "You're fond of me?"

Gwen's unplanned confession demanded honesty. "I thought you knew that I am."

His voice husky, Ben replied, "The feeling's mutual."

When Gwen didn't respond, he kept talking. "I've got an idea. Because I might be the reason for Parker's resistance, we should call his name together. If jealousy is keeping him away, he might make an appearance to challenge me. Think about it and let me know what you decide."

Staring into the flames, Gwen mulled over Ben's offer.

When she turned, Ben held up his empty mug. "Any chance for another cup?"

Together, they walked to the kitchen, where she busied herself brewing another pot, all the while debating whether Ben's involvement would be helpful or detrimental to Parker's appearance.

Her decision remained elusive.

Chapter Seventeen

...mid-morning, Wednesday

After Gwen rinsed the coffee filter, Ben lifted it from her hand and placed it in the machine, saying, "Putting aside your anxiety about Parker's absence, has anything else happened while I've been in Albuquerque?"

"Quite a bit. Early Monday morning, Shirley nearly tripped over her cousin Hank at the bottom of the Victorian's front steps. He was bleeding in the snow from a knife sticking out of his back. She dialed 9-1-1, then called me. I rushed over there to provide moral support."

Ben's scrunched brows almost touched. "Is her cousin recovering?"

"No. Yesterday afternoon, Sgt. Rossini paid me a visit. While we were talking, he received a call that Hank died during surgery to relieve the pressure from his head injury."

"Head injury?" Ben questioned. "Not from the knife wound in his back?"

"That's what I asked Rossini. He explained that after Hank escaped out the front door, he tumbled from the veranda and hit his head on a concrete step. The impact caused a brain-bleed. During surgery, his heart stopped."

The seconds ticked by until Ben reacted. "I'm guessing the initial stabbing incident has been upgraded to a homicide investigation?"

"That's what Sgt. Rossini shared before he and Cole Martin rushed off to the hospital. And now Shirley's worried she'll be arrested."

"Because she's the one who called 911?" Ben asked, his experiences as a long-time detective surfacing.

"Exactly."

Ben eased onto an island stool. "That's been a ploy in the past. The guilty party tried to cover his or her involvement in the crime by pretending to be a good Samaritan."

"That's what Shirley explained."

"Do you think she arrived earlier than she claims and stabbed her cousin?"

Gwen shook her head. "I can't imagine her going to that extreme. Granted, she blamed Hank for his mother's fatal accident twenty years ago, but, still, I don't want to believe that Shirley's capable of attacking anyone."

"Could have been a crime of passion," Ben suggested. "Even the gentlest person has a breaking point." His head shot up. "Hold on a sec. Why did Rossini and Martin knock on your door yesterday?"

"Rossini wanted to apologize for his dismissive attitude at the Tucker Victorian on Monday."

Ben scowled. "What changed his tune?"

"Other detectives mentioned my C.I. status with you."

"Did Rossini suggest you get involved in the Hank Payne investigation?"

"The call came in before he had a chance. But even if that's why he stopped by, I'd refuse to join his team."

Ben drummed his fingers on the granite countertop. "Good to hear. You've landed in harm's way too often. In hindsight, I regret that I allowed you to snoop for me."

"I don't need your apology, Ben. I barged into your first case to protect a friend from wrongful suspicion."

His hand covered his mouth to stifle a yawn.

Gwen leaned across the counter. "You probably haven't slept well for days. You endured the red eye flight. Exhaustion has caught up with you, Ben. Go home and get some well-deserve sleep."

He swallowed a final sip of coffee and slipped off the stool. "You do *best friend* very well, Gwen."

In the foyer, he slid his arms into his coat sleeves, shoved his feet into his boots, and squatted down to tie the laces.

Because Ben no longer blocked Gwen's view of the foyer table, she spotted Parker grinning at her from the treasured beach walk photo as he always did.

She now regretted telling Ben about her conversation with Betty. Not only her admitted fondness for him but Betty's suggestion that Gwen's growing affection for Ben could be the reason for Parker's no-shows.

Was Parker's absence pushing her toward Ben?

Or was Ben the reason Parker hadn't been responding to her calls?

Only Parker's spirit could answer those questions.

Ben grunted as he straightened, kissed Gwen's cheek, then reached for the antique door handle, saying, "I'll call you later about dinner.

Mired in conflicting contradictions, Gwen watched his red Corvette ease around the village green, careful not to lose control on the snowy surfaces.

She valued Ben's friendship, but she wasn't ready to abandon or endanger her connection with Parker's spirit.

In that instant, she decided to call Parker without Ben's involvement.

Chapter Eighteen

...late morning, Wednesday

With Jenna embroiled in classes, and Ben returned to his condo, Gwen headed upstairs and sat on a cushion at the bank of windows.

When Amber hopped up and snuggled against Gwen's thigh, she let her hand rest on the cat's soft fur.

Filling her lungs, she released the air then called, "Parker, can you hear my voice?"

Her focus slowly roved the sitting room, but Parker's shimmering form did not materialize.

With each successive repetition of his name and a plea to show himself, her volume and desperate tone ramped up. Easing away from Amber, Gwen got to her feet and circled the entire mezzanine, all the while calling Parker's name.

What was she hoping for? A stronger satellite signal?

Warm tears collected but didn't spill.

What would she do if Parker's spirit never appeared again? Could she tuck her deep love into the recesses of her heart and welcome Ben more fully into her life?

Could she?

Would she?

How did other widows justify moving on with a new man? Some re-married once, twice, even three or four times. Did they feel a sense of disloyalty to each previous husband?

Suspending her attempt to connect with Parker – at least for now – she returned to her cushion and pulled her cell from her pocket. She searched for local grieving groups and found several. Her imagination took flight. Wouldn't it be fascinating if she met a widow with a ghost husband?

Making a mental note to visit a meeting soon, she drifted downstairs. The instant she added another log to the fire, her doorbell chimed. Had Ben left something behind? Glancing around the living room, she noticed nothing out of place so hurried through the foyer to open the front door where she found Det. Sgt. Ryan Rossini and Officer Cole Martin.

"Good morning. Another visit so soon?"

Rossini's expression appeared as inscrutable as her cat's.

"If you'll invite us inside, Mrs. Andrews, I'll explain."

Both men again removed their boots before she led them into the living room.

When Rossini took up a position at the mantle, Cole stood to one side.

"I'll get straight to the point," Rossini began. "Yesterday afternoon, we again interviewed the Tuckers and came away with the strong impression that they're protecting one of their own for the stabbing of Hank Payne. To use an old phrase, they've circled their wagons."

Gwen opted to remain standing so she wouldn't encourage them to stay any longer than necessary.

"That's interesting."

Lifting an eyebrow at her vapid response, Rossini spoke again. "Based on your behind-the-scenes assistance for Det. Snowcrest, Chief Brown suggested we involve you in the Tucker-Payne investigation."

There it was, Gwen fumed. Though the satisfaction of untangling a mystery enticed her, she respected Ben's reminder that she'd found herself cornered during previous sleuthing exploits and placed her own life at risk. He'd also warned her against getting more deeply involved with Shirley's family troubles.

To forestall her reaction to Rossini's proposal, Gwen asked, "Is there evidence against a Tucker family member?"

Rossini shifted his weight. "The fingerprints on the knife handle most likely belong to Filomena Tucker. The lab report will confirm."

Sliding behind the sofa to create a barrier between herself and the brusque Rossini, Gwen recalled the block of knives near Filly's stove and couldn't imagine the stately woman stabbing anyone. To Rossini, Gwen said, "No surprise if that knife came from her kitchen. The attacker could have worn gloves."

Rossini's expression remained arrogant. "In addition to Mrs. Tucker, I'm also suspicious of Shirley Knapp. Though she claims she stumbled upon Hank Payne bleeding in the snow, she could have arrived earlier than she says and stabbed her cousin."

Ben had asked the same question. Gwen had objected.

Before Rossini had a chance to continue, Gwen again forestalled him by asking, "How about Norman Tucker's statement?"

Rossini began to pace back and forth at the hearth. "He woke up and was released from the hospital late yesterday."

"Does he recall any details about Monday's incident?"

Coming to a halt, Rossini regarded Gwen as if she were a precocious child, but still he responded. "He claims no recollection of why he was lying on the floor or who stabbed his grandson."

Gwen muttered, "That's convenient."

"It is," Rossini surprisingly agreed.

Though Gwen had liked Norman Tucker, she could easily imagine the gruff old man protecting a family member from arrest.

Rossini kept talking. "As we were checking backgrounds, we came upon news about Hank Payne's recent activities."

Goosebumps pimpled Gwen's arms. "What was that?"

"He's suspected of robbing a convenience store last Saturday, injuring the owner and his wife before fleeing on his motorcycle."

Gwen drew in a sharp breath.

Rossini waved at Cole Martin. "Did you bring that bulletin?"

Nodding, Cole withdrew several printouts from a deep pocket of his police parka, holding one out for Gwen to see.

"This frame is from the store's security camera. There's a definite resemblance to the face of Hank Payne that we viewed at the coroner's office."

Rossini said, "Tell her the rest."

Cole separated a second printout from the first. "A subsequent frame showed this same man speeding away on a motorcycle. We concluded that he'd been eluding capture by hiding out with his Tucker relatives in Harbor Falls."

The fact that these two policemen were sharing case details only emphasized the reason they remained in her living room. Gwen's internal debate about joining their investigation raged, her decision teetering. To delay her response, she asked, "Was Hank by himself?"

Cole glanced at Rossini. "Should I answer, sir?"

Rossini waved his hand as permission.

Cole continued. "The range of the store's security camera is limited, but see the shadow of a second person inside the store?"

Moving around the couch to Gwen's side, Cole held the grainy printout so she could follow along, pointing to the left of the man they'd identified as Hank.

Gwen asked. "And did this other person also speed away on a motorcycle?"

"Not that the security camera captured," Cole replied. "But the two of them could have split up and gone in opposite directions."

Envisioning dire consequences if she agreed to work with Rossini and Cole, Gwen opted to put them on the defensive. "So you have no idea if this potential second thief was a threat to the Tucker family or Hank himself?"

Rossini furrowed his forehead. "If he was involved in the robbery and assault on the owner and his wife, plus is aware of Hank's relatives in Harbor Falls, that shadow person might have already shown up and eliminated Hank."

Gwen's nerves on end, she reacted. "So you're saying that someone besides Filly Tucker or Shirley Knapp could have stabbed Hank."

"That's correct," Rossini answered. "In addition to those two suspects within the Tucker family, there's a potential third out-of-towner. We held back the detail of Hank Payne's death from the local media. If his accomplice roars into town, we'll capture and arrest at least for the robbery."

Gwen stared at them both. "Your theories are based on grainy frames from a security camera." She paused while her comment registered. "You both need to understand that my sleuthing for Ben did not include a potential run-in with a career criminal."

Rossini tried and failed to reduce her concern.

"Don't panic, Mrs. Andrews. Our patrolmen have been alerted to watch for any suspicious strangers, with or without a motorcycle."

Crossing her arms, Gwen glared first at Rossini and then at Cole Martin. "For one thing, you don't have any details about that shadow person. And for another, I'm not experienced or equipped to deal with ruffians."

Gwen didn't offer that she'd defended herself in the past with whatever weapons were handy. Once a cast iron skillet, another time a 2x4 length of lumber.

"And we don't expect you to," Rossini promised. "We only need you to determine if one of the Tuckers is our more likely culprit." He paused. "Or eliminate all of them."

Gwen suspected he'd dangled that last comment to give her hope that neither Shirley nor her Aunt Filly were guilty of the stabbing.

Playing his game, Gwen came back with, "Now you seem convinced that the stabber was a family member."

"Investigations always follow several paths of possibility until the truth is uncovered," Rossini declared, stretching his hand toward Cole, palm open. "Your interview notes."

Cole dug into the other deep pocket of his police parka and pulled out folded papers, handing them to Rossini.

Rossini passed them to Gwen. "These are the interview

notes from Monday morning, and again yesterday."

When she didn't reach out for the pages, Rossini leaned down and placed them on the low table, then pointed at them. "Read through the responses from the family members to prepare yourself for personal conversations with each of them."

Without giving her a chance to either agree or refuse his instructions, Rossini half-turned toward her foyer.

After a single step, he pivoted back. "I don't think a Confidential Informant arrangement is necessary in this case, so if you unearth any significant clues, pass them along to Officer Martin."

Without another word, they both exited.

Speechless at his assumption that she was cooperating, Gwen slammed the door shut.

Chapter Nineteen

...mid-afternoon, Wednesday

Swiping condensation from her living room window, Gwen watched the police sedan crawl around Library Lane.

Reluctantly, she retrieved Cole's photocopies, spread them out, and flattened the creases with her fingers.

She wondered if Cole had been relieved that she hadn't mentioned his interest in Jenna in front of Rossini. Given Cole's goal to become a member of the detective squad, he must have worried that Rossini would consider Cole's pursuit of Jenna a conflict of interest.

Was Cole aware that Jenna intended to keep him at arm's length? Gwen almost felt sorry for the young man but knew better than to involve herself in their personal business.

Turning her attention to the interview notes, but still conflicted about snooping on the Tucker family, Gwen gained no clues from the scribbled questions and answers.

She tossed the photocopies onto Parker's recliner.

Snooping for Rossini did not interest her. The man still rubbed her the wrong way. Was she put off by his general pompousness or him turning a deaf ear to her objections where the Tucker family was concerned?

Rossini was no Ben Snowcrest.

Because Gwen did her best thinking while distracted by mindless cleaning, she rushed up the staircase and changed into tattered jeans and a frayed sweatshirt.

Returning to the kitchen, she located her spray bottle of white vinegar water under the sink and grabbed a package of microfiber clothes. She moved from one ground-floor window to the next, spraying, then wiping away the excess moisture while making each windowpane sparkle.

The downstairs finished, she proceeded up the staircase and repeated the process until all the glass glistened.

While she'd been removing the condensation, Gwen's mind revisited the events of each day since Annabelle knocked on her door early Sunday morning to deliver Shirley's summons.

By the time Gwen stored the remaining solution beneath the kitchen sink, she'd decided to refuse Rossini's suggestion that she join his investigation. She'd do her best to deny his request as tactfully as possible without insulting the man.

**

Finding she had little appetite, Gwen ate only a few forkfuls of rotisserie chicken salad while Amber delicately nibbled on cat food.

As Gwen chewed, she watched the midday news on the kitchen's small TV screen, paying close attention to each segment. No mention of Hank Payne's stabbing or his death during surgery. Rossini had indeed kept the Tucker family out of the public eye. For the time being anyway.

Aware that cat hair needed to be sucked up again, Gwen wrestled her vacuum from the closet. Amber stared at the monster and raced upstairs.

Gwen had considered buying an iRobot. But the open levels of the converted library eliminated that idea. The poor i-Robot would either tumble down the staircase or get stuck beneath the mezzanine railing.

***

The afternoon flew by until Ben called around four, telling Gwen, "I slept like a baby and now I'm famished. If your appetite matches mine, we don't need a reservation for the early bird specials at The Wharf."

With such a light lunch, Gwen was indeed hungry. Plus she was anxious to share her decision to refuse Rossini's plan for her to spy on the Tucker family.

To Ben, she said, "I'll be ready in fifteen minutes. But I need to clear my head, so let's walk."

"Fine with me. A winter stroll sounds refreshing after the Albuquerque desert. I'm on my way."

Looking down at her housework garb, Gwen hurried to her bedroom and changed into black leggings, an oversized sweater, and thick wool socks to keep her feet warm.

When the roar of Ben's Corvette announced his arrival,

she opened her front door, welcoming the fresh winter air.

As Ben approached, a half-smile parted his lips.

Resisting the urge to again reach out and stroke his soft beard, she said, "I'm so glad you're back from New Mexico."

His grey eyes searched hers. "Has something happened since I left after breakfast this morning?"

"Your sixth sense is as perceptive as ever. I'll explain while we stroll. Ready?"

He nodded, and Gwen locked the door behind her.

As they entered the postcard-perfect village green, the glow from the tall lamp lights bordering the pathways reflected off the mostly undisturbed snow.

As they each placed one booted foot in front of the other, Ben said, "So tell me what's happened."

Before Gwen could say a word, her usual sure-footedness deserted her and one boot skidded. She windmilled her arms to regain her balance.

In an instant, Ben reached over and kept her on her feet.

As he held onto her, she imagined a bruised tailbone or sprained wrist if he hadn't acted so quickly. "Thanks. I'll be more watchful about where I'm stepping."

Still gripping her, he met her eyes. "Could happen to anyone. Should we go back and drive to The Wharf?"

His body heat warmed her. "No, no. Let's keep going. But if you don't mind, let's hold onto each other."

"Don't mind at all. If one goes down, we both go down?"
She chuckled at his quip. "Hopefully neither."

Chapter Twenty

...late afternoon, Wednesday

By the time they entered the restaurant, Gwen had finished telling Ben about the second visit from Rossini and Martin.

Settling at a window table with a view of the flickering harbor lights in the late day dusk, she ordered broiled scallops. Ben opted for steak tips.

While waiting for their meals, Ben leaned his forearms on the white tablecloth. "You mentioned Officer Martin's notes. If I'm not interfering, I'd like to review them when we get back to your place."

Gwen was quick to reassure him. "Ben, you're the last person I'd accuse of interfering. If I didn't want you to know about Rossini and Martin's plans, I wouldn't have mentioned their two visits."

"I'm flattered that you respect my opinion."

"Of course I do."

After a female server delivered their meals, they ate in affable silence, focused on the food and their thoughts.

When Gwen ate the last crumb, she crossed her knife and fork to signal the server that she'd finished her meal.

Glancing at Ben, she said, "Shall we skip dessert?"

"My thoughts exactly," Ben agreed. Signaling their server, he handed her his credit card then signed the charge.

Guiding Gwen out the restaurant door, they encountered bone-chilling January air.

"The temperature must have dropped at least ten degrees while we ate dinner," she declared.

"We should have driven down, Gwen."

"Or I could have cooked us a nice meal."

"Too late now. Let's go before it gets any colder."

Treading up Harbor Hill arm-in-arm, they retraced their earlier path through the village green and entered Gwen's home before most people had prepared their supper.

She reached for Cole's photocopies in Parker's recliner and handed the initial set to Ben. "These are the notes from the first interviews on Monday after Shirley discovered Hank in the snow."

"Give me a sec to review these," Ben murmured, scanning the questions and answers.

While he absorbed the details, Gwen laid a fire and struck a match.

When she settled beside Ben on the sofa, he tapped the photocopy. "These first interviews gathered basic facts from the family who reside in the Victorian." He ran his finger down the notes, reading out loud:

...name, phone number, address

...relationship to the family

...what time had they last seen Hank Payne
... same question about Norman Tucker
... had Hank or Norman mentioned expecting a visitor?
...did they hear a disturbance early Monday morning?

Ben peered at Gwen. "You're not included here."

"That's right," Gwen confirmed. "Rossini had told me to go home. But I hung around on the front sidewalk until he waved Shirley inside. There was nothing more to hear."

Ben laid down the first notes and picked up the second batch, scanning quickly. "These are dated yesterday when Rossini and Martin returned to the Victorian."

When he finished reading, Ben spoke. "It says here that they gathered the family in the kitchen but interviewed each person in the dining room. You've been inside that house. Could the people waiting in one room hear the conversation in the next?"

Gwen thought back. "I think there was a pocket door between those two rooms. I assume Rossini or Cole pulled it closed for privacy, but I'm only guessing."

Returning his attention to the notes, Ben said, "Only Daryl Whitcomb offered a suggestion about the sequence of the injuries. These other two couples contributed little."

Gwen leaned closer for another look at Cole Martin's scribbles. "What did Daryl say exactly?"

"That Norman Tucker fell out of his hospital bed trying to stop Hank's attacker," Ben supplied.

"That's one possible scenario," Gwen commented.

"I agree. But unless Norman's memory returns, the pieces of this puzzle will be difficult to connect."

Ben shook his head. "These unhelpful answers support Sgt. Rossini's assumption that the family is protecting one of their own. How many people from Rossini's second interviews did you meet?" He handed her Cole's notes.

Gwen reached across and picked up a pencil from her reunion planning. Running her finger down the notes, she placed a checkmark beside the Tuckers she'd met, saying each name out loud. "Filly and Norman Tucker. Daryl and Doris Whitcomb. I don't recognize the names of these other two couples. They must not have come down on Sunday."

She flipped the photocopy to the other side and back again. "On Sunday morning, Lawrence Tucker, his daughter Jennifer, and her baby, Olivia, walked in from a snowy stroll. Jennifer took the baby upstairs to change her diaper. Lawrence didn't mention where he lives, but they're not included in these notes from the second interview group."

Ben said, "Shirley's name isn't listed either."

"I noticed that, too, but I haven't heard from her since Monday, so I have no idea why she wasn't there."

Ben pushed himself up from the leather sofa, striding toward the hearth before reversing his stance. "You said Martin showed you other documents this afternoon?"

"He did but didn't leave me a copy."

125

Gwen described the bulletin about Hank being suspected of robbing a convenience store plus the printout from the security camera of the shadow person.

Adding more detail, she continued. "Rossini labeled the shadow person as Hank's potential partner-in-crime, and possibly on his way to Harbor Falls to eliminate Hank as a witness to the robbery and assault."

Ben paused for a second. "Cole Martin might have downloaded the footage from the store's security camera. I can't believe Rossini wants to pull you into an investigation that could involve a second criminal. And you say Chief Brown suggested that Rossini approach you?"

Gwen was equally concerned about her vulnerability if she agreed to infiltrate the Tucker family. "That's what Rossini told me. I didn't agree to join his team, but I didn't actually refuse either. I need to inform him that I'm not going to risk it. Plus, he wants me to sleuth behind the scenes without a Confidential Informant agreement."

Glancing at his watch, Ben said, "Chief Brown might still be in his office.. I'm going to the station and find out what he's thinking about Rossini. I'll call you later."

Gwen stood in her doorway and watched Ben approach his Corvette, only then realizing she hadn't mentioned Rossini withholding Hank Payne's death from the press.

Such a cover-up might not be possible these days.

Especially when a member of the family *is* the press.

Chapter Twenty-One
...late afternoon, Wednesday

Ben frowned at his Corvette. The reflection of Gwen's security light drew his attention to the muddy snow splashes marring the sports car's shiny red paint. Fortunately, after retiring the previous summer, he'd moved into a condo with a heated two-car garage, where he could handwash and wax his Corvette any time. He'd take care of that chore after he returned from speaking with the chief.

Perhaps it was time to buy a second car or maybe a pick-up truck for driving in New England's inclement weather.

He opened the car door, buckled into the leather form-fitting driver's seat, and turned the key. There was nothing more satisfying than the purr of the eight-cylinder engine.

Shifting into low gear, he drove at a safe speed until pulling into the visitor parking lot at the police station.

He entered through the front door for the first time – he'd always used the officers' entrance around back – and strolled to the tinted glass reception window.

Though Ben hadn't retired that long ago, he couldn't recall the name of the female officer gesturing toward the microphone encased in the thick glass.

Smiling, she asked, "May I help you?"

Ben felt a bit awkward as he leaned down to answer. "I'd like to see Chief Brown if he's in the building."

"Your name, please."

"Benjamin Snowcrest."

As she jotted his name on a clipboard, she lifted her eyes and studied his face. "I'm so sorry, Detective Snowcrest. I didn't recognize you with that white beard and mustache. Very professorial."

Her name popped onto Ben's tongue. "Thanks for the compliment, Patsy. Great to see you, too."

"Hold on and I'll check if the chief's available."

Pushing buttons on the desk phone, she spoke, then listened, then jumped to her feet to unlock the side door, waving Ben through. "The chief said to send you up."

Ben thanked her, entered the elevator, and pressed the button for the second floor.

When the doors slid open, Chief Mike Brown was quickstepping toward Ben, his right hand outstretched.

"Ben, you old coot." After a quick shake, Mike tugged Ben's neatly trimmed beard. "What's this white stuff?"

"The ladies seem to like it," Ben bragged.

The two men had known each other for decades as they chased criminals in Harbor Falls until Ben retired the previous year. Their relationship remained easy, their mutual respect unwavering.

"Let's go to my office," Mike said, passing the open area of the detective squad. One of the men looked up at Ben, grinned and waved.

Ben returned the greeting then veered into Mike's office.. He sat in one of two hard uncomfortable guest chairs, meant to keep visits short.

Settling behind his desk, Mike rested his folded arms on the blotter. "To what do I owe the honor?" Stretching closer, he added, "Bored with retirement?"

"Not at all. I just returned from a trip to Albuquerque."

"Another gig as a consultant?"

Ben opted not to explain his father's death. "Keeping tabs on me, are you?"

Mike raised one eyebrow. "Did you think I wouldn't? Smart to apply for your PI license when you retired. Would hate to see your talents wasted."

"Nice to know you've still got my back."

"Always, my friend."

Mike tapped a pencil on the desk blotter. "If you didn't come to see me because you're bored, tell me the reason you're sitting across from me."

Wanting to tread lightly about Rossini's suggestion that Gwen should sleuth for him, Ben said simply, "The stabbing at the Victorian on South Street."

"Do you know the Tucker family?"

When Ben shook his head, Mike held up his hand like a

traffic cop. "I know why you're bringing up that incident."

Ben waited for the chief to complete his prediction.

With an assessing glance, Mike said, "You're uneasy that Sgt. Rossini asked for Gwen's assistance with the case."

"Good guess, Mike."

"Hold on. Let me see if Sgt. Rossini's left for the day."

Mike paused at his office door and scanned the detective den across the hall, then walked off.

While Ben waited for the chief's return, he listened to the familiar buzz of the police station. Phones ringing, computer keys tapping, plus animated conversations competing with each other.

Within minutes, footsteps echoed outside the door and the chief re-entered, followed by a tall beefy man in an expensive-looking suit, his face weathered, a manila case file clutched in one hand.

"Ben Snowcrest, meet Detective Sergeant Ryan Rossini. He came on board after you retired."

Getting to his feet, Ben extended his hand, studying the man who'd taken his place as lead detective.

With a brief handshake, Rossini said, "Good to meet you, Snowcrest. The older detectives have mentioned you."

Ben stiffened. Was that a comment about his age? Rossini was hardly a spring chicken.

Mike waved to the second guest chair. "Have a seat."

After he sat, Rossini repositioned his trouser creases.

Chapter Twenty-Two

...late afternoon, Wednesday

Chief Brown glanced at Ben, then back to Rossini. "I'd like you to update us about the Tucker-Payne incident."

Though Ben knew many of the details from Gwen's limited perspective, he was interested to hear Rossini's official version.

Pushing back his chair, the sergeant stood and opened his case file, then looked down his nose at Ben.

"Very early Monday morning, *Gazette* reporter Shirley Knapp claims she came upon her cousin Hank Payne near the front steps of the Victorian house on South Street. He was bleeding from a knife wound in his back."

Rossini waved his hand as if he were a renowned lawyer addressing a jury.

"Knapp dialed 9-1-1. Very convenient and the reason she's one of my two suspects for the stabbing."

Chief Brown nodded his agreement. "Understandable."

Ben remained silent to hear the rest of Rossini's report.

"After Payne was rushed to the emergency room, Officer Cole Martin noticed the front door stood ajar and walked inside. He found Norman Tucker lying on the floor beside his temporary hospital bed, his wife cradling his head in her lap. Martin called for a second ambulance and then me."

Rossini flipped to the next page of notes. "Mrs. Tucker accompanied her husband to the emergency room. Martin and I spoke with other residents at the Victorian, all members of the family. None of them claim knowledge of the stabbing."

Rossini again glanced down at Ben. "On Tuesday afternoon we dropped in on Mrs. Gwen Andrews."

Chief Brown held up his hand. "Explain your reason."

"Certainly. One of the older detectives in my squad mentioned that Mrs. Andrews had been a valuable asset as Snowcrest's Confidential Informant. Unaware of her status, I dismissed her out-of-hand at the scene on Monday morning and I felt I should make amends."

When the chief didn't interrupt, Rossini kept talking. "While we were at her home, a call came to my cell that Hank Payne had died during surgery and our stabbing incident was elevated to a murder investigation. Yesterday, Officer Martin and I arranged a second round of questions with the relatives who had been on the property Monday morning. We took fingerprints for background checks."

Shifting his weight, Rossini focused on the chief. "By the way, the *Gazette* reporter Shirley Knapp, who lives in her own apartment on the other side of town, didn't attend the second interviews so we didn't get her fingerprints. I've contacted her to report to me here." He glanced at his watch. "She should be arriving soon."

Without commenting, the chief said, "Tell Ben why you arranged a second conversation with Gwen Andrews."

"Of course," Rossini replied. "Because I suspected the Tuckers were protecting one of their own and was now aware of Mrs. Andrews solving a few of your cases, Snowcrest," Rossini tossed a cocky expression at Ben, "I thought we should make use of her ability to uncover important clues behind the scenes."

Stiffening, Ben resented Rossini's implication of incompetence but said nothing.

The chief must have noticed Ben's physical reaction. "Ben, I agreed with Rossini that Gwen could be a valuable asset. But I want him to share the rest of his investigation before we hear your input about Gwen's involvement."

Though Ben had a lot to say about them roping Gwen into helping them identify Hank Payne's attacker, he followed Mike's suggestion and kept his mouth shut.

The chief waved his hand. "Please continue, Sergeant."

Rossini removed a document from the manila file and extended it to the chief. "I asked Officer Martin to search the law enforcement websites for background information. This wanted poster came up."

Accepting the printout from Rossini, Chief Brown murmured, "Hmmm. Hank Payne is wanted for robbing a convenience store last week and injuring the owners."

"Can I see that?" Ben asked then studied the image. The man's head was bowed, so the camera angle from a higher elevation didn't capture his facial features, but the unruly black hair and long scruffy black beard matched Gwen's description. Ben now understood her negative reaction to the oversized Hank Payne.

Reaching for the wanted poster, the chief said, "Anything else in your case file, Sergeant?"

"Yes, sir. When Martin came across the wanted poster, there was a link to footage from the store's security camera." He retrieved another printout and handed it across the desk. "This expanded recording shows the robber leaning over the check-out counter, his arms stretched as if reaching for the cash drawer. This face was used on the wanted poster."

The chief inspected the image, asking, "Does this photo resemble the stabbed man?"

Rossini cleared his throat as though nervous. "I didn't arrive on the scene until Payne had been rushed to the emergency room. But when I accompanied Mrs. Tucker to the morgue yesterday, she identified that man as her grandson. He's the same guy."

The chief passed the printout to Ben.

Pulling another sheet from the folder, Rossini explained, "This frame shows him speeding away on a motorcycle."

Rossini pulled a fourth printout. "This is the most

important frame that takes us beyond Hank Payne's identification. This one shows the shadow of another person to his left, implying a possible accomplice."

Leaning forward in his chair, the chief spread out the four prints, concealing his blotter. "Have you spoken with the store owner and his wife about this shadow?"

"Not yet," Rossini admitted, his cocky expression fading.

"Have you touched base with the detectives in the town where the robbery took place?"

Rossini's face reddened as he repeated, "Not yet."

Struggling to maintain his professionalism, Ben had expected at least phone calls to gather more details.

Before Rossini had a chance to excuse his delay, the chief mentioned an earlier comment. "You suggested a second family suspect for the stabbing. Who is that?"

Rossini opened the empty folder and quickly closed it. "That would be Filomena Tucker, Norman Tucker's wife."

"Why do you suspect her of stabbing their grandson?"

"During the initial interviews, when she was with her husband at the emergency room, one of the relatives murmured that she wasn't very happy to have Hank Payne staying under their roof."

"Did you ask that relative to expand his statement?"

"No, sir, because whoever mumbled those words wouldn't come forward with more detail. Then one of the women pointed out that a knife was missing from the wooden block in the kitchen. I suspect it's the same knife removed from Payne's back. The lab will confirm Mrs. Tucker's fingerprints on the handle."

Straining to contain his impatience at the unverified leap to suspicion, Ben studied Rossini. How competent would this detective prove to be?

The chief collected the four printouts covering his blotter and handed them to Rossini. "Are you expecting any more documents?"

Rossini appeared grateful that he could provide a positive response. "Yes, sir. The lab report on the knife plus additional background checks on the family members."

Chapter Twenty-Three

...early evening, Wednesday

When Ben heard the chief address him, he forced himself to stop staring at Rossini. The sergeant's efforts had been mediocre at best.

"Sorry, Chief," Ben said. "I was absorbing the details of this case. What did you ask me?"

The chief smirked at Ben. "Do you have any comments about Gwen joining Rossini's investigative team?"

Finally able to upset Rossini's apple cart, Ben said, "To begin with, Rossini told Gwen that a C.I. Agreement won't be necessary."

The chief focused his hooded glare on Rossini. "That's incorrect, Sergeant. All CIs need to be registered."

Rossini sniffed. "Then I'll have her sign one."

The chief again turned to Ben. "Anything else?"

Ben debated whether his next comment would be considered petty, deciding he needed to place all his cards on the table. "Yes. Gwen didn't agree to work behind the scenes for Rossini."

His face again reddening, Rossini stammered, "But, but, before we left her home this afternoon, I outlined her infiltration of the Tuckers and instructed her to report all findings to Officer Martin."

"She heard you loud and clear," Ben confirmed, "but she didn't say that she'd do it."

"Snowcrest," Rossini blustered. "You need to convince her to help us solve this case, just like she solved yours."

Irritated by Rossini's demand plus his repeated implication that Ben had relied on Gwen's sleuthing to solve his own cases, Ben shot back, "I won't convince Gwen to do anything that makes her uncomfortable."

The chief interrupted. "Hold on there, Ben. Do you know why Gwen is hesitating? This won't be the first time she's assisted with an investigation. All of them yours, as Rossini pointed out."

Ben repositioned his weight on the uncomfortable chair and rested his forearms on his thighs, interlocking his fingers to control his simmering anger. "Gwen has worked behind the scenes for *me* because a friend of hers was suspected of wrongdoing. She's always had a personal reason for getting involved."

"The Tuckers aren't her friends?" the chief asked.

Ben shook his head. "Hardly. On Sunday morning, Shirley Knapp renewed her acquaintance with Gwen by calling her to the Victorian and introducing her to an aunt and uncle and a few other relatives. Hank Payne – who's arrival stirred up old resentments among the family members – lumbered into the kitchen while Gwen was sitting with a few members of the family, bragging that he'd stayed overnight. Shirley had thought that Gwen's even-keeled nature could calm everyone's nerves. Prior to that, Gwen had never met any of the Tuckers."

"Well, there you go, Snowcrest," Rossini blustered. "When the unfailing Mrs. Andrews uncovers the real culprit, she'll clear her revived friend Shirley Knapp from my suspect list."

Still on his feet, Rossini lifted his chin and repeated his stare down his bulging nose at Ben. "If Shirley Knapp is innocent, that is."

Trying hard to ignore Rossini's snide remark, Ben added fuel to the simmering firestorm. "In addition to Gwen's lack of connection to the family, she's not trained to defend herself from that possible accomplice in the robbery."

The chief switched his focus to Rossini. "That's a valid resistance, Sergeant. Gwen isn't qualified to deal with career criminals. Don't you agree?"

Rossini shifted to his other foot. "I suppose so. If the shadow is an accomplice, he'd want to tie up loose ends."

Ben spoke up. "A confrontation at the Tucker home could turn ugly in a split second. I don't blame Gwen for withholding her sleuthing skills."

As if sensing Ben's growing irritation with Rossini, the chief stood and circled his desk, positioning himself between the standing Rossini and the seated Ben. Reaching sideways for the knob, he opened his office door. "That'll be all for now, Sergeant. I'll hold onto that case file for now. Thanks for your report."

Rossini reluctantly placed the file in the chief's hand and skulked out the door.

Chapter Twenty-four

...early evening, Wednesday

Observing Rossini's shocked expression at the chief's rather abrupt dismissal, Ben waited for the office door to latch before asking, "Where did you find this guy, Mike?"

The chief shrugged. "I needed someone to take your place, Ben, and manage the detective squad. Rossini made a good first impression and his credentials held up."

"Why not promote one of my detectives?"

"None of them felt qualified to fill your shoes."

Shaking his head, Ben rested his forearms on the front edge of Mike's desk. "A different alternate scenario of the stabbing has occurred to me."

"Enlighten me," Mike encouraged.

Ben's hands gestured as he shared his imagined scene. "What if that possible accomplice snuck into Harbor Falls early Monday morning to eliminate Hank Payne? The guy could have arrived under cover of darkness and spotted Hank coming out the Victorian's kitchen door. Seeing his angry accomplice, Hank ducked back inside. The guy chased after him, grabbing the kitchen knife on his way past the wooden block. The commotion woke Norman Tucker, who tried to intervene but his cast got hung up in the bed sheets. He fell out of bed and his head smacked the hardwood floor, knocking him unconscious. As Hank opened the front door, the accomplice caught up with him and plunged the knife into his back. Hank stumbled across the veranda and tripped, his head clipping the concrete step before he landed in the snow where Shirley found him."

Raising one eyebrow, Mike murmured, "You have a vivid imagination, Ben. If that's an accurate scenario, don't you think the accomplice would have stuck around to be sure Hank was dead?"

Ben shrugged. "Grasping at straws, Mike. Maybe Mrs. Tucker screamed when she came upon Norman and the guy fled. He could still be hiding in town."

Mike drummed his fingers on the blotter. "Got any other theories to contribute?"

Getting to his feet, Ben crossed his arms and paced as he hypothesized. "Norman Tucker claims no memory of his fall from his bed. The family members claim they saw nothing. At this point, no one knows what actually happened. Boot prints would have been helpful, but I'm guessing the EMTs trampled the snow around Payne as they tried to keep him alive. Checking for a second set of motorcycle tire prints, plus conversations with the store owner and the other police department could clarify some of the details."

Mike waved at the guest chair. "Sit down, Ben."

His curiosity peaked, Ben sat. "You gonna say I'm crazy?"

"Hardly. You've always thought outside the proverbial box. You're right – there are unasked questions and a lack of follow-up. I'm thinking to reassign Rossini and hire you as our consulting detective."

His pulse quickening, Ben leaned closer. "Won't that embarrass him?"

"Not if I convince him that a different crime is more urgent than this one."

Not expecting this turn of events, Ben considered Mike's offer. "Is there any detail Rossini skipped over?"

"Only one. He's been keeping Hank Payne's death under wraps to increase our chances of catching the second criminal – if there was one. If the other guy arrived early Monday morning to eliminate Hank, that would support your alternate scenario."

Ben nodded. "But if I'm wrong, the shadow accomplice could still be on his way to Harbor Falls to search for Hank. A confrontation at the Tucker home could turn very ugly very quickly. Is Gwen aware of Rossini's tactic?"

"I don't know if he told her or not," Mike answered. "Do you want me to ask him if he mentioned this detail?"

Ben rose to his feet. "No, I'll ask her myself."

"I'm hoping you'll consider working this case for us, Ben. Should I submit the paperwork to hire you?"

143

"Not yet, Mike."

Ben paused and pointed at the case file. "Can I have copies of those printouts and the wanted poster?"

"Sure. In fact, take the entire case file while you're debating my offer." Mike held out the manila folder. "You know, Ben, that white beard and mustache doesn't give the impression that you're a topnotch investigator."

Ben smoothed his beard, still surprised to find it on his face. "An unintended bonus, Mike."

Chapter Twenty-Five

...late afternoon, Wednesday

Soon after Ben left to confront Chief Brown about Rossini's request for her assistance, Gwen opened her front door to discover Shirley Knapp standing on the top step, punching furiously at her cell phone.

Beyond Shirley, snowflakes created tiny shadows as they passed through the pale light of the lanterns in the village green.

Gwen moved aside. "Come in. I see it's snowing again."

"Very observant," Shirley snipped as she stepped over the wide oak threshold.

Wondering the reason for Shirley's unexpected visit, not to mention her curt attitude, Gwen hung the reporter's coat while Shirley removed her boots.

Gwen settled Shirley in the chair nearest the fire, saying, "Would you like a cup of hot something?"

"Thanks but nothing. Sorry about my bad mood, Gwen. It turns out I can't stay long."

Not sure she wanted to know the reason, Gwen lowered herself onto Parker's recliner and asked, "Why's that?"

Shirley held up her cell.

"Sergeant Rossini texted that he wants me to *'drop over'* to review my Monday morning statement. I should have known I'd hear from him again."

"Because..." Gwen prompted.

Shirley snapped, "Because I didn't show up at Aunt Filly's yesterday afternoon for Rossini's second round of questions. Damn it, Gwen. I've been worried he'd target me for stabbing Hank because I dialed 9-1-1."

Trying her best to remain an outsider, Gwen didn't feel it her place to confirm Shirley's status as a suspect in Rossini's eyes. Nor would Gwen mention his additional skepticism of Filly's innocence based on his assumption that the lab would identify her fingerprints on the knife handle.

Gwen didn't take her eyes off Shirley. "And you think that's why Rossini is calling you to the station?"

"Why else would he request a review? I hate to think someone in my family stabbed Hank, but I didn't do it, Gwen. That means one of the cousins or an aunt or an uncle must have. They all hated Hank."

Gwen opted not to reveal her insider knowledge of the shadow person on the convenience store security recording. The connection between that person and Hank was still pure speculation. No need to muddy the waters.

"Before I go, Gwen, I need to ask a favor."

Unable to prevent the obvious reaction, Gwen asked, "What favor is that?"

Shirley first stared into her lap, then raised her eyes to focus on Gwen's. "First of all, I'm aware of your prior behind-the-scenes sleuthing for Ben Snowcrest."

Shocked that Shirley was privy to the identity of Confidential Informants, Gwen hurried to uncover the connection. "Your *Gazette* articles about the investigations when I assisted Ben never mentioned my involvement."

Shirley smirked. "Of course they didn't. I never reveal the name of any citizen who helps catch a criminal."

Though Shirley had hinted there were other C.I.'s in the Harbor Falls Police Department, she hadn't revealed if she knew their identity. Still, relief coursed through Gwen's veins and she decided to dig no further. As a reporter, Shirley would most likely claim she couldn't reveal her sources.

And so Gwen reverted to Shirley's earlier request. "So tell me about your favor.'

Stretching her hands toward the warmth of the flames, Shirley spoke sideways. "Would you be willing to help me zero in on the relative who stabbed Hank?"

When Gwen hesitated, Shirley jumped to her feet and stood with hands on hips, her short legs planted in a wide stance, stopping short of wagging her finger at Gwen. "I'm telling you here and now that I did not – and I repeat *DID NOT* – stab my cousin Hank."

Fortunately for Gwen, Shirley's cell buzzed and she punched the button to answer, ignoring the fact that Gwen hadn't reacted to the declaration of innocence.

Shirley exchanged a few words on her cell then disconnected. To Gwen, she said, "Aunt Filly has called a family meeting tomorrow. I'd like you to come with me."

Gwen's original perception that Shirley might have protested too much vaporized. If the reporter had indeed stabbed Hank, why would she risk that one of the relatives would reveal witnessing the attack?

"Did your aunt tell you the reason?" Gwen ventured.

"Yes, to discuss burial arrangements for Hank. Will you come with me?"

"Hold on, Shirley. Give me a second to think." Kneeling before the fire, Gwen poked at the logs, sending embers up the chimney.

The few details known to date whirled around inside Gwen's head. Shirley wasn't aware of Hank's potential accomplice. But if that shadow person on the security footage was eliminated, they'd be back to suspects inside the Victorian.

Needing more information, Gwen asked, "Who else will be attending Filly's meeting?"

"Cousins, uncles, aunts. You met a few who live in the Victorian on Sunday morning. Other relatives are driving from their own homes."

Despite Ben's cautionary words and Gwen's own reluctance to get more deeply involved, her penchant for solving mysteries urged her to take advantage of this opportunity. Plus, she'd much rather snoop on Shirley's behalf than for Rossini.

Shirley's voice interrupted. "I'm begging you, Gwen, to identify the relative who stabbed Hank. Because as I've told you repeatedly, I'm not the one who did it."

"Several times," Gwen confirmed. "All right, I'll go with you. Though I don't think your family members will appreciate me sticking my nose into their discussion."

Shirley reached over and hugged Gwen. "Thanks so much. I'll figure out a logical reason why I asked you to sit in. And I think I know why you're no longer resisting my request of a favor."

"Tell me, please."

"You can't resist meeting the unfamiliar relatives for the first time and the familiar ones for the second time. While you're sleuthing to nail one of them for stabbing Hank, you can accidentally bump into those who seemed willing to talk about the rest of them."

Shirley glanced at the mantel clock. "Listen, I'd better hightail it to the police station. Don't want Rossini to think I've left town to avoid him."

As Shirley headed for the front door, she turned back to Gwen. "Tomorrow morning's meeting is scheduled at ten. I'll be here at quarter 'til and we can walk over together."

Waving goodbye to Gwen, the reporter rushed out the

door and hustled toward her car parked at the curb.

Gwen stared after Shirley's departing figure.

The *Gazette* reporter seemed well versed about Gwen's sleuthing technique. Had Shirley read Gwen's reports filed for each of Ben's cases? She was tempted to ask him if Shirley rated access to the C.I. files.

Closing the door, Gwen intended to exit the foyer. Instead, she again picked up the framed picture of Parker's final photo, his cheerful expression unchanged. "I could really use your input, Parker. I've called your name so many times over the past few months. Why haven't you come to me? Parker? Parker?"

Once again, his spirit remained in the clouds.

Chapter Twenty-Six

...early evening, Wednesday

Setting Parker's photo back on the foyer table, Gwen wondered if it was still snowing outside. The persistent storm had eased only briefly since Sunday. Though she loved watching the white flakes flutter to the earth, the slippery conditions for both cars and pedestrians could turn treacherous within minutes.

Reopening the door to check the weather, Gwen nearly crashed into Ben as he bounded up her front steps.

He stopped short. "How did you know I'd return after my visit with our police chief?"

"I didn't. I'm just checking if the snow has stopped."

Ben glanced behind him. "It's tapering off."

When he faced her again, Gwen couldn't resist touching his beard. "What did our chief think about your new look?"

Ben beamed. "He says it gives me a misleading advantage when talking to witnesses and suspects."

Gwen grinned. "I think he's right."

He tapped his boots against the edge of the top step before crossing the threshold, hanging his coat, and aiming his boots toward the drip tray.

"I thought you'd be interested to hear about my conversation with Chief Mike."

"I am. Let's sit in the kitchen while I brew a pot."

A few minutes later, she handed him a mug of half-caf, then poured one for herself and settled on the opposite stool.

After blowing on the hot brew, Ben downed nearly half before saying, "Mike called Rossini into the office to report on the Hank Payne investigation."

"What a treat," Gwen wise cracked. "What do you think of Rossini?"

Ben hesitated as if searching for the right words. "I don't like to find fault with another detective, but Rossini's been slow to follow-up on several details."

"Did he happen to mention that he thinks I'll be snooping for him?"

"He did and was shocked when I told him you hadn't agreed. When I told the chief that Rossini didn't think a C.I. agreement would be necessary, Mike scolded him for ignoring department policy. Then Mike asked me why you resisted Rossini's request because you were willing to work with me on several of my cases."

Gwen held up one hand, fingers splayed. "Hold on, Ben. My involvement was only because a friend was wrongly suspected. So if the chief asked you to talk me into snooping for Rossini, don't waste your breath. That man has rubbed me the wrong way since the moment I met him."

"Relax, Gwen. Mike made no such suggestion. Besides, I'd never talk you into doing anything you don't want to do."

She locked eyes with him. "Good to know. Keep talking."

Ben took another sip. "Also, Rossini admitted he hadn't contacted either the store owners or the other police department about the robbery and possible accomplice. At that point, Mike dismissed Rossini but kept the case file."

"How did the sergeant react?" Gwen asked.

"Deflated is the best description."

"So you and Mike continued without him?"

Ben nodded. "That's when Mike suggested an unexpected solution to Rossini's lack of attention to details."

"What's brewing in the chief's head?"

Ben lifted his mug in salute. "Clever choice of verb."

She play-slapped Ben's free hand. "Stop stalling."

"All right, all right. So impatient." Ben grinned at her. "Mike's thinking to re-assign Rossini to a different case and hire my consulting services to continue the investigation."

Because Gwen respected Ben's detecting talents more than Rossini's, she asked, "Are you going to accept?"

"Only if you'll agree to be my unofficial sidekick."

"Funny you should ask."

Ben's forehead crinkled. "Why funny?"

"Did you notice Shirley driving away as you pulled up?"

"No, but only because I don't know what she drives."

"Give me a second to resurrect our conversation."

"Now who's stalling," Ben teased.

She grinned at him. "And look who's impatient."

"That makes us even." Ben waved her on. "I'll sit here patiently until you're ready to share."

Gwen wrapped her hands around her warm mug. "Shirley couldn't stay long because Rossini had texted her to report at the police station. And listen to this, Ben. She told me that she knew about my CI work for you."

He sat up straight. "How did she find out?"

"She didn't tell me and I didn't ask but she said she'd never reveal the identity of any C.I. when drafting articles about apprehended criminals. Then she swore again she wasn't the one who stabbed Hank and asked me for a favor."

Stepping to the other counter, Ben held the carafe aloft in a silent question to refill Gwen's mug. She hovered her hand above the still-steaming coffee, signaling she didn't need him to top it off. "So what's Shirley's favor?"

"First of all, I didn't mention Hank's possible accomplice, so she's still assuming one of her relatives stabbed him. She wants me to figure out which one as her personal C.I."

"Interesting quandary, Gwen. How did you react?"

"Before I could decide, Filly called Shirley's cell to announce a family meeting tomorrow morning. Shirley begged me to go with her to begin my sleuthing efforts.

154

She'll re-acquaint me with the relatives I met Sunday morning and introduce me to the others who show up to discuss Hank's burial."

"Let me guess: You agreed to go with her?"

"Yes, I did."

"So you're no longer worried that the unknown shadow person at the convenience store might show up at the Victorian looking for Hank?"

Gwen waved her hand in dismissal. "I can't explain why, but I don't think Hank had an accomplice. He struck me as more of a lone wolf."

"If your instincts are right, we'd be back to either Shirley or one of her relatives as Hank's stabber."

"That does bother me, but there's something else."

"What's that?"

"If I help Shirley snoop on her family and if you accept the consultant job for our police chief, does that create a conflict of interest?"

"I wouldn't think so, Gwen. If I accept the chief's offer – and I'm thinking I will – you and I will both be seeking the identity of Hank's attacker, regardless of who requested our assistance. What's Shirley's timing for tomorrow?"

"She's coming here before ten and we'll head over."

"Good. That will give you a chance to ferret out family details from Shirley on the way."

"Exactly," Gwen confirmed.

Ben reached over to cover Gwen's hand with his. "Far be it from me to suggest sleuthing tactics. In the past, you've zeroed in on the guilty party, putting yourself in harm's way, so be watchful."

His hand atop hers, neither of them said a word.

And then Ben broke the silence. "You realize that my investigation might lead to Shirley's arrest based on Rossini's suspicion of her timing."

Gwen stared at Ben. "Her 9-1-1 call isn't nearly enough reason to prove she's guilty."

"Of course not," Ben agreed. "I'd need more evidence."

"I should hope so," Gwen quipped, pulling her hand from beneath his. "I believe Shirley when she says she didn't do it."

Ben sat back. "Understood, but when all is said and done, you might end up saving Shirley from me."

When Ben winked at her, Gwen recognized he was only half-teasing and paused as she formed her comeback.

She thrust out her hand for a shake. "Challenge accepted, Detective Snowcrest."

Chapter Twenty-Seven
…early-morning, Thursday

The next morning, as Gwen puttered around her kitchen, a sleepy-eyed Jenna wandered down from the guestroom and plopped onto an island stool.

"You came in rather late last night." Gwen knew the exact time because she'd lain awake until hearing the front door open and close before the lock snicked back into place.

"Sorry if I woke you," Jenna said. "Cole invited me to supper after my last class. I met him at The Bayside Café."

Gwen commented, "Good choice for a casual meal."

"After we ate, he suggested a stroll around town."

"So you enjoyed your time with him?"

Jenna nodded and said, "He's quite funny, you know. But like I told you the other day, I'm not interested in a serious relationship until I finish my degree."

Accepting Jenna's claim as genuine, Gwen changed the topic. "No early classes today?"

"Not this morning. I need to edit a paper that's due this week. I can't believe I'm in my final semester."

Jenna's comment reminded Gwen of her own plans. "I have a question related to your graduation."

Jenna grinned. "I'm intrigued. What's your question?"

"If none of your classmates has made plans with you, I'd like to host your graduation party in my back yard. If you're interested, of course."

Jenna threw her arms around Gwen's neck. "That sounds great! Thank you. With grandpa down in Florida, I didn't think I'd have my own party up here."

"Do you think he'd travel up for it?" Though Gwen had long ago dismissed Hal Jenkins' unwelcomed advances to move their platonic friendship to something more serious, she still worried that seeing him again could be awkward.

Jenna's voice interrupted. "He's planning to fly up for my graduation. Do you want me to mention the party?"

"Why don't you wait until we solidify the details?"

"Good idea." Jenna slid off the stool. "I'm going to shower and head over to the library."

Gwen's opportunity to suggest adding her family reunion to Jenna's party had come and gone so she decided to reconsider the idea of combining the two events.

To Jenna, she said, "Do you want breakfast?"

"I'm not hungry but I should be back late this afternoon. Why don't you let me help you make supper?"

"We haven't cooked dinner together for a while, so that would be fun. I'll dream up a menu and gather the ingredients."

"Perfect. I'll see you later."

Jenna bounced up the split staircase, followed closely by Amber, who'd appeared out of nowhere.

***

Half an hour later, Jenna shouted goodbye as she opened the front door, instantly followed by, "Gwen, guess who's here."

Gwen rushed from the kitchen to hear Jenna say, "Good to see you again, Ben. I'm off to the college library."

"Have fun," Ben said in his baritone voice.

Stepping over the threshold, he spotted Gwen and his grin widened. "Good morning."

"Good morning," she echoed.

After he removed his boots, he traipsed to her kitchen in his stockinged feet, waving a document. "This is my consulting contract for the chief to sign."

Gwen dropped onto the adjacent stool. "I've been thinking about our odd partnership."

His white eyebrows shifted. "Why do you call it odd?"

"Because I've agreed to help Shirley prove her innocence while you'll be trying to prove her guilt."

"I guess that qualifies as odd," Ben said. "But just because Rossini liked her for the stabbing doesn't mean I agree with his assessment."

Gwen studied Ben. "When we've worked together in the past, we weren't proving or disproving the guilt of a particular person. We were only seeking the real culprit."

"And we will be doing exactly that this time."

She harumphed. "With opposite intentions?"

Ben moved to sit across from Gwen and concentrated on her eyes. "This isn't a competition. There's no winner or loser, except for the person we identify as Hank's attacker."

He sat back and tapped the granite counter as he spoke. "It's true we'll be working opposing angles, but I expect to share details I uncover and I hope you'll do the same. Otherwise, our odd partnership – as you call it – won't work out very well."

"I have no problem sharing information, Ben. Are you going to tell our police chief that we're working together?"

"Only if Mike asks and maybe not even then. You'll be working with me, not directly with the detective squad."

"In that case, since I'm not official, I don't need to sign a confidential informant document."

"That's right," Ben confirmed. "We should avoid being in the same place at the same time while we investigate. Don't want to arouse suspicions."

"We can text our destinations as we move from clue to clue," Gwen added.

"Deal." Ben offered a firm shake.

Gwen smiled at his faux formality and gripped back.

And then he said, "Seriously, Gwen, be careful. Shirley hasn't yet been eliminated as Hank's attacker."

Straightening, Gwen couldn't let his words go

unchallenged. "Yes, yes. Shirley's 9-1-1 call. But I believe her story about nearly tripping over the bleeding Hank. Did Rossini check her winter coat for blood splatter?"

Distracted by a glance at his watch, Ben didn't respond to Gwen's question, saying instead, "What time is Shirley coming here this morning?"

"A little before ten."

"Then I'll finish my coffee – delicious as usual by the way – and deliver my contract to Chief Brown." He gulped the final sip, then placed his mug in the sink.

A minute later, as Ben struggled with his boots, he said over his shoulder, "I have no doubt we'll expose Hank Payne's attacker in record time."

Gwen commented, "If only Norman Tucker would regain his memory, he could solve the case in the blink of an eye. But maybe he's holding back."

Without commenting on that unlikely event, Ben stood up and grinned at her. "I'm glad to be back in Harbor Falls and investigating with you at my side."

His lips touched the top of her head, then he pushed her to arm's length. "Good luck at the Tucker home."

She indicated the consulting contract clutched in his hand. "How soon will that be processed?"

Ben shrugged. "I've never had an arrangement like this with the Harbor Falls police department, so I have no idea."

Reaching up and straightening his woolen cap atop his

161

white hair, she said, "Which means you don't know where you'll be going today."

"Not yet," he supplied. "After I settle with Mike, I'll determine my best course of action and text you."

She reached behind him and yanked the door open. "And I'll text you after the meeting at the Victorian."

"We have a plan, Gwen." He tipped his cap and out the door he flew.

Chapter Twenty-Eight

...mid-morning, Thursday

A few minutes before Shirley was due to arrive, Gwen tucked an oversized chicken breast with bone into her crockpot with broth and an assortment of dried herbs that she titled 'Scarborough Fair,' all the while humming the Simon & Garfunkel recording from the '60s. *'Parsley, Sage, Rosemary, and Thyme.'*

The doorbell chimed, announcing Shirley's arrival, and Gwen hurried through the foyer.

"Ready to go? Aunt Filly's a nut for punctuality."

It seemed that her Aunt Filly was a nut for several guidelines for living one's life. That past Sunday, her rules had included good manners and cleanliness. Now Shirley added being on time. What were Filly's other decrees?

Gwen still harbored doubts about letting Shirley draw her more deeply into the hunt for the Tucker family member who'd stabbed Hank. What if Ben wasn't approved as a police department consultant for this case? She'd already promised her sleuthing efforts to Shirley.

Too late to back-out now. Gwen would simply proceed by herself. After all, she'd snooped on her own long before

163

she teamed up with Ben. She could do it this time if necessary.

After donning her hooded coat, Gwen slipped her feet into winter boots and pulled a warm knit cap onto her head. "I'm ready."

The two women emerged into bright sunshine sparkling off the snow that blanketed the landscape. For the first time in days, no white flakes drifted from the clear blue sky onto the coastal town of Harbor Falls.

"You okay to walk?" Shirley asked.

"Sounds perfect to me. It's a winter wonderland."

Gwen hooked arms with Shirley. "Step carefully. I nearly went down when Ben and I walked to The Wharf."

They descended to Gwen's front walkway without incident.

As their boots broke through the crusty surface of the village green's nearly untouched pathways, Shirley asked, "How is Ben? I only knew him as a police department source when I was gathering background for an article. He and I never spoke on a personal level."

If Shirley's claim were true, she'd eliminated Ben as the officer who'd leaked C.I. identity to a *Gazette* reporter.

Pushing aside her curiosity, Gwen said, "You probably wouldn't recognize him. This past fall, he let his whiskers grow and is now sporting an impressive white beard and mustache, along with white hair that touches his collar.

During the holidays, my friend Liz hired him as Santa Claus for Kris Kringle Day at her bookshop."

Shirley's mouth dropped. "Annabelle and I stopped in at *Fiction 'n Fables* for a photo spread about her Santa event. You're right: I didn't recognize him."

They veered onto a second undisturbed path, winding through the village green and soon approached the Sugar 'n' Spice Bakery.

Shirley moaned. "The scent of yeasty breads and sugary desserts certainly sweetens the air. You must walk over here every day to buy their goodies."

Shaking her head, Gwen snickered. "Heavens, no. I have to limit myself to once a week or I'd be as big as a house." She pointed to the second-floor windows. "Annabelle's apartment is dark. Is she on assignment?"

"No idea," Shirley commented. "I requested personal time this morning so I could attend Aunt Filly's meeting."

Gwen followed that thread. "Has the *Gazette* assigned you to write Hank's story?"

Shirley snapped, "No," her tone sharp.

"Because you're related to the Tuckers?"

"That's not the half of it," Shirley's voice wobbled. "Would you mind if I unburden myself about my situation?"

Clueless about Shirley's career status, Gwen halted at the South Street traffic light and pushed the button for the crossing sign. "Go ahead, I'm all ears."

Shirley tucked her hands deeper in her coat pockets. "For the past few months, I've sensed that the new editor is attempting to force me to retire earlier than I planned."

"How so?"

Shirley huffed. "My assignments have become more and more frivolous. I've always reported on political stunts, uprisings at town hall meetings, or criminals brought to justice. Compare those topics to my current assignment about the effect of snowstorms on sales at the harbor shops."

In an attempt to ease Shirley's stress, Gwen said, "I'd be interested in that story. It could encourage residents to shop at the waterfront businesses more often during the blustery winter months."

Shirley glanced sideways, her eyes narrowing. "Nice try, but your sympathy doesn't sooth my ego. The younger reporters are covering the more in-depth stories and haven't even noticed my unannounced demotion. They also have the advantage of being more tech savvy than I am."

The traffic lights all turned red, halting cars and trucks before flashing the crossing sign.

As they hurried to the opposite sidewalk, Shirley continued her gripe session. "In a few more months, I'll satisfy the longevity required for full pension. The new editor has already mentioned budget cuts. He could hand me a pink slip at any moment and blow up my pension."

Shirley's money worries brought Gwen's own financial

situation to mind. She and Parker had paid off the mortgage on their library home years before his premature death. The interest from their investment portfolio combined with her pension from Baylies provided a steady flow of cash to support Gwen in her post-widowhood lifestyle.

But it seemed that Shirley was not so comfortable. Had the reporter ever married? Gwen had no idea. With no financial contributions from a spouse, income for retirees could be unreliable at best. Shirley was depending on that full pension from the *Gazette*. Gwen couldn't imagine the feisty reporter asking any of her relatives for financial assistance. Another Aunt Filly guideline for life would probably appear, like never loaning money to a relative.

Walking at Gwen's side, Shirley pronounced, "Don't panic, Gwen. I wasn't expecting you to offer a solution."

"That's good," Gwen joked, "because I don't have one." A second later, she hoped her unhelpful remark hadn't offended Shirley.

But Shirley didn't seem perturbed. "I just needed to blow off some steam. It's enough that you listened. You seem settled in your retired life. What's your secret?"

With the Victorian fast approaching, Gwen debated how much to share. Before she had a chance to decide, a man's deep voice called them. "Shirley? Gwen?"

They both looked ahead to see Lawrence Tucker waving as he hurried from the opposite direction.

***

When Ben walked through the police department visitor's entrance a second time, Patsy looked up from her phone call and grinned at him, holding up one finger. A second later, the side door clicked open. He saluted her before pushing through and entering the elevator. Upstairs, officers passed in the hallway, but none of them seemed concerned to see Ben approaching Chief Brown's office.

Mike jumped to his feet, pointing at the document in Ben's hand. "Morning. Is that your consultant contract?"

Ben handed it over and Mike studied the details. "Your stipend is reasonable." He signed on the acceptance line, then made a copy for Ben. "I'll send your original to the accounting office for processing."

Sliding the copy into the case file he'd brought back with him, Ben asked, "Do you need approval from anyone else?"

"Nope," Mike replied. "I have the authority to hire and fire. Have a seat." Mike opened a drawer and slid a Harbor Falls detective's badge across to Ben.

Then Mike's cheeks reddened. "Unfortunately, Sergeant Rossini left the building before I had a chance to re-assign him to what I'll call a more urgent case. That's something I want to do in person."

Quiet for a moment, Ben eventually spoke. "What are the chances he'll be visiting the convenience store owners and the other police department this morning?"

"Are those your intended destinations?"

Nodding, Ben retrieved the security camera photo of a shadow beside Hank at the register. "I need to determine whether this shadow was Hank's accomplice or just another customer. What I discover will settle the potential threat to the Tucker family."

And Gwen, he thought but didn't say out loud.

"Makes sense," Mike said. "I'll contact Rossini to come back in so I can officially take him off your case."

Ben stood and extended his hand. "It'll be good to work with you again, Mike. I'll report to you when I find something important."

Another officer knocked on the chief's door jamb, ending their conversation. Ben got to his feet, nodded at the entering officer, and wound his way to his Corvette in the visitor's lot.

Chapter Twenty-Nine

...late morning, Thursday

A woman's voice ordered, "Get in here. You're all late."

Gwen, Shirley, and Lawrence all looked up from the walkway to see Aunt Filly leaning against the Victorian's doorframe, her usually perfect hair a bit disheveled.

Rushing up the steps and across the veranda, Lawrence held the door open for Shirley and Gwen to enter.

The family matriarch said, "Lawrence, I'm glad you're joining us. Jessica and Olivia are in the kitchen."

"Thanks, Mom." Lawrence slid past Shirley and Gwen, quickly disappearing inside.

Next in line, Shirley kissed her aunt on the cheek. As the older woman leaned into the affection, her gaze landed on Gwen. "I see that you've brought your friend again."

Filly's tone of annoyance combined with her raised eyebrows indicated she was waiting for a believable reason.

Without hesitation, Shirley said, "I hope you don't mind. I thought Gwen could contribute ideas for Hank's final arrangements from a different perspective."

Because they hadn't discussed a cover story for Gwen's presence, she was impressed with Shirley's quick thinking.

Stepping to the reporter's side, Gwen added, "If you feel my presence will be disruptive, I'll head back home."

Despite giving Gwen the stink eye, Filly Tucker relented. "No, no, that won't be necessary. You're here now, and I won't be rude, so let's join the others."

As they passed through the dining room, raised voices in the kitchen shouted over each other:

'Did Hank leave any money for his burial?'

'He mooched-off us, so I'm not paying one red cent.'

'He doesn't deserve a pricy funeral.'

'For all I care, they can bury him as a pauper.'

'How about cremation?'

Disturbed by the negative attitudes, Gwen paused beneath the archway, reluctant to involve herself in the nasty direction of the family discussion.

Grieving loved ones usually planned funeral and memorial services. Gwen had organized a grand service for her Parker, well attended by scores of friends and associates. But, then, Gwen had deeply loved her husband.

It appeared that every Tucker had hated Hank.

As Gwen considered the best way to flee, Shirley waded into the middle of the fray, shouting, "Shut up, all of you! You're being disrespectful to Hank and embarrassing me in front of my friend Gwen, who graciously offered to contribute some ideas for our planning."

At that moment, baby Olivia let loose a wail, breaking

up the tension around the kitchen table.

Jessica gently rocked her daughter. "I hope you're happy. You've upset our youngest Tucker. Shame on you."

With that, Jessica handed her child to Lawrence.

In the stunned silence that followed, the slightest whisper would have bounced off the walls. Shirley used the quiet to introduce additional family members to Gwen. As each name was spoken, the person nodded or waved.

Introductions completed, Filly took the floor. "Now that we're all calmed down, let's have a civilized discussion about arrangements for Hank's burial."

The earlier bickering made it obvious to Gwen that more than one Tucker possessed enough anger to do away with Hank. From her remote spot at the archway, she gazed from one person to the next, wondering how she'd manage to bump into each one for a private chat.

A tall elderly female emerged from the group and quick stepped to Gwen's side, extending her wrinkled hand. "I'm Minnie, Filly's younger sister, aka the family spinster." The woman chuckled at her self-deprecating comment. "I didn't realize you're a friend of our Shirley."

Gazing into the pleasant face, Gwen said, "Shirley and I go back a few years." Failing to pull forth a connection to this woman who seemed to know her, Gwen continued. "I'm sorry, but have we met?"

"Not officially. I hide in the back at the garden club

meetings and leave before the snacks. You're usually front and center. That's why I recognized you."

"I'm sorry," Gwen repeated, "but I never noticed you."

"Don't feel bad. Most people look past me, I've lived in this house all my life but only developed an interest in flowers late last summer. I'm hoping the garden club will help me choose the best flowers and bushes to spruce up our surroundings when spring arrives."

Gwen couldn't imagine this flower lover harming Hank.

Norman banged his fist on the table. "Let's get back to our discussion. Has anyone stayed in touch with Hank?"

When no one admitted contact with the black sheep, Lawrence spoke up. "Why don't I touch base with his most recent landlord and ask if he left anything behind? There could be some cash hidden in a pocket or something."

Norman called down the table. "Excellent suggestion, son. I'll contact the coroner's office to keep Hank's body in the freezer until we advise final arrangements."

Norman said to the group. "Can any of you contribute a useful suggestion?" When no one spoke up, he struggled to his feet, balancing on his crutches. "We're done for now. After Lawrence locates Hank's belongings, we'll call another meeting."

Chapter Thirty
…mid-day, Thursday

With tensions eased, family members pushed arms into coat sleeves before venturing out into the sunny but chilly day. Those who lived upstairs headed toward the front staircase.

Sensing that Minnie hadn't moved from her side, Gwen considered that their garden club connection provided a perfect reason to arrange a visit with Filly's sister.

"Minnie, would you like to get together and discuss appropriate flowers you could plant?"

A smile brightened Minnie's face. "I'd love that."

"Let's exchange numbers and I'll text you."

Details registered in cell phones, Minnie thanked Gwen and moved toward the kitchen door, saying goodbye to those who were heading out.

Standing at the stove, Shirley appeared embroiled in a conversation with her aunt, so Gwen turned to leave.

But Lawrence blocked her way as he jiggled baby Olivia in his arms. "Sorry you witnessed that ugly shouting match."

"Not your fault," she offered.

And then Shirley slid next to them. "Great idea to search for Hank's belongings. Let's hope he stashed some cash."

Lawrence shrugged. "Seemed like a logical next step."

"When will you start?" Shirley wanted to know.

Lawrence shrugged again. "No idea. Right now, I need to carry Olivia upstairs to Jessica's rooms and settle my granddaughter for a nap."

Before he had a chance to leave, Shirley placed her hand on his sleeve. "I've got an idea. Gwen here has always enjoyed solving mysteries. Why don't you let her help you search for Hank's belongings?"

Gwen feared that Shirley had come dangerously close to revealing their plan to either eliminating or identifying Hank's likely attacker from within the family. However, spending hours with Lawrence would be another opportunity to learn about the other family members.

Gwen looked up into his face. "I didn't come with Shirley to butt into your family's business, but I must admit Shirley's suggestion makes sense. I've always found that unraveling a mystery is easier with someone who's equally interested. I'm willing to help if you'll let me tag along."

Lawrence studied Gwen for a moment. "If cousin Shirley thinks you can speed up my hunt for money to pay for Hank's burial expenses, I welcome your involvement."

Shifting Olivia to his other arm, he pulled out two personal cards and a pen from his pocket. Handing all to Gwen, he said, "Here's my contact info. Keep one and write your cell number on the other one and hand it back to me."

Gwen complied, then returned his pen and one card. "Let me know when you want to head out. My calendar is flexible these days."

"You'll hear from me soon." He hurried to the staircase, making Olivia laugh when he bounded two steps at a time.

As Gwen walked out with Shirley through the dining room archway, heels clicked on the floorboards behind them. Gwen turned to see Filly Tucker.

"Don't rush off without saying goodbye, Gwen. I apologize if my family's bickering is chasing you away."

Gwen smiled at her. "I didn't want to interrupt your conversation, Filly."

"You seem a kind soul, Gwen, so I understand why our Shirley is relying on you for support during this crisis. Do you have a big family?"

"Not nearly as big as yours," Gwen hedged.

Filly paused. "You no doubt noticed that my relatives aren't afraid to speak their minds."

Stating the obvious, Gwen said, "Your grandson's burial expense seems to have unearthed old resentments."

Collapsing on the nearest dining room chair, Filly released a breath. "I don't want you to think unkindly toward them, so let me explain Hank's history."

Curious if Filly's version would match Shirley's story of the other day, Gwen dropped into the chair opposite Filly and Shirley sat in the adjacent one.

Filly toyed with a placemat as she spoke. "Hank was like every other mischievous boy until he reached his teens and his father died in a work accident. Hank's mother – our youngest daughter Theresa – became a single parent but couldn't control her son's anger. Some of us thought he abused her, though Theresa never admitted it. A few years later, she died in a car accident during a raging storm."

Though Shirley had shared these same details, Gwen respected Filly's need to unburden herself so she sat quietly and listened. *Did any of the others share Shirley's suspicion that Hank had been the reason his mother drove to the ATM that night and ended up dying?*

Eyes glittering with unshed tears, Filly resumed. "Norman and I tried to step in, but the boy's anger ran too deep to accept our guidance. He fell in with the wrong crowd and was arrested several times. In between stints in jail, he found his way to Harbor Falls and mooched off every relative who lives here. No one sitting around that table intends to contribute even one more dime."

A booming voice called, "Filly, come here."

Swiping at her eyes, she struggled to her feet. "Gotta go. Norman's not in the best of moods. Forgive me if I shared too much. You're welcome here anytime, with or without Shirley." Patting Shirley's cheek, Filly stood up and walked slowly through the kitchen archway.

Gwen tucked Filly's open invitation in the back of her

mind. Dropping in unannounced could be rather useful.

After saying nothing for quite a while, Shirley blurted, "Gwen, I need to retrieve my car and check-in at the *Gazette*. Let's head back to your place."

Exiting the Victorian, they said little as they retraced their steps, soon arriving at Gwen's front curb.

Shirley broke the silence. "I hope you're not upset that I volunteered you to accompany Lawrence."

"You made me nervous for a second," Gwen admitted.

"What?" Shirley responded, a bit of roughness in her tone. "You thought I was about to tell him you'll be solving the mystery about which Tucker stabbed Hank?"

Not backing down from the reporter's irritation, Gwen replied, "That was my reaction exactly."

After a brief hesitation, Shirley chuckled, "Well, now you know I still have my wits about me."

"Glad to hear it. You said you need to check in at the *Gazette*, but can you stay for a few minutes?"

Shirley waved her hand in dismissal. "I was only making our departure sound urgent in case anyone else tried to delay us leaving. So, yes, I have a little time."

"Good. I'd like you to make a list for me."

Inside, Gwen guided Shirley to an island stool, then grabbed her legal pad from the living room and flipped past her jotted ideas for her family reunion to a blank page, which she placed in front of Shirley with a pencil.

"Tell me what you need on this list."

As Gwen ticked off her requests, Shirley created columns with headers of the topics:

... *name of each family member*

...*when did Gwen meet that person.*

... *brief description for recognition purposes*

... *where each one fits into the Tucker family tree.*

... *phone and address*

"Begin with Minnie," Gwen requested.

"Why Minnie?"

"Because I'll be meeting with her to suggest flowers to plant around the Victorian this spring."

"I wondered why she sidled up to you. Good thinking." After filling the first cell of the table with Minnie's name, Shirley added the requested details.

Shirley paused and said, "This'll take more than a few minutes."

"I won't hover," Gwen promised. "When you're finished, call my name. I'll be close enough to hear you."

Twenty minutes later, as Gwen closed an old address book, Shirley's voice called, "I'm done. Take a look."

Gwen rushed to the kitchen, perched on the adjacent stool, and reached for the legal pad. "Looks great. Thanks."

"Tell me if I missed anything," Shirley instructed.

Gwen scanned the chart then slid the legal pad back to Shirley. "One more detail. Put a checkmark at ones in the

Victorian Sunday night into Monday morning."

Shirley sunk her teeth into the pencil, leaving indentations. "That's a detail I can't guarantee. The ones who live upstairs might have gone out the night before and maybe weren't back by morning."

"Good point," Gwen agreed, "but having these specifics will be enormously helpful when I'm snooping."

"Okay, I'll do my best." Skipping some names, she added checkmarks sporadically until she reached the bottom of her graph. "By the way, everyone confides in Minnie and she keeps secrets like a bank vault."

That bit of trivia left Gwen wondering how to urge Minnie to share a few of those secrets, which might or might not reveal a potential connection to Hank's stabbing.

Shirley glanced at Gwen's kitchen clock. "Okay, now I really have to report in at the *Gazette*. Keep me updated about your hunt with Lawrence, and your time with Minnie."

"I will," Gwen promised, escorting Shirley to the front door. After Shirley's car pulled away from the curb, Gwen sent a text to Ben: *Home from the Tucker family meeting. Info to share.*

Chapter Thirty-One

...mid-day, Thursday

As Ben drove out of Harbor Falls, he mentally reviewed his plan. First, he'd interview the convenience store owner and his wife, then drive to the local police station to speak with the detectives who handled the robbery report.

His cell buzzed through his Corvette's radio, the screen ID reading Police Chief Mike Brown.

Ben answered, "Hey, Mike. You miss me already?"

"Don't be daft. Are you close enough to come back?"

Glancing up at the *'Thank You for Visiting Harbor Falls'* sign, Ben said, "Sure. Be there in a few minutes," and pulled to the side of the road to make a U-turn.

Curious about Mike's reason for the callback, Ben soon parked in the still-empty space he'd vacated earlier. Assuming Mike's summons involved the Hank Payne stabbing, Ben grabbed the case file and headed inside.

Patsy again waved him through, and he hurried to Mike's office, standing in the doorway until the chief finished his phone conversation.

"That was quick, Ben."

"You call, I come," Ben teased. "What's up?"

"I've reassigned Rossini."

"Good to hear but you could've told me that on the phone, so there must be something else."

"There is." Stepping to the window, the chief pointed toward the visitors parking lot.

"When you pulled away earlier, I noticed you're driving your Corvette."

"That's right. Until I buy a second vehicle, my sports car is my only transportation. Are my wheels a problem?"

The chief waved Ben to sit, then he sat in the other guest chair. "It could be. A town councilman stopped by, and I mentioned hiring you. He cautioned me that our insurance policy won't cover a personal vehicle if damage is sustained while you're employed by the department."

"That applies to a temporary consultant?" Ben asked.

"Apparently, it does. I want you to team up with Officer Cole Martin. Riding in his department vehicle solves the insurance problem. I had paired him with Rossini as my liaison for this case. I see no reason to change his assignment. Have you met him? He wants to work his way into a detective position."

During Ben's phone call from Albuquerque, Gwen had mentioned Cole Martin's investigation of her backyard boot prints and then showing a personal interest in Jenna.

To Mike, Ben said, "I'm aware of him, but we haven't been introduced."

Getting to his feet, Mike stepped to his doorway.

"Martin," he called across the hallway. "I need you in my office. Bring your research for the Hank Payne case."

Ben heard the reply. "Be right there, chief."

Because Gwen hadn't described the detective, Ben was surprised when a young blonde man entered.

"Officer Cole Martin," Mike began, "please meet retired Detective Benjamine Snowcrest."

Martin stretched his hand to shake Ben's. "Pleased to meet you. I've heard many stories about your career."

Mike interrupted. "Are you aware, Martin, that Sergeant Rossini is no longer working the Hank Payne murder investigation?"

Martin replied, "Yes, sir. He stopped by to tell me."

"Good. I've hired Ben here as our consultant on that case, and I'd like you to team up with him."

Returning the handshake, Ben decided no time like the present to establish the pecking order in their partnership. "Have you gathered any more research on this case?"

Holding up a manila folder, Martin replied, "I have, sir."

"No need to call me sir. Ben will do."

The chief's phone rang. He answered and asked the caller to hold before placing his palm over the microphone. "It appears you two are off to a good start. The conference room is unoccupied, so I suggest you take advantage of the privacy to review the investigation and the additional

183

research." Without waiting for a response, the chief swiveled in his chair and apologized to his caller.

Ben caught Martin's eye and jerked his head toward the door. They filed out, soon spreading the contents of their separate folders on the conference table.

"You're familiar with the details to date?"

"I am, sir, I mean, Ben."

"Good, then you know what's in the official case file. What have you collected since then?"

"For one, the photos taken by the *Gazette* photographer." Martin handed the stack to Ben. "She dropped them off early this morning."

After sifting through the photos, Ben said, "Have any of these boot prints been eliminated as belonging to the ambulance service EMTs?"

"Not yet. I requested impressions of their boot soles but they haven't been sent over yet."

Ben pushed the prints toward Martin and stood up. "I'm not sure any of these images will be helpful. Keep them in your folder, and we'll review them later. Do you need to tie up any loose ends before we head out?"

"The Payne stabbing is the only investigation assigned to me right now, so I'm ready when you are."

"Lead the way, "Ben said, then followed Martin down the elevator and out the back door of the station. As they approached one of the department SUVs, Ben grinned at the

ID number painted on the door and laughed. "What do you know. This is my old ride."

Martin chuckled. "I'd call that good luck for us both."

"Let's hope that's true. I'll program the address of the convenience store into the GPS and we'll be on our way."

Though Ben preferred to work alone, he was relieved by this new arrangement for two reasons. For one thing, driving his sports car on slippery winter roads always presented the threat of fishtailing. And second, the red Corvette could give a too-casual impression when witnesses saw him arrive.

Exiting the station property, they soon passed the *'Thanks for Visiting Harbor Falls'* sign, heading south.

Comfortable enough in the passenger seat, Ben opened the case file and removed the security camera photo of Hank at the register to study the shadow on the floor.

Would he and Martin uncover an accomplice or discover there was no connection to the theft?

Chapter Thirty-Two

...early afternoon, Thursday

When Gwen received a text from Ben that he and Cole Martin had driven down to the convenience store three towns south of Harbor Falls, she quickly dialed his number rather than get caught in a texting frenzy.

As soon as he picked up, she said, "Can you talk?"

"Not for long. Cole Marti is outside filling his gas tank."

"I thought you'd be working alone."

"So did I. I'll explain when I see you."

"Any idea how late you'll be back in Harbor Falls?"

"Not yet. After our interview with the store owner and his wife, we'll be stopping at the local police station for a conversation with the detectives who handled the robbery. Why do you ask?"

"Because Jenna and I will be preparing a crockpot chicken dinner. Plus I have info to share from this morning's Tucker meeting."

"Sounds good. I'll text our ETA when we're on our way back to Harbor Falls."

"Will Cole be coming here with you? There should be enough chicken for an extra serving."

"Not this time. I'll retrieve my Corvette at the police station, then drive to your place. Gotta go. The tank's full."

***

As Ben led the way into the store, he waved Cole to check the aisles for customers.

Approaching the cash register, a woman with her arm in a sling looked up, her eyes reminiscent of a deer in the headlights.

As he removed his wool cap, Ben held up his badge to signal he was no threat. "Good afternoon. I'm Detective Ben Snowcrest from the Harbor Falls Police Department."

The woman leaned over the counter to inspect his badge.

Coming up beside Ben, Cole shook his head that no suspicious characters lurked in the aisles, holding out his own badge, saying, "Officer Cole Martin, ma'am."

Taking charge, Ben said, "We're investigating your robbery of last week. I see your arm was injured."

She turned toward a half-open door a few yards away and yelled, "Phil, come here. Two policeman want to talk."

A powerfully built man with a bandage obscuring his receding hairline rushed over to stand beside her, eyeing Ben with suspicion. "What do you want?"

Again, Ben held up his badge. "Mr. Gibbs?"

When the man nodded, Ben added, "As I told this lady..."

Mr. Gibbs sneered, "Wanda's my wife."

"Sorry, your wife. We're here to ask about your robbery."

"I filed a report with the local police."

"We're aware, but we have a few questions."

Phil Gibb's face distorted with anger. "That grizzly son of a bitch better not show his ugly face in here again. He tossed my Wanda to the floor and broke her arm. When I tried to wrestle our cash from his filthy fist, he whacked me on the head. By the time I found my balance, he was out the door with our cash and zooming off on his motorcycle."

Ben pulled the wanted poster of Hank from his jacket pocket. "Can you confirm this man was the robber?"

Wanda backed away.

"Don't worry," Ben soothed. "You'll never see him again."

"Why is that?" Phil asked. "Has the slimy bastard been locked up?"

"Not in jail. He was killed in Harbor Falls, which is why we drove down here to speak with you."

"What for? Case closed," Phil blustered.

"Not quite," Ben said, turning to Cole. "Hand me that printout of the shadow person."

After sorting through the case file contents, Cole extended the requested photo to Ben, who angled it so both Wanda and Phil could see the grainy image.

"Hey," Phil said, "that's from our security camera."

"Yes, it is." Ben pointed to the shadow on the floor next to Hank at the cash register. "We need to identify the person standing next to the robber. Was he or she an accomplice?"

"Bastard came in by himself as far as I could tell," Phil answered, his facial features relaxing. "The local cops still have our security footage if you want to doublecheck."

Pulling the photo closer to his face, Phil said, "I think that's me rushing out here when I heard Wanda scream. Just before the son of a bitch clobbered me."

By claiming the shadow was himself, Phil Gibbs had just eliminated an accomplice, reducing the pool of suspects.

Ben was relieved that Gwen didn't need to worry about a dangerous outsider showing up in Harbor Falls. But now his pool of suspects was most likely a Tucker relative.

Reaching out to shake the store owner's hand, Ben said, "Thank you for clearing up this detail, Mr. Gibbs."

"No problem." The gruff man grasped Wanda's free hand. "Thanks for telling us that he won't walk in here again. We can relax until the next thief tries to rob us."

As Ben turned to leave, he noticed Cole placing a bag of peanuts on the counter, reaching toward his back pocket.

Wanda Gibbs waved him off. "No charge, officer."

Cole thanked her and followed Ben outside to the SUV.

Chapter Thirty-Three

...late afternoon, Thursday

After Gwen's brief phone conversation with Ben, she concentrated on her family reunion project. Having no idea which of her remaining relatives would be making the trip to Harbor Falls, she knew that preparation and planning were essential. Would Jenna agree to combine this reunion with her graduation party, or would Gwen be planning her gathering as a standalone event?

To stay busy, she jotted menu ideas and created a blueprint for backyard table locations in her gardens. She could only hope for pleasant weather, but with the events months away – whether combined or separate – it was much too early to check forecasts.

***

Around four o'clock, the front door banged open. Jenna whirled into the living room, plopping down next to Gwen.

"My research paper is finished. I'll submit it to my professor tomorrow for a grade."

Gwen pushed her party files to the far side of the coffee table. "That'll give you some down time this evening."

"Sure will," Jenna agreed, nearly bouncing up and down.

190

"We should play a game after dinner. By the way, as soon as I walked in the door, I smelled your delicious crockpot chicken. Do you think it's ready for the final touches?"

"Let's go check."

In the kitchen, she pointed at the light panel, which indicated *'warm.'*

"Chicken is cooked and waiting for the next step."

"What are we making?"

Gwen laughed. "You'll think me silly but I've always called this dish Scarborough Fair Chicken Stew." She went on to explain the herbs from the Simon & Garfunkel song.

"Not silly at all," Jenna objected. "I've heard that song on the oldies stations and love it. Tell me what I can do."

Gwen grabbed a bag of russet potatoes from the pantry. "You're in charge of cooking these for mashies."

Leaving Jenna to peel and boil the potatoes, Gwen turned her attention to the stew.

First, she strained the crockpot juices into a large glass measuring cup, then deboned and chunked the chicken breast. Next, she sauteed portobella mushrooms, followed by a thickening roux to which she stirred in the crockpot broth until it thickened. Lastly, she added diced pimentos, the sauteed mushrooms, and the chicken meat.

Jenna sniffed. "Hmmm, smells so good."

"Let's sauté zucchini slices. If Ben doesn't return in time to join us, I'll reheat a plate for him when he gets here."

"Where is he?"

"Cole Martin drove them both down the coast to pursue an investigation."

Jenna's forehead wrinkled. "What investigation?"

Because Jenna had been preoccupied with her studies, she hadn't been present for Gwen's conversations with either Ben or Shirley, so Gwen shared a bare bones summary of Hank's stabbing plus Ben being hired as a consulting detective. She didn't mention her own involvement on Shirley's behalf.

Jenna frowned. "I had no idea. Is Cole coming, too?"

Gwen countered with a two-pronged question. "Are you wishing he does, or hoping he doesn't?"

Pausing for a split second, Jenna delayed her answer. "I wouldn't mind seeing Cole again. I enjoyed our supper at the Bayside Café, and our two walks. He's interesting and funny, too."

Gwen hadn't been exposed to the humorous side of the young officer's personality but wouldn't stand in the way of Jenna's budding friendship. "When Ben texts his ETA, I can ask him to invite Cole."

Jenna's smile spoke volumes to the observant Gwen.

Returning to the stove, Gwen stirred the stew and studied the resulting bubbles. Determining it was hot enough, she stirred in a bit of light cream and slid the pot to the stovetop's warming burner.

As Jenna finished mashing the potatoes, Gwen said, "If Ben doesn't text soon, you and I will dig in."

As soon as she said those words, her cell buzzed. Sure enough, the expected text from Ben had arrived.

'Heading to HF now. ETA 20 minutes.'

Gwen typed, *'Jenna asked if Cole would like to join us.'*

'Let me think about that as we get closer. [Smiley face].'

Verbally editing Ben's text, Gwen told Jenna he'd ask Cole and left it at that.

***

Though the sun had set, and the road surfaces were beginning to re-freeze, Cole proved a cautious driver.

Ben limited their conversation to a rehash of their actions and what they'd do next. When they passed the *'Welcome to Harbor Falls'* sign, Ben made his decision. "Gwen and Jenna invited me for dinner. You're welcome to join us."

Cole kept both eyes on the bright lights coming toward them in the opposite lane. "Thanks. I never turn down a dinner invitation."

Not surprised by Cole's answer, Ben added, "Gwen also told me you inspected boot prints in her back yard."

"Yes, I did. She was relieved to know her basement entrance hadn't been breached." Smacking the steering wheel, Cole said, "That reminds me. I want to compare my cell phone pics to Annabelle's photos at the Victorian."

Impressed with Cole's plan, Ben said, "A comparison

would eliminate the local EMTs. It's a good place to start."

"I'll do that next time I'm at my desk." Cole took at quick glance at Ben. "Did Mrs. Andrews tell you that my grandparents own the house next door that's for sale? I'm thinking about buying it if I can arrange the financing."

"I hope that works out for you," Ben said.

Reaching the village green, Cole turned the SUV onto Library Lane and parked at Gwen's curb. He exited the driver's seat and gazed at the old library's brick and brownstone façade. "When I was little, and visited my grandparents next door, I was fascinated by the abandoned library. Such a clever conversion into a private home."

"Vacant libraries don't come along very often," Ben commented, then took the lead up the walkway to press the doorbell. Glancing to his left, he noticed Jenna peeking out the front curtains. Seconds later, the door flew open.

Her eyes shining, Jenna said, "Ben, glad you made it back, and you, too, Cole. Get in here before you freeze."

Ben sniffed. "Something smells awfully good."

"Sure does," Cole agreed. "Anything I can do to help?"

"Dinner is ready and waiting. Boots off, gentlemen."

Following Jenna to the kitchen, Ben halted, watching Gwen place small salads on the island counter before saying, "Looks like we made it just in time."

"You did," Gwen confirmed.

Chapter Thirty-Four

…early evening, Thursday

Coming into the kitchen, Cole said, "Good to see you again, Mrs. Andrews. Thanks for inviting me to dinner."

"Jenna suggested we include you, and you're welcome."

"Any more curious boot prints in your back yard?"

"Not that I've noticed. A fresh snowfall would make new indents easier to spot among all the bird and squirrel tracks."

She waved toward the lidded pots and cast-iron skillet of sauteed veggie. "We're eating buffet style, so scoop what you want, then choose your stool."

The last to serve himself, Ben spooned steaming stew onto his mashed potatoes and added the zucchini. Gwen spoke in a low voice, "Did you have a successful day?"

"Sure did. Cole and I eliminated a potential threat."

"Can't wait to hear the details."

She took her seat at the island and joined the chit-chat.

As Jenna finished eating, her fork clanged to her plate, her eyes wide. "Gwen, I forgot to tell you the news about my graduation."

"Drumroll, please," Ben said, tapping two fingers on the edge of the granite in a rhythmic beat.

Tossing Ben a look, Jenna added, "I'm set to graduate with high honors."

Cole clapped and yelled, "Congratulations!"

Giving Jenna a thumbs-up, Gwen said, "I'm so proud of you. All your hard work is paying off. You know, it's never too late to begin planning your graduation party."

Gwen's comment reminded her that she hadn't yet asked Jenna about adding her family reunion to the party. She needed to approach the idea soon, but not during dinner.

"I can't thank you enough for hosting my party." Jenna came around the island and hugged her sort-of grandmother.

Ben asked, "What are your plans after graduation?"

Shrugging, Jenna replied, "Haven't decided. I applied for two positions at Baylies. Plus I'm exploring options for my master's degree in Vermont, New Hampshire, and Maine. I'd like to stay in New England if I can."

Gwen had wondered if Jenna would relocate to Florida, where her grandfather now resided.

The excitement of Jenna's announcement dying down, Cole pushed aside his plate. "That was delicious, Mrs. Andrews. Can I help you clean up?"

Waving off his offer, Gwen replied, "No need."

"In that case," Cole began, turning to Jenna. "I could use a brisk walk to settle that food. Want to come with me?"

Before Jenna could respond, Gwen tossed her a grin and said. "You two go on. Enjoy your walk."

Hopping down from his stool, Cole extended his hand to Jenna. "How about we take a last look at the holiday lights decorating the village green before they disappear?"

After the front door closed, Gwen touched Ben's sleeve. "Now tell me why Cole drove the two of you today."

Ben held a dirty plate in mid-air. "Mike didn't want me driving my Corvette. The department insurance wouldn't cover damage to my personal car while I'm his temporary employee. He teamed me up with Cole to drive me in an official vehicle. Turns out, we're in my old ride."

"That must have amused you." Gwen placed the lidded pot of chicken stew in the fridge. "Let's put another log on the fire and share our day's successes. Want coffee?"

"Always. You brew and I'll tend the fire."

Gwen poured two mugs and carried them to the living room, placing Ben's on the coffee table before sitting.

Ben settled next to her on the sofa. "You go first."

"Such a gentleman," she joshed. "But all right. This morning's kitchen meeting at the Victorian proved that every Tucker resented Hank for his mooching. If I can find reasons, I'll arrange to bump into each of them using the list Shirley gave me this afternoon."

"What list is that?"

She explained the detailed chart for her sleuthing efforts.

"So you made no headway at the meeting?"

"Patience, Ben, patience."

197

Ben smirked at her gentle reprimand. "Sorry. Go on."

And so she did. "When the family uproar subsided, Filly's sister Minnie – the family spinster – approached me. She'd seen me at garden club meetings but had never said hello. Anyway, gardening provided a good reason to meet with her. I'll text her tomorrow morning and invite her to come over for a discussion of flowers for the Victorian."

"Is she mobile enough to come here?"

"She seems as spry as her sister Filly."

"You're calling Mrs. Tucker Filly now?'

Gwen nodded. "That's right. She asked me to after I first met her. This morning, she also invited me to visit anytime."

"That should come in handy," Ben commented. "I take back my earlier comment. You made headway today."

Holding up one finger, she said, "And I'm not finished."

"Well, excuse me," Ben teased. "Please continue."

"Shirley also told me that Minnie is keeper of all the family secrets."

Ben eyebrows wrinkled.

"And," Gwen added, "when Lawrence Tucker offered to hunt for Hank's stuff, hoping to find cash to put toward the burial expenses, Shirley suggested I go with him."

"That was cocky of her. Did he suspect you two were colluding to probe into the family members for clues connected to Hank's stabber?"

"He didn't seem to and welcomed my assistance."

"How soon will his hunt begin?"

"No date yet. We exchanged numbers. He'll text me."

She tapped Ben's hand. "You said that you and Cole eliminated a potential threat. Tell me how you did that."

Ben recounted their visit with the gruff store owner and his timid wife, their confirmation that Hank had been the thief, and relief to hear that he was dead. Then Phil identified himself as the shadow when he rushed from the back room after Wanda screamed.

Gwen studied Ben's expression. "So I shouldn't worry about an accomplice showing up at the Tucker home?"

"For now at least, we've narrowed the suspect pool to the family members."

"Should I be relieved or more concerned?"

"A bit of both, I imagine," Ben said. "Are you unhappy that a Tucker will likely be uncovered as the guilty party?"

"Yes, I guess that's it." Gwen dreaded learning that Shirley had been the stabber despite the reporter's insistence that she's undeserving of Rossini's suspicion.

Ben turned to face Gwen directly. "Whichever one stabbed Hank won't want to be exposed."

"I'm aware of the danger, Ben." Looking to shift his attention, Gwen posed a different question. "Any other progress this afternoon?"

"Yes. After leaving the convenience store, Cole and I stopped at the police station and updated their detectives that

Hank was confirmed as the thief but had been murdered so they could close their robbery case."

"Fast work, Detective Snowcrest," Gwen teased, partly jesting and partly concerned where their dual investigations would lead the two of them.

"Just the facts, ma'am," Ben retorted, mimicking an old TV crime show.

The front door opened to the laughter of Cole and Jenna. They hurried into the living room and stood before the fire, hands stretched toward the warmth of the flames.

"Did you enjoy the lights?" Gwen asked.

"Sure did," Jenna and Cole answered at the same time.

"But now we're chilled to the bone," Cole added, changing position to face Ben. "When do you want to retrieve your Corvette?"

"Whenever you're ready."

"I'm ready now."

Chapter Thirty-Five

…early morning, Friday

The next morning, not knowing if Minnie was an early riser, Gwen waited until eight to send a text:

'Minnie, Sorry if I'm texting too early. Are you available to come to my home at ten to discuss flowers? Gwen'

Within seconds, Gwen's cell buzzed an incoming text. Thinking that octogenarian Minnie was indeed out of bed, Gwen was surprised to see Shirley's name as the sender.

'Good news, Gwen! Can I stop over now to share?'

If Minnie arrived around ten, Gwen figured that two hours should be more than enough time for Shirley to share her news. Gwen typed a short response:

'Sure. See you soon.'

Just in case Shirley hadn't yet consumed enough coffee, Gwen scurried to the kitchen to brew a pot.

201

Hearing a car pull up out front, she hustled through the foyer and opened the door to see Shirley chugging up the front walkway.

Before the reporter had even stepped across the threshold, Gwen asked, "What's your good news?"

"I need coffee while I tell you. Let me in."

Gwen guided Shirley toward the kitchen and eased her onto an island stool. When the coffee brewer beeped, she filled a mug and set it in front of Shirley, then sat on the opposite stool to watch Shirley's animated expressions.

Her hands wrapped around the hot mug, Shirley's eyes opened wide. "I'm so excited to tell you this."

"Did one of your relatives confess to stabbing Hank?"

Shirley puffed air from her nostrils. "I wish. Sergeant Rossini would have to drop his suspicion of me."

It occurred to Gwen that Shirley was unaware of Rossini's re-assignment and Ben's hiring to work the case, opting to keep that tidbit to herself for now.

"But that's not my news." Shirley announced.

"So don't keep me in suspense. What's happened?"

"All right, all right. This morning, when I arrived at the *Gazette*, the receptionist said to report to the editor's office."

Gwen's hands reached over to cover Shirley's. "Judging by your expression and tone of voice, I'm guessing he didn't force you to retire."

Shirley's huge smile signaled there was more to share.

"Nope. He advised that I could stay until the end of this month, finish the story I've been developing, and then I'm officially retired with full pension. Did you hear that, Gwen? Full pension!"

Hopping off her stool, Gwen hurried around the island and wrapped Shirley in a tight hug. "Wonderful! I'm so relieved for you."

"Trust me, you can't possibly be more relieved than I am. But listen, Gwen, a few days ago, you were about to share your retirement experience but we were interrupted. I'd still like to hear how you maneuvered the transition. Do you have time now?"

Knowing that she'd have to keep one eye on the clock for Minnie's potential arrival, Gwen replied, "If you think my experience will help you shift from the 9-5 grind to a leisurely lifestyle, I have a little time."

Shirley held up her empty mug. "A refill first?"

After topping off Shirley's mug, Gwen returned to her stool and interlaced her fingers.

"I'll give you the abbreviated version of my transition."

Shirley blew on the steam. "That should be enough."

"Okay, here goes. While I was still teaching at Baylie College, my husband Parker was struck by lightning on the golf course and passed away a few days later."

"I remember that tragedy," Shirley said, her hand quickly gripping Gwen's arm. "My belated condolences."

A hitch in Gwen's throat threatened to steal her voice but she managed to say, "Thanks," and regained her composure.

"As you can imagine, I was shattered by Parker's death but did my best to maintain focus on my students. Still, the head of the Baylies music department gently suggested I retire. For a long time, I mourned Parker's absence in the privacy of the home we created together."

Trying not to lose control of her emotions again, Gwen sat up straight. "Are you aware that after Parker and I purchased the abandoned library, his architectural ingenuity converted the building into this?" Gwen waved her hand to include the entire transformation.

Shirley glanced around the open spaces and up to the skylights far above them. "Amazing talent, your Parker."

Gwen nodded her agreement. "Sorry to distract myself from telling you about my transition."

"Understandable," Shirley said. "The floor is yours."

Clearing her throat, Gwen picked up where she left off.

"Two springs after Parker died, my good friend Betty Owens convinced me to participate in the garden club's autumn tour. As I resurrected our gardens, Mother Nature stepped in as my grief counselor. And then one evening, Parker's ghost appeared to me right over there."

Gwen pointed through the Ficus trees beneath the open staircase to Parker's recliner beside the fireplace. "After the shock wore off, my mourning subsided."

"So the return of Parker's spirit helped you emerge from your sadness and settle into your retirement," Shirley summarized. "And his appearance also explains why you hosted the séance re-scheduled from Liz's smoke-filled bookstore to here. How much later did that take place?"

Gwen paused to think. "I believe that was the following year. But Liz neglected to tell me that she'd hired Annabelle to record the evening's success or failure."

"And I'm glad Annabelle suggested I come along," Shirley said. "You know, I squinted to see your Parker's ghost, but I never did."

"Neither did Liz or my sister Tess," Gwen said. "Fortunately, the other attendees not only could see Parker's transparent form but made their own connections."

"Has your Parker appeared to you since that séance?"

Before Gwen could frame a reply to reveal his absence for the past few months, her cell buzzed with a text.

Minnie: *'Thanks for the invite. See you at 10am.'*

"Excuse me, Shirley, I need to respond to this."

"Go right ahead." Shirley collected both mugs and rinsed them in the sink.

After sending a thumbs up emoji to Minnie, Gwen joined Shirley at the sliding glass door to the deck, both gazing out onto Gwen's back gardens, entrancing even in their snowy winter incarnation.

Shirley spoke first. "You know what, Gwen? An article about your love story with Parker would make a heartwarming tale as my final contribution before retiring from the *Gazette*."

"Gosh, I don't know," Gwen hedged. "Only a handful of people in Harbor Falls are aware of Parker's ghost. I'd rather not make our love story public."

"In that case, I won't pester you about it."

"I appreciate that. By the way, that was Minnie who texted. She's coming here at ten."

"That was quick work. Your garden club connection was a clever way to arrange your chat. Like I told you, Minnie is the keeper of family gossip so she may share a few tidbits."

"We'll have to wait and see, Shirley."

"Well, best of luck. Thanks again for agreeing to help figure out who stabbed Hank. Will you let me know if Minnie is helpful?"

"Of course. And Lawrence, too. I'm waiting for his text to hunt down Hank's belongings. Then I'll try to arrange chance encounters with the other family members."

"My Aunt Filly's open invitation should come in handy for the ones who live in the Victorian."

"That's true. And your list with addresses etc. for the others will be helpful as well."

"I'd better skedaddle before Minnie gets here." Shirley donned her coat, boots, and mittens, then hustled to her car.

Chapter Thirty-Six

…mid-morning, Friday

When Shirley's car pulled away from the curb. Gwen typed a quick text to Ben: *'Shirley just left. Minnie at ten'.*

Ben's nearly instant reply: *'While you're chatting with Minnie, I'll be introducing myself to the Tuckers as Rossini's replacement.'*

Not long after, Gwen opened the door to find Minnie on her doorstep. Noticing no car either at the curb or pulling away, she turned to Minnie. "I see you walked over."

The elderly woman's expression revealed surprise at the comment. "I stroll the village green pathways every day."

Gwen glanced toward the cloudy sky. A brisk icy breeze blowing off Massachusetts Bay was swooping across the village green, swaying the tree branches.

"You're a hardy woman, Minnie. Please come in."

As Minnie stepped across the threshold, she glanced at the boot tray. "I see you agree with my sister – footwear off. Eliminates cleaning up what visitors track inside."

Shivering, Gwen quickly latched the door closed.

Though a tall woman, the elderly Minnie had no problem

bending down to remove her practical black boots. Hanging her coat, she pulled a pair of slippers from her oversized tote and slid her oversized feet into them.

"There we go," Minnie proclaimed as she stretched to her full height and grinned down at Gwen. "Thank you for inviting me over this morning. I've been anticipating our discussion of flowers that will add some color to Filly's Victorian when the weather warms."

Gwen waved Minnie from the foyer and toward the living room. "Let's make ourselves comfortable near the fire. These old walls were insulated during the conversion, but on frigid days, the chill manages to find its way inside."

"Same in my sister's house," Minnie commented, settling at one end of the leather sofa. She noticed the horticultural books placed on shelves and side tables.

Hoping their conversation didn't backfire, Gwen indicated her teapot on a tray. "Would you like a cup?"

With a twinkle in her eye, Minnie chirped, "Tea would be a lovely change from what I've been drinking this morning, so thank you." She snickered at her misleading and non-specific joke.

Gwen's manners kept her from asking Minnie what she'd been drinking. Instead she filled China cups she'd inherited from her mother.

Passing one to Minnie, Gwen said, "This is a delightful herbal blend I discovered recently. I've been reducing caffeine, which tends to give me heartburn."

Accepting the cup and saucer, Minnie stirred a small amount of sugar into the pale beverage. "Very wise of you."

As Minnie sipped, Gwen continued the heartburn topic to solidify a pleasant relationship. "I can't totally abandon coffee, but I do mix a caffeinated blend with a decaf."

Placing her cup and saucer on the low table, Minnie repositioned herself, resting her arm on the sofa back before placing her cheek atop one curled fist. "I confess to a chocolate addition, which gives me the same heartburn."

Gwen laughed. "I can't believe we're both chocoholics. You'll laugh that I sent an email to the largest chocolate company about removing the caffeine from cocoa beans."

"You're a hoot, Gwen. Did you get a reply?"

"I sure did. The email read something like this." Gwen faked a haughty voice as she recalled the words:

'Mrs. Andrews, thank you for your inquiry. At the moment, our R&D department has no plans to pursue the decaffeination of cocoa beans.'

Minnie chuckled. "You know what that means?"

"I'd love to hear your best guess."

"Well," Minnie continued. "The day you discover decaf chocolate bars on the store shelves, you should expect a big fat check for your suggestion."

Gwen's turn to laugh, delighted that her connection with Minnie seemed to be warming with each passing second.

"I hope to live long enough to see that day."

"You and me both," Minnie agreed.

"Time to talk flowers, Minnie. Are you ready?"

"I was ready the moment I received your text invitation."

Reaching into her tote, Minnie retrieved a spiral notebook and pen. "Now I'm really ready. My memory is shot, so I need notes for everything."

Enjoying Minnie's easy-going nature and sense of humor, Gwen strolled to the closest bookcase and selected two photo albums, placing one on her lap, the other on the coffee table. "First, these are pictures of the perennials that bloom around my property each season. You can decide which blossoms and colors you like best."

Flipping from one page to the next, Gwen identified each flower by name, sun or shade exposure, and bloom time as Minnie recorded each detail.

When Gwen closed the final page of the second album, Minnie again reached into her tote and withdrew several photographs. "I brought these to show you the minimal landscaping around Filly's Victorian, which nearly disappears in the winter months. I'd like your opinion."

"Of course." Gwen flipped from one picture to the next, then pointed at a line of bushes. "These look like forsythia. If you prune them, they'll thicken and create a hedge."

Minnie made a note and looked up. "Maybe we should add a patio."

"Great idea," Gwen agreed. "A narrow flower bed along the base would add texture and color. Before you install new plants, be sure to enhance the soil then water."

Gwen continued her advice. "Perennial beds will need a good clean-out before the new shoots begin to emerge next year. When the stalks die down, you can add annuals for a colorful summer display. I can let you know when I begin my clean-up if you want to watch how I do it."

"I'll keep that in mind."

Minnie added a few more comments, then tucked her notebook and photographs into her tote bag. "I can't wait for the warmer spring days so I can start beautifying the Victorian for Filly."

"She'll love it, Minnie."

Minnie's focus traveled around the living room, seeming to absorb the decor. "I hope you won't think me rude, but I'd love to see the rest of your home."

Hoping Minnie would segue from the décor to the family's upset about Hank's demise and burial expense, Gwen pushed herself off the sofa. "A tour is included with your flower lesson. Follow me."

Chapter Thirty-Seven

...mid-morning, Friday

At half past ten, confident that he wouldn't bump into Gwen at the Tucker home, Ben asked Cole to drop him off.

"You sure you don't want me to go in with you?"

Cole sounded disappointed, and Ben regretted turning down the young officer, but he had a good reason. "Sorry, but I need to approach this family in a non-threatening way, the polar opposite of Rossini. Plus, they've already seen you with him. Whoever's here this morning could be intimidated if we both are present."

"Makes sense, Ben. Good luck."

Before closing the SUV's passenger door, Ben leaned in to add, "I'll text you later to come and get me."

"No problem," Cole said. "This'll give me a chance to follow up on Mrs. Andrews' boot prints."

Again impressed by Cole's work ethic, Ben closed the passenger door as quietly as he could and remained on the sidewalk until the SUV drove out of sight.

There was no way for Ben to know if the arrival and departure of the police vehicle had been spotted by anyone inside the house, so he steeled his nerves then stepped along the front walkway. His keen sense of observation picked out the rapidly disappearing indentations in the snow, the largest one where Shirley had nearly tripped over Hank Payne less than a week earlier.

Approaching the concrete steps, Ben glanced briefly at the red-tinted step that had caused Hank's brain to bleed.

After ascending the steps and taking several strides across the veranda, Ben lifted and dropped the antique knocker mounted on the frame of the stained-glass door. Seconds later, the door opened to reveal a youthful female staring back at him.

She held the door partially closed. "Can I help you?"

Pasting on his friendliest smile, Ben held out his Harbor Falls Police Department badge for her inspection. "My name is Detective Benjamin Snowcrest. I'm investigating the Hank Payne stabbing."

She studied his badge, then waved him inside. "Please remove your boots. You can place them on that rug."

After doing as he was told, Ben stood upright and waited.

Through an archway into the next room, a stately older woman strolled toward him.

"I heard the knocker, Jennifer. Who is this?"

"A police detective, Grandmother."

Ben assumed the older lady must be Filomena Tucker. "I have only a few questions, Mrs. Tucker. I won't take much of your time."

She squinted at him. "You know who I am?"

He tossed her a half grin. "Doesn't everyone?"

She chuckled at his flattery. "Come in, Detective. What's the reason for your visit?"

Mrs. Tucker hadn't moved more than a foot or two, so they remained just inside the front door.

Ben explained, "The police chief asked me to wrap up the investigation into Hank Payne's stabbing."

She leaned sideways to peer beyond Ben's shoulder, though the stained glass blocked her view. "Is that unpleasant Detective Rossini with you?"

"No, ma'am," Ben replied. "He's been assigned to a more urgent case." Ben purposely downplayed the importance of his follow-up, hoping she'd be more forthcoming with information.

"Excellent," she said with obvious relief. "The entire family found him quite irritating."

Ben let her critique slide past. "My condolences that your grandson died from complications."

With no hint of sorrow, she responded, "Thank you," then turned to Jennifer. "I can handle things from here. Why don't you go upstairs and check on Olivia."

Mrs. Tucker watched her granddaughter mount the staircase before turning her attention back to Ben. "There aren't many of us in the house this morning but whoever's here will answer whatever questions remain unanswered."

"I appreciate your cooperation." Ben focused on her still attractive face. "Where do you suggest I conduct my interviews?"

"My kitchen is the heartbeat of this old house. This way."

Ben followed her across the entrance hall and living room, noting Norman Tucker's empty hospital bed at the far end, the location of his assault, but by who?

As they passed beneath one archway into the adjacent dining room and then a second into the kitchen, Ben noted the flat latch of a pocket door between the two rooms.

In the kitchen, Mrs. Tucker waved him to an oversized farm-style table, its surface well-worn from decades of meals and discussions.

"Sit anywhere you like." Without asking, she moved to a coffee maker and poured two cups, setting one in front of Ben. She was obviously used to waiting on her family.

"Do you take sugar or cream?"

"Neither. Just black, thank you."

She eased into a chair on the opposite side of the table. "Now tell me about those unanswered questions."

Hearing no noises echoing in the expansive house, Ben felt confident they wouldn't be interrupted any time soon.

Opening Cole's wire bound notebook, Ben flipped through the notes scribbled during Rossini's two interviews,

"Give me a moment," he said to her, reviewing the written words for his benefit and hers.

Mrs. Tucker noticed him arriving at the next blank page.

He looked up to see her fidgeting with the handle of her mug. "Sorry, these questions won't take very long."

She flicked her fingers for him to get on with it.

"Here we go. What time did you come downstairs last Monday morning?"

Pausing, she finally spoke. "Oh, at my usual time, I expect. That would be somewhere between five and six."

He jotted the question and her answer.

"Did you descend using the front staircase?"

Her eyebrows lifted. "Oh, no. I always check on Jennifer and Olivia before taking the back steps." She got to her feet and strolled to the rear corner, indicating a flight of steps. "My ancestors added this set of steps to serve as an exit from the living quarters upstairs in case of a fire."

"Clever of them," Ben commented. "And did you come down because you heard noises?"

Her forehead wrinkled as she returned to the table. "Noises? Oh, you mean by whoever entered this house and attacked my dear Norman then stabbed Hank?"

Finding her return question of interest, Ben dove deeper. "So you think someone broke in from outside?"

She tossed her head and not a single hair moved out of place. "Isn't that the most obvious conclusion, Detective? I can't imagine you'd think anyone in my family injured Norman and Hank."

Ben returned to his question that she hadn't answered. "So you didn't come down because you heard a disturbance?"

Again, she shook her head. "The insulation in this old house was upgraded years ago. Noises downstairs cannot be heard through the bedroom doors upstairs. I came down simply to start breakfast."

Adding her statement to the notes, Ben looked over at her. "At what point did you realize something had happened down here?"

She stood and walked to the kitchen door to the outside, pointing out its window. "When lights from an ambulance lit up my kitchen wall, and I heard voices out front, I rushed to the living room and found Norman unconscious on the floor. A young policeman came through the front door, which seemed to be open to the elements. My niece Shirley entered behind him. He called for an ambulance and I accompanied my husband to the ER."

She stared at Ben, her expression challenging. "Does that resolve your issue?"

"It does, thank you. Sorry to make you relive the upsetting event." Again, Ben made a note, then said, "Just a couple more questions. Before you rushed to your husband, did you notice anything amiss in this kitchen? The door ajar? A missing knife?"

"A missing knife?" she asked.

217

"Yes. Were you aware that Hank had been stabbed?"

She jerked back in surprise. "Not until later. I was too concerned with my Norman to be aware of anything else. I'm sorry, but the rest of that morning is a blur."

"Understandable," Ben said in his most soothing voice, knowing that he'd be interviewing her again. "That's enough for now. May I return if any other details need to be clarified?"

"If you find that necessary."

Chapter Thirty-Eight
…mid-morning, Friday

Before giving Minnie the tour, Gwen gathered the photo albums and returned them to particular shelves.

Waiting patiently, Minnie wandered around the living room, her fingers stroking the wood, her feet abandoning the slippers so her stockinged feet could toe the area rugs, her hands repositioning knickknacks into an arrangement only she understood.

When Minnie made eye contact, Gwen pointed up and Minnie tilted her head back. "Oh, my. I didn't notice the mezzanine is still exposed. Your home retains the essence of the original library. Filly and I used to spend hours in the children's section."

Gwen nodded that she understood. "I've been told many similar stories. Childhood memories are so charming."

Easing around the fireplace wall, Gwen led Minnie into the music studio dominated by a baby grand piano. Flames flickered from this side of the double-sided fireplace.

Gwen explained, "I offer piano and flute lessons to the local youngsters."

Minnie pressed a few piano keys. "Do you teach adults?"

"On occasion. You sound interested."

"I am. When I was a youngster, I refused piano lessons but would love to learn now. There's an old upright piano in a storage room of Filly's house where I could practice."

"Then let's find a date for your first lesson. What day works best for you?"

After adding Minnie to the lesson calendar, Gwen said, "Congratulations. And don't worry, I won't force you to participate in a student recital."

Pretending to swipe sweat from her forehead with the back of her hand, Minnie joked, "What a relief."

Not expecting Minnie's playfulness, Gwen led her from the music studio, pausing at the sliding door to the back deck, sweeping her hand to indicate the landscape. "My winter-weary gardens."

Minnie peered through the glass. "I'm trying to imagine how it looks with your flowers in full bloom. I missed out on the last garden club tour."

Gwen commented, "The winter months are interesting in their own way, but frustrating to an avid gardener who can't wait to plunge her hands into the warming soil."

She waved Minnie into the open kitchen, circling the center island before continuing past the formal dining room to pause at the bottom of the swooping staircase. "Second level next."

Ascending beside Gwen, Minnie glided her hand along

the gleaming wood. "I don't recall anything this fancy in the original town library."

Memories of the conversion flooded Gwen's mind. "My husband found this salvaged staircase in New Hampshire."

"I can't imagine the labor to install it."

"It was quite a project with lots of strong backs."

Gwen didn't speak again until they reached the mezzanine level. "This sitting room is my favorite space."

Minnie stepped to the row of window seats and gazed down for an elevated view of the gardens. "Oh, Gwen, you must sit here often to read a book or just get lost in thought."

Before Gwen had a chance to respond, Amber appeared and leaped onto the cushion next to Minnie.

Reaching over, Minnie stroked the golden head, murmuring, "Aren't you just the sweetest kitty?"

Her eyes glistening, she turned toward Gwen. "Your little beauty looks similar to one I rescued years ago. Mine had the same golden coloring but with a white bib. Unfortunately, when a relative with allergies moved into the Victorian, I had to return my Goldie to the shelter."

Gwen took the cushion on the cat's other side. "This mischievous feline is named Amber."

"Perfect choice. May I use your facilities before we continue? All that tea you know."

"Certainly. The guest bathroom is around the mezzanine curve. Let me show you."

When Minnie rejoined Gwen, they peeked into Jenna's guest room but didn't venture inside. Moving along the front edge of the mezzanine, they entered Gwen's gable bedroom.

Minnie strolled to the window at the head of Gwen's bed. "The village green looks so New England from this angle."

They soon found themselves returned to the sitting room and descended the staircase.

"Delightful," Minnie gushed as they reached the first floor. "Thank you so much for an entertaining morning."

Because Minnie hadn't mentioned Hank's stabbing, a segue to a bit of sleuthing had yet to emerge. Gwen touched Minnie's arm. "Would you like to stay for a light lunch?"

A smile brightened Minnie's face. "Yes, I'd enjoy that."

***

As their simple midday meal progressed, Gwen and Minnie chatted about everything except Hank until the opening Gwen had hoped for finally made its appearance.

Minnie lowered her soup spoon. "I'm so glad we finally met, Gwen. It was unfortunate that Shirley invited you to the family meeting about the cost of poor Hank's burial. I was quite embarrassed by their bickering."

Gwen recognized that Minnie was the first Tucker to express a modicum of sadness about Hank's death.

Reminding herself not to ask direct questions that Minnie might consider too nosey, Gwen offered a platitude. It's difficult to say goodbye to a younger family member."

"That wasn't the only problem. They all resent Hank for his mooching. Filly and I are hoping the others will become more forgiving after we lay Hank in his final resting place."

Gwen offered a second platitude. "Life goes on, Minnie, and I suppose all we can do is accept what has happened."

"Another truism," Minnie agreed.

Not wanting to inadvertently expose her collaboration with Shirley, Gwen decided silence was her best response, so she picked up her egg salad sandwich and took a bite.

As expected, Minnie couldn't resist the urge to fill the empty air with her thoughts.

"Filly and I choose to believe that no one in our family is bold enough to stab another relative within the walls of the family home."

"Do the others agree with you?" Gwen regretted her too-targeted words as soon as they left her tongue.

When a frown dented Minnie's forehead, Gwen feared she'd delved too deeply too quickly.

Fortunately, Minnie didn't seem to notice. "I hear that Sergeant Rossini is determined to blame one of us. Even our Shirley is on his hit list. Now that we've met, I understand why she turned to you for support. You have such a calming nature."

Encouraged that Minnie didn't seem to suspect the real reason Shirley had reached out to Gwen, she reversed Minnie's previous statement as a question.

"You and your sister both think someone came into your home from outside?"

"We do." Minnie upturned the Vintage lapel watch pinned to her bodice. "Oh, dear, how the time has flown."

Minnie's abrupt intent to go home came as a surprise. Gwen's hope to hear family secrets dashed, she was powerless to change Minnie's mind about leaving.

Moving around the island, Minnie placed one arm across Gwen's shoulders and squeezed. "Thank you for the flower suggestions, a delightful tour, and a delicious lunch."

Though elderly, Minnie moved at a quick pace toward the foyer, soon fully dressed to brave the winter weather, including multicolored mittens on both hands.

When Gwen unlatched and opened the front door, a brisk breeze blew inside. Again she shivered as she scanned the darkening sky, spotting nearly invisible white flakes swirling against the tree skeletons in the village green.

Minnie paused on the threshold. "Another snowstorm?"

"Seems so," Gwen answered. "Are you okay to walk home? It's not a bother to give you a ride."

"Don't worry about me. This is not my first snowstorm." Minnie grinned at her play on words. "Let's get together again. Next time, you come to the Victorian for lunch."

"Sounds wonderful. Text me when you're safely home."

Gwen watched Minnie's figure hunched against the wind and snowflakes as she faded into the distance.

Chapter Thirty-Nine

…late morning, Friday

Waiting patiently at the Victorian's kitchen table, Ben anticipated the return of Shirley's Aunt Filly – with or without other family members in tow.

To fill the minutes, he scanned the decor. Appliances had been upgraded over many decades of Tuckers while other features appeared original including the flowered wallpaper, the linoleum floor, and the glass-fronted cabinet displaying delicate China cups and saucers.

Those features reminded Ben of his grandmother's kitchen, where he'd eaten many mouthwatering meals when his mom was working to pay the rent.

Forcing himself back to the investigation, he'd been struck by Filly Tucker's firm assertion that no one in the family could have possibly been involved in her grandson's stabbing. She insisted that an unknown outsider – one of her grandson's unsavory acquaintances? – had snuck inside with murderous intent.

After speaking with Phil and Wanda at the convenience store, he and Cole had eliminated that shadow person as a possible accomplice. So far, no clues had emerged that an enemy of Hank's had broken in to seek revenge for some past grievance. Ben stepped to the kitchen door and bent down to examine both the mechanism and the door jam. No sign of damage. His mind whirled back to the family members as the only logical suspects.

Was Filly Tucker protecting a family member, whether a resident or someone living elsewhere in Harbor Falls or a nearby town?

To re-create the sequence, Ben paced the linoleum floor, mentally reconstructing events before, during, and after the personal interviews.

1. *Shirley arrived near dawn to discover Hank's bleeding body in the snow and called 9-1-1.*
2. *Cole Martin responded and questioned her.*
3. *EMTs rushed Hank to the nearest ER.*
4. *Noticing the front door ajar, Cole entered and found Filly Tucker cradling her unconscious husband. Cole called for a second ambulance.*
5. *Rossini arrived. After a brief review of the scene, he labeled Shirley and Mrs. Tucker as his prime suspects.*
6. *Shirley called Gwen to come to the Victorian for support.*
7. *Gazette photographer Annabelle showed up, claiming that Gwen was her assistant. Rossini called her bluff and told Gwen to go home, which she didn't.*

8. *Rossini ordered Annabelle to take photos. [Ben noted he needed to review her photos.]*
9. *Surgeons failed to ease Hank's brain-bleed. His death eliminated him as a witness.*
10. *Rossini hadn't called in a forensic team because Hank was only injured and not dead which left the knife in Hank's back the sole source of timely fingerprints. Too late now to collect untainted evidence within the crime scene.*

Ben massaged his forehead. If one of the family members had witnessed Hank's stabbing, he or she was keeping their secret carefully guarded. Perhaps not even sharing with the other Tuckers.

With virtually no clues to guide them, Ben and Cole – along with Gwen – needed to ferret out the Tucker who'd stabbed Hank in some other way. Unless Filly Tucker was right about someone else being involved. But who had motive and opportunity? Those questions needed answers.

The sound of a key unlocking the kitchen door interrupted Ben's concentration.

The door opened and a man stiffened in the doorway. "Who are you?"

Ben pulled out his ID and shoved it forward. "Detective Benjamin Snowcrest."

Startled, the man pushed his hands out to his sides,

indicating no weapon. "I'm Lawrence Tucker."

"Sorry to alarm you," Ben said, tabling his badge.

Lawrence stepped closer, his eyes never leaving Ben's.

Ben considered that every member of the family might possess a key to that kitchen door. If a non-resident Tucker stabbed Hank, breaking in wouldn't have been necessary, so no evidence.

The echo of footfalls descending the main staircase reached Ben's ears. Seconds later, Filly Tucker appeared in the kitchen archway, staring at him and Lawrence.

"Good morning, son." Filly strolled toward him and placed a peck on his cheek. "I see you've met Detective Benjamin Snowcrest."

"Just now, Mother," Lawrence responded.

Filly transferred her focus to Ben. "I'm sorry, but almost everyone is out running errands. Only Jessica and little Olivia are in their rooms."

The screeching cry of a baby verified Filly's claim.

When Lawrence moved toward the dining room, Ben got to his feet. "Before you go, Lawrence, I'm here to interview everyone who was on the premises Sunday night into Monday morning."

"Sorry, Detective," Lawrence challenged. "I can't talk with you right now. My daughter's worried about baby Olivia and called me to come over."

Before Ben could object further, Filly said, "Detective

Snowcrest, you'll have to come back some other time."

Ben reached for the notebook and his badge. "I'd really like to close this case, Mrs. Tucker. If you can gather everyone who was here last Monday morning, I'll return this afternoon for my interviews."

Her expression remained impenetrable. "After supper would be more convenient. Return around seven."

Ben felt duly chastised for daring to dictate her schedule but needing her to fully cooperate, he caved. "In that case, I'll see you this evening. Goodbye for now."

Without acknowledging Ben's agreement, she followed Lawrence through the archway toward the front staircase.

Ben exited out the kitchen door, surprised by the snowflakes that greeted him.

Chapter Forty

…noon, Friday

Gwen grinned at Ben's text, *'Coast clear?'*

Instead of texting back, Gwen called his cell. "Minnie left a few minutes ago. What's your next move?"

"I'm thinking to walk over to your place if that's okay."

"More than okay," Gwen responded.

A millisecond later, his intent registered. "You're walking here? Where are you?"

"Under a huge tree across the street from the Victorian."

"Then you must know that it's snowing."

Ben chuckled. "Yep." He paused. "Wait. That must be Minnie scurrying across the street at the light. On the tall side? Black coat? Brightly colored mittens?"

"That's Minnie. Even if you had passed her, she wouldn't have known who you are. You'd better hustle to my house before the snow gets any heavier."

"On my way."

***

Before Ben texted, Gwen had been writing notes about Minnie's visit in the back of her legal pad, the page next to Shirley's chart of Tucker family information. She now added some final details, questioning her impression of Filly's elderly sister. Minnie seemed like a sweet old lady, but Gwen had misjudged more than a few people over the years, eventually paying for her mistake.

Gwen considered her initial opinions this early in the investigation. Were her evaluations premature? Her exposure to many of the Tuckers during the heated discussion about burial expenses had provided most of them with a motive, only one prong of probable guilt. The knife was the means. The opportunity remained elusive.

In fact, Minnie – Gwen's first private conversation with a family member other than Shirley – had been adamant that Hank's attacker came from outside the family.

Positioning herself near the front windows to watch for Ben, Gwen justified her scrutiny of the family as a means to clear Shirley of Rossini's suspicion, which was included in the case notes. As Gwen worked her way through each Tucker, would she discover that all of them – like Minnie – were an impenetrable vault of secrets?

But if Gwen eventually broke through their attempts to hide the guilty party and pointed her finger at the Tucker who'd plunged that kitchen knife into Hank's back, her success would bring her no pleasure.

Her cell buzzed. A text from Lawrence. How timely, as he was the next Tucker on Gwen's list. As she finished reading his last sentence about them searching for Hank's belongings, she spied a lone figure fast walking along the perimeter of the village green and opted to delay her reply to Lawrence's day and time suggestion.

Ben was so covered with snow, she could barely distinguish between his white beard and mustache from his sheepskin collar.

She rushed to the front door, holding it open as he bounded up the outside steps. Like a dog leaping from a summer pond, Ben shook himself to cast off the clinging flakes before stepping inside.

"Get in here, Ben. Don't worry about dripping on the floor. That's why Parker laid porcelain tile."

She helped his arms slide from his sleeves and hung the heavy coat to drip dry as the remaining snow melted.

"Brr," he roared. "Did I smell welcoming smoke drifting down from your chimney?"

"You did. I lit one during Minnie's visit. Go in and warm up. I'll fix us some hot chocolate." Before she turned away, she added, "With marshmallows," and grinned at him.

He beamed back at her and hurried into the living room.

Several minutes later, Gwen entered with two steaming mugs to find Ben on the raised hearth warming his hands.

"Thawed out yet?" she asked, handing him a mug.

"Almost. I added a few more logs."

Trying not to spill her own drink, Gwen eased into Parker's recliner and dared a cautious sip, moaning at that first taste of chocolate. "Why didn't Cole drop you off?"

"I'll explain after I've thawed."

The doorbell chimed, startling Gwen. She glanced at Ben. "Who can possibly be out in this storm?" She pushed herself off Parker's recliner and soon opened the front door.

Shirley stood on the top step, her face tucked into the folds of her hood, her hands tucked beneath her armpits.

"Shirley, what are you doing out in this weather?"

"Not my choice," Shirley barked, barging past Gwen. "I stopped at the Sugar 'n' Spice for something sweet and when I got back in my old car, the engine wouldn't turn over. I called AAA but the operator said the trucks are all out on emergency calls and won't arrive for at least a half hour. On top of that, the bakery is closing and Annabelle's apartment is dark. Any chance I can stay with you until AAA arrives?"

"Of course. First, get out of that wet coat."

Ben came up behind them. "Hi, Shirley."

"Hello, Ben. I didn't know you'd be here."

"Got caught in the storm, like you," he fibbed.

The three of them made their way to the roaring fire.

Ben said, "Did I hear you say you're waiting for AAA?"

"You heard right."

"I might be able to speed up your rescue. I've been hanging around with Police Chief Brown. Maybe one of his officers can stop by and give you a jump start."

Anxiety eased from Shirley's face. "Great. Thanks."

"I'll make that call." He walked around the fireplace wall, dialing Cole from the privacy of Gwen's music studio.

Shirley crossed her legs. "I need your bathroom, Gwen."

"Use mine upstairs. It'll be more private."

Shirley bounded up the staircase in stockinged feet as Ben rejoined Gwen.

"Very chivalrous of you," she murmured.

"I'm always willing to help a damsel in distress." His soft grey eyes looked down on her. "Cole will be here in a few minutes. He said the roads are already treacherous, but their SUVs are equipped to handle bad weather."

She touched his arm. "I don't like the idea of you driving your sports car in this storm. The Corvette's powerful engine could land you in a ditch before you reach your condo."

When her cell buzzed, she glanced at the caller ID and pushed the answer button. "Jenna, are you okay?"

"I'm fine, but I wanted to tell you that Samantha suggested I stay with her in the dorm tonight. I've accepted."

"Thoughtful of her. Now you won't risk falling on the icy sidewalks. Will you be back in the morning?"

"I can't say."

"Well, call or text when you know," Gwen said.

Promising she would, Jenna disconnected.

Turning to Ben, Gwen said, "Well, that settles it. I strongly suggest you remain here tonight. Jenna's staying on campus so the guestroom will be available."

"Now who's being chivalrous?" Ben teased. "I accept your offer. Cole can retrieve me tomorrow."

Shirley flew down the staircase and wiggled her eyebrows at Gwen, a veiled indication that she'd overheard Gwen's invitation for Ben to stay the night.

While waiting for Cole to rescue her, Shirley took a seat beside Ben on the leather sofa. "I understand you were in New Mexico to visit with your father before he passed on. My condolences."

"Thank you," Ben responded, "and I hear you'll be retiring soon. Any plans to travel?"

Still distracted by Minnie's visit, Gwen let Shirley and Ben discuss destinations while she scribbled more notes.

Chapter Forty-One

…mid-afternoon, Friday

Ben escorted Shirley down Gwen's snowy front walkway to Cole's SUV and assisted her into the passenger seat.

"Are you sure you're okay to drive, Shirley?"

"Don't worry about me, Ben. My car may be old, but it's a tank in the snow. Thanks for everything."

Ben looked across the passenger seat at Cole, "And thanks for the rescue. I'll touch base tomorrow morning when the roads are more Corvette-friendly."

"Fine." Cole focused on Shirley. "Point out your car."

Retreating inside, Ben and Gwen stood at the front windows to watch Cole's SUV inch slowly around the village green until he stopped near a green sedan in front of the bakery's dark windows.

While Shirley brushed off the snow, Cole connected his cables. Within seconds, dark smoke blew from the exhaust.

Seconds later, Ben pointed. "Cole must have offered to follow Shirley home."

"I think you're right. He seems to be following her," Gwen agreed. "He's a nice guy."

Ben turned toward her. "Why don't I shovel for you?"

Grinning, she touched his arm. "That's sweet of you, but I pay a young man who likes to earn his own money."

As if to confirm her snow day arrangement, the sound of metal scraping against concrete leaked through the quickly disappearing windowpanes.

Glancing beyond Ben, she pointed toward a young man tossing snow to the side of her walkway. "He'll have to shovel again after the storm ends, but I'm willing to pay him as often as it snows."

***

Ben settled across from Gwen as they shared what they'd each learned about the Tuckers, analyzing their progress.

Suddenly, Ben jumped to his feet. "Damn. Filly Tucker agreed to assemble her family at seven this evening so I can finish my interviews. Not a good idea with this weather, I need to cancel."

Gwen pushed herself up from Parker's recliner. "You go ahead and make that call. I'll check what's in my fridge for our supper."

Ben watched her stroll toward the kitchen and was overcome by the image of them as a real couple. But no matter how much he wished that could happen, he was keen enough to understand that Parker's ghost maintained a strong hold on her heart, despite his failure to appear since late October.

Ben would have to be satisfied with their limited time

together in a platonic friendship with Gwen.

Pushing aside his fantasy of a deeper relationship, Ben picked up his cell and dialed the Tucker Victorian.

He was jolted from his musing when an unfamiliar voice answered, "Who's this?"

Taken aback by the brevity of the speaker, Ben replied. "Detective Benjamin Snowcrest. May I speak with Mrs. Tucker, please?"

"She's right here."

Ben listened as voices whispered and feet shuffled until the phone was picked up. "This is Filly Tucker, Detective. I hope you're calling to cancel your interviews this evening."

"That's right, Mrs. Tucker. With this unexpected snowstorm, we'd be smart to reschedule."

"Very intuitive of you. Several family members have already called to say they can probably meet with you sometime tomorrow. That assumes the roads are plowed and my driveway shoveled. Is that satisfactory?"

Again using the tactic to let potential suspects have a hand in the arrangements, Ben said, "We'll give that a try. I'll call tomorrow after the roads are passable so we can agree on a time."

As Ben ended the call, Gwen walked back in. "I heard most of that. So tomorrow's interviews will depend on the snowplows? Good thing you're staying here tonight – short walk tomorrow."

"A bonus of your invitation. I'll try not to be underfoot."

She threw back her head and laughed. "It'll take more than an overnight emergency to get tired of your company."

Their eyes met for an elongated moment until she broke the trance. "Do you mind a repeat of last night's chicken stew? We'll eat over toast if you're agreeable."

"Comfort food at its best," Ben answered.

"Good. The stew's reheating on the stove, ready in a half hour or so."

"Fine with me," Ben said, getting to his feet. "I'd like to hear your opinion of the Tuckers you've met so far."

"Okay. Let's move to the kitchen."

Seconds later, he stood beside her near the stove. "How can I help prepare our supper?"

"How about you stir the chicken stew."

As Gwen slid bread slices into the toaster, she spoke over her shoulder. "You never did say why Cole dropped you at the Victorian this morning."

"Oh, that. I explained that the family might be more open with me if Cole wasn't there because he was with Rossini. Besides, I like to write my own notes so I wouldn't need him for that. I promised to include him tomorrow and sent him back to the station."

"That all makes sense," Gwen commented.

I'm debating where we should eat – island counter or the dining room table."

"I've never had a meal on your antique maple table."

"Perfect. That belonged to my grandmother."

Gwen's cell buzzed so Ben didn't comment.

She glanced at caller ID before connecting. "Hello, Lawrence," then winked at Ben.

Lawrence's voice spoke into her ear, "Hi, Gwen. I was planning to hunt for Hank's belongings first thing tomorrow morning, but now I think we'd be smart to wait until the roads are plowed. I should have asked first if you're still willing to help me, not to mention available."

"I'm still willing," she echoed. "And I'm available."

"Good. I'll call you when my street is cleared. Minnie said you live in that converted library on the village green."

"That's right. I'll wait to hear from you."

Confirming that her cell call with Lawrence had disconnected, she waved a thumbs up at Ben. "My trip with Lawrence will begin sometime tomorrow. Ready to eat?"

In answer, Ben waved through the steam of the stew and sniffed. "You bet. This smells even better the second time."

They spooned the stew over toast, added canned corn with nutmeg, and carried their plates to the maple table.

As they ate, they reviewed Shirley's list of Tuckers. Gwen retold her encounters with the few she'd met.

"All we can do," Ben suggested, "is chip away at the Tuckers – me official, you more casual. Let's hope that eventually, one of them will slip and tell the truth."

***

After cleaning up their few soiled dishes and confessing that they were both tired from their exhausting day, Gwen led him to the guest room so they could change the sheets on Jenna's bed.

Finished, Gwen slid her hand over the top coverlet then flipped back all the layers to create an invitation.

"There you go, Ben. Jenna's bathroom is right there. I placed a new toothbrush on the vanity. I'll see you in the morning."

Chapter Forty-Two

…mid-morning, Saturday

Into his cell phone, Ben said, "Good morning, Mrs. Tucker. This is Ben Snowcrest, calling to settle on a time for my interviews with your family members."

"Detective," she said as a greeting, an edge to her voice.

When she offered no further conversation, Ben resumed speaking. "The storm blew by and the plows have been busy since sunrise. Have the others arrived?"

"The last two are on their way," she answered curtly.

"Good. How about I come over in about an hour to finish up my final questions?"

Mrs. Tucker didn't respond right away. Voices murmured in the background until she finally said, "Eleven should work."

Ben disconnected and looked at Gwen. "I'll be meeting with the rest of the Tuckers at eleven this morning."

"So I heard. Same time Lawrence will pick me up."

"Apparently he doesn't feel the need to be there for the family interviews."

"Didn't you ask for only the people who were in the house on Monday morning?"

Ben covered her hand. "You're right. Give me a sec to touch base with Cole. I'll have him arrive here earlier so we don't cross paths with Lawrence."

Later, Ben waved goodbye to Gwen and settled into Cole's passenger seat, glancing over at the rookie officer. "I hope you're not miffed about yesterday's interviews."

Cole said, "I admit I'd hoped to participate, but I don't whine. I figured you'd involve me at some point."

"As it turned out, only Mrs. Tucker and her granddaughter with a screaming baby were in the house, so I asked her a few questions and rescheduled for this morning. You didn't miss much."

When Cole only nodded, Ben added, "After we finish with the rest of the potential witnesses, "let's return to the station and take another look at Annabelle's photos."

"They're sitting on my desk. And, by the way, Chief Brown has requested an update."

"Well, let's hope we'll be able to give him something."

Proceeding at a slow speed to avoid the smaller plows, Cole drove them to the Victorian and parked behind several cars in the partially shoveled driveway.

Ben led the way to the kitchen door and knocked.

A middle-aged man opened the door. "You must be Detective Snowcrest."

"I am," Ben confirmed, then indicated Cole. "And this is Officer Cole Martin."

The man nodded. "I'm Daryl Whitcomb. Come in."

Closing the door behind them, Daryl helped Ben and Cole out of their coats, indicating a nearby drip tray. "Boots off, please."

Ben tried and failed to absorb the multiple conversations of the people mingling in the kitchen. Standing in his stocking feet, he spotted Filly Tucker regarding him without expression and approached her. "Thank you for gathering your relatives."

She didn't smile as she said, "We'd like you to finish your interviews quickly so we can resume our lives."

"That's my hope as well," Ben promised. "Is there a room where we can speak privately with each of you?"

She waved her hand. "The front parlor has a door."

"Perfect." Ben scanned the faces staring at him. "Who wants to go first?"

Reaching for the hand of the woman standing next to him, Daryl Whitcomb glanced at the others as he took a step forward. "If no one minds, Doris and I will start this off. Follow me." He led Doris, Ben, and Cole through the adjacent dining room.

Hearing a soft snore, Ben spotted a large man asleep in the hospital bed. He presumed Norman Tucker.

Without stopping, Daryl led them past the stained-glass front door and into a small room. He and his wife sat on an old-fashioned sofa, waving Ben and Cole to the side chairs.

Finding his seat stiff and uncomfortable, Ben shifted to find the least offensive spot. "Let's start with basic details. Your full names, your family connection, and your whereabouts last Sunday night into Monday morning."

Cole flipped open a new wire-bound notebook, recording both questions and answers.

The initial details handled, Ben concentrated on Daryl. "Since you were in residence last Monday morning, what time did you come downstairs after hearing a ruckus?"

Doris lowered her head as Daryl answered. "I heard nothing until the siren of an ambulance. Our apartment is halfway back on the third floor. Their flashing lights wouldn't have come through our windows."

"Who else lives on the third floor?"

Daryl answered, "Filly's sister Minnie occupies two rooms at the far end near the back stairs."

Ben glanced over at Doris Whitcomb. "Did you hear any noises or footsteps?"

She glanced sideways. "If anyone passed our door, they weren't loud enough to wake me."

After a few more unhelpful answers, Ben sensed he'd get no useful details from either husband or wife. "Thanks for your input. Please send in another relative."

Agreeing they would, Daryl guided Doris toward the parlor door, then turned back. "I have a theory if you're interested in my opinion."

"I'm interested," Ben said. "What is it?"

"I think that Uncle Norman was yanked from his bed when he attempted to stop the guy with a knife."

"So you think there was a single attacker," Ben restated.

"It's a possibility," Daryl said defensively, shrugging his narrow shoulders. "When Hank was running from the guy with the knife, he bumped Uncle Norman's bed and woke him up. The stabber wouldn't want any witnesses so he tossed the old man to the floor, knocking him unconscious."

Cole scribbled the theory as Ben absorbed the possibility. "You have quite the imagination."

Surprisingly, Doris spoke up. "All my husband does is read mysteries."

Seeming to ignore her comment, Daryl expanded his theory. "There could have been two. One fought with Uncle Norman and the other stabbed Hank."

After Ben thanked Daryl a second time, the couple exited into the entrance hall, Daryl quietly chastising Doris for her snarky remark.

Waiting until the two of them were out of earshot, Cole closed his notebook. "If you don't mind my input, Ben, I think a chat with Doris Whitcomb alone would be useful."

"My same thought, Cole."

They sat quietly as they waited for the next Tucker.

An idea popped into Ben's head. "You know, Cole, a sketch of the floor plan to locate everyone could be useful.

Can you create a rough diagram? I'll take over the notes."

"Sure thing." Cole ripped out several pages from the back of his notebook before handing it to Ben.

Drawing a rough outline of the third floor, he printed the names of Daryl & Doris in their approximate location, then Minnie's name in the space behind them.

Chapter Forty-Three

… early afternoon, Saturday

After riding with Lawrence through two towns, Gwen admired his expertise as he parallel-parked in front of a worn-down apartment house. "Your parking skill is becoming a lost art. Nice job."

"Thanks," he said. "Years of practice. This way."

He didn't seem worried about tracking muddy snow into the dilapidated building, so Gwen wasn't mindful either.

She followed him up one flight of rickety stairs, avoiding treads that she feared might collapse beneath her weight.

Lawrence stopped at an unpainted door, the number 13 dangling sideways from a crooked nail threatening to fall to the floor. Apparently the owners paid no mind to the bad luck associated with the number.

Surprised when Lawrence pulled a key from his pocket, Gwen leaned closer. "You have a key?"

"For emergencies," Lawrence claimed without explaining how or why he possessed it.

Struggling with the lock, he finally gave the door a hard shove and almost tumbled into the room when it opened.

He suggested they'd save time by searching separately.

She began with the dresser and checked the contents.

Minutes later, she walked over to the closet, where Lawrence was rummaging through other stuff. "I found Jocky shorts, socks, and tee shirts."

"My big find is dirty jeans and oily motorcycle parts." He nodded toward the bed. "Help me slide the mattress onto the floor."

They found no papers or cash hidden on the bedsprings.

A fist pounding on the door startled them both. An instant later, it sprung open to reveal a grizzled old man, his expression aggressive. "Who are you and why are you rifling through my tenant's belongings?" he growled.

Lawrence placed himself between the man and Gwen. "I'm Hank Payne's uncle. We're checking the personal items he left behind."

"I'm his landlord. Did he authorize you to do that?"

"Are you aware that he died earlier this week?"

The landlord appeared surprised, then switched his attitude. "In that case, you may as well pack up his stuff and haul it out. I have others waiting to rent this room."

Gwen could imagine the variety of characters populating that waiting list. "Do you have any packing boxes?"

The landlord grunted. "I think there's a few in the basement. You stay here. This'll take me a minute."

Leaving the door open, she waited for the landlord's steps to fade before looking up at Lawrence. "I hope you don't mind me stepping in about boxes."

"Not at all," Lawrence replied. "As we're packing, we might find something we missed."

Gwen pondered if Lawrence – on his own – would have simply left everything and walked away. Deciding to give him the benefit of the doubt. Gwen touched his arm. "Do you think Hank owed any back rent?"

"If there's money due, I'll take care of it."

Not expecting his generosity, Gwen considered the relationship between Lawrence and his nephew. "It appears you were closer to Hank than anyone else in the family."

Shrugging, Lawrence paused before answering. "I felt bad for my nephew after my sister's husband died. A few years later, she died in a car accident. Hank was still a teenager. It seems my influence wasn't strong enough to keep him from going down the wrong path."

Lawrence kept talking. "I don't know why I bothered to lecture him when he barged in during the family dinner last Saturday. I'm surprised he didn't ask me to return his extra key." Lawrence dangled the spare. "Of course, then he would have had to explain why he was at the house when he had a place to stay."

The sound of footsteps in the outer hallway signaled the return of the landlord. He entered carrying two packing boxes in each hand, none of them with lids.

"By the way, Hank's Uncle," the cranky man began, "he

owes rent for three months." He let the phrase linger.

"How much?" Lawrence asked.

Gwen watched the landlord calculate in his head, wondering how much he'd padded the total. "Four hundred dollars. I only take cash."

Reaching into his pocket, Lawrence removed a money clip and counted fifties and twenties into the landlord's outstretched hand.

"You want a receipt?"

"Don't bother. Here's the spare key."

The landlord snatched it. "Don't close the door."

After the grumpy guy shuffled off, Gwen reached for one of the packing boxes and carried it to the dresser, making short work of the few clothing items.

In the closet, Lawrence tossed the dirty jeans and greasy motorcycle parts into separate boxes.

And then he did something that brought Gwen up short.

He yanked each dresser drawer out, flipped it over, then tossed it aside. On the bottom of the lowest drawer, he ripped a manila envelope secured with duct tape.

"Here we go," Lawrence exclaimed, winking at Gwen. He flipped the envelope back to front. "No writing on the outside. We'll check what's inside when we're someplace more private. Let's haul these boxes down to my car."

Two trips later, Lawrence placed the final box in his trunk, slammed the hood closed, and turned to Gwen. "You up for a bite of lunch? I know a decent diner in a less seedy part of this town."

"Sure," Gwen answered, climbing into his passenger seat, relieved as they drove away from the depressing apartment building.

Choosing a booth at the back of the diner, Lawrence placed the envelope on the bench seat beside him.

They ordered sandwiches, ate them in record time, then waited for the server to clear the table and walk away.

Lifting the manila envelope, Lawrence eased open the clasp and slid the contents onto the table. "Let's see what Hank taped on the bottom of that dresser drawer."

He plucked out a fat envelope, removed several bulky documents and flattened the creases. A few others he slid across to Gwen. "You look through these."

After he scanned the words on each sheet, Lawrence muttered, "Hmmm. These all have to do with Hank's release from jail, conditions for retaining his freedom, meetings with his parole officer, etc. None of this matters now. I'll let them know he won't be showing up."

Gwen detected a slight hitch in Lawrence's voice. She wondered if he lamented his futility to guide his nephew.

"What have you got in your pile?" Lawrence asked.

"An electric bill for one. And here's an envelope addressed to you." She slid a hand-written envelope across the table until it touched his hand.

252

Lawrence eased open the sealed flap and withdrew a preprinted document plus a handwritten note.

Beginning with the note, he read the words in silence then laid the note on the table. Next, he positioned it sideways so Gwen could read at the same time.

After a quick glance, she said, "This is a boiler plate Power of Attorney. Does this penmanship match Hank's note?" She stopped short of calling the style of writing a childlike scrawl.

Lawrence compared the two papers. "I'd say it's the same. Hank may have become a wild one, but he must have sensed his life would be shorter than most. His note and this document are dated four months ago, before he was jailed for nearly killing a guy in a bar fight. He never mentioned giving me his power of attorney."

As Lawrence stared at the document, his eyes glistened.

Gwen pointed to the bottom of the POA. "Your signature is missing."

A frown creased Lawrence's brow as he followed her finger to the blank line. "You're right. If we can find this attorney, he can tell me if I can sign it now."

"I'm not sure that's allowed but it won't hurt to ask." She pulled her cell from her purse and punched-in the attorney's address. Seconds later, she'd located the office.

For some reason, she glanced at the diner's menu taped to the side wall and noticed the address. "Hey, Lawrence, the attorney's office is located on his street. We could leave your car here and walk there just in case his parking lot hasn't been plowed."

Chapter Forty-Four

... midafternoon, Saturday

A parade of Tucker family members filed in and out of the Victorian's front parlor. As Ben asked questions, he received less than helpful answers, nonetheless adding each response to the case notebook.

Since each relative resided within the Victorian, Cole noted the name within their location on his sketches.

As one person left with instructions to send in another family member, Ben found it difficult to grasp that Hank's stabbing and subsequent death had happened less than a week ago. The time between then and now seemed longer.

The moment Ben didn't think he could tolerate one more second on the uncomfortable chair, Jessica arrived with baby Olivia. To give his backside a break, Ben stood up and stepped toward her, waving her to the settee.

After acquiring her basic information, he asked about her early morning actions that previous Monday.

"For one thing," she answered, "Olivia here was crying. She's teething if you haven't guessed. I didn't know anything had happened downstairs until I heard the ambulance sirens."

Ben glanced at the adorable baby staring at him. "Your little one seems much calmer."

"Do you have grandchildren, Detective Snowcrest?"

"No, I don't," Ben admitted. "But I've been around many babies over the years. I have to say, your Olivia is cute as a button."

"Thanks. I think so, too."

Opting not to ask what happened to the baby's father, and needing to finish his interviews, Ben said, "Thanks for your cooperation. Please ask your grandmother to join us."

"Of course," Jessica agreed, snuggling her child, who cooed at Cole as they passed through the door.

In a short span of time, footsteps echoed as they crossed the hardwood floor and Filly Tucker swept into the parlor.

When Ben indicated the settee, she shook her head. "I'll stand, thank you. That damn thing has outlived its usefulness. Are you satisfied with your interviews?"

"For the most part," Ben answered. "Just a few more details. Where are your quarters in this lovely house?"

She glanced down to see Cole's pencil poised above his three pages of crude floor plans. "I see you're very diligent." She pointed at his sketch of the second floor. "We converted several rooms into our apartment decades ago. There's no elevator, which is why Norman is confined to the first floor until his cast comes off."

She shuffled Cole's sketches until she plucked the first-floor sketch. "When Norman's hospital bed is removed, this entrance hall will revert to our formal living room. I see you've already added the dining room and the kitchen. On this side, there's a half-bath beneath the staircase plus a hallway to storerooms in the back."

Filly slid Cole's first-floor sketch aside to find his rendition of the third floor. She pointed to the space directly above her apartment. "This is the guest room where Hank slept for one night."

As Filly Tucker watched Cole pencil the labels into the spaces, Ben observed her demeanor, making note that she lacked visible emotion about her grandson's demise.

Another topic that Sergeant Rosetti hadn't considered relevant popped into Ben's mind. "One more question, Mrs. Tucker. When you heard the early morning scuffle, is that when you came down to see what was going on?"

Her head shook side to side. "Not a scuffle, but the squeak of Norman's hospital bed wheels just before the frame banged against the wall. I rushed down the stairway and found him unconscious on the floor."

Ben suspected that this was a different answer from the one provided the day before. He'd compare them later. Eyeing her, he said, "You have excellent hearing."

"It's a gift and a curse," she replied with a coy grin.

"Detective Cole found you cradling your husband's head in your lap. Were you aware that your niece Shirley almost stumbled over your grandson in the snow out front?"

Filly Tucker winced. "Not until I returned from the ER."

"Now that you know what happened to Hank," Ben pressed, "do you think there's a connection between Norman's fall and Hank's stabbing?"

"I'd only be guessing, Detective. My son-in-law Daryl thinks the person who stabbed Hank had probably fought with Norman first."

Daryl had obviously been sharing his theory.

"For all we know," Filly Tucker continued, "there could have been two attackers. I guess we'll never know."

Daryl's expanded theory or her own guesswork?

Ben made direct eye contact. "Thank you for your time.

As she turned to leave, Ben asked, "Is anyone else waiting in your kitchen to be interviewed?"

"Yes, my sister Minnie plus my niece Shirley. She popped in as you summoned me."

In the distance, a bristly voice called, "Filly, is that you?"

She swiveled in the open parlor door, then looked back at Ben. "That's Norman. I need to find out what he needs."

Sensing Filly would provide no more details, Ben said, "You go check on your husband. You've been quite helpful."

Without commenting, she rushed out.

Through the open door, Ben heard the elderly couple murmuring but could catch none of their conversation. If only he possessed Gwen's keen sense of hearing.

258

Alone with Cole in the parlor, Ben pushed the door until it snicked shut to muffle their own conversation. He had a theory, but instead of revealing it to the hopeful rookie, he asked, "Any comments?"

Cole's forehead wrinkled. "Daryl's two theories are interesting. And she mentioned the possibility as well. Do you give his suggestions any credibility?"

"Tough to say," Ben murmured. "None of the other Tuckers admitted witnessing someone tussling with Norman or stabbing Hank, so we have no statements about the number of attackers."

Cole came back with, "They're a closeknit family. Did you find it odd that none of the other residents heard anything until the rescue sirens blasted them awake?"

"And even then," Ben mused, "some hid in their rooms, while others gathered in what we now know as the third-floor guest room to watch the action viewable beyond the veranda roof. After we speak with these last two, we'll review everything back at the station. And, if possible, I'd like to find out if Norman remembers anything."

Chapter Forty-Five

...mid-afternoon, Saturday

Gwen and Lawrence exited the diner then strolled carefully along the partially shoveled sidewalk. They hadn't gone far when Gwen spotted the lawyer's sign swaying above street level. She nudged Lawrence and pointed.

"Good catch" he said, then guided her up the slippery steps to the door and stretched his finger toward the rusty doorbell button.

They waited for at least a full minute – debating whether to give up and return to his car – when the door opened partway to reveal an older man dressed in a tailored but well-worn suit.

"Can I help you?" he asked, a smile on his face.

"Yes," Lawrence replied, extending Hank's Power of Attorney. "Are you the lawyer who assisted my nephew on this document?"

Grasping the paper, the man slid reading glasses into position before squinting at the details, then handed it back. "Yes, this was prepared by my office. Is there a problem?"

Gwen stepped forward. "It's rather brisk out here, sir. May we come inside while we explain?"

"Yes, yes, of course. Where are my manners?"

He backed inside and opened the door wide. "Please forgive the condition of my office. My secretary recently retired and I haven't found her replacement. She used to keep everything more organized."

Gwen glanced around at the scattered boxes and stacks of papers atop filing cabinets. She could only hope that this lawyer was at least proficient in his chosen career.

The attorney indicated a door. "Let's talk in my office."

Circling several cartons, Gwen entered and sat in one of two chairs positioned in front of a huge desk that had seen more prosperous days.

Lawrence settled in the other.

"Now," the lawyer began, "tell me what you need."

Flattening the POA plus Hank's personal note on the attorney's desk blotter, Lawrence added his driver's license then pointed at the blank line across the bottom. "Here's my problem. I wasn't aware my nephew intended to give me his power of attorney. You can see he never asked me to sign."

The attorney inspected both documents and Lawrence's driver's license. "I remember this client. If you don't mind me saying, he was a bit down on his luck."

"The family is well aware of his situation," Lawrence mumbled. "Can I sign this now to make it legal?"

The lawyer focused over the rims of his glasses. "I'd feel more comfortable if your nephew joined us."

"I'm sure he would if he could," Lawrence began. "Unfortunately, he passed away earlier this week. I came upon this POA and note while cleaning out his apartment."

"Oh, my," the lawyer uttered. "Please accept my sympathies for your family."

"Thank you," Lawrence said. "Does his death impact my delayed signing of his Power of Attorney? This is the only way we'll be able to settle his estate."

Taking another look at Lawrence's license, the lawyer said, "Concerning the legality of your situation, I recall that your nephew spoke very highly of you, Mr. Tucker. After I explained the various versions available to him, he chose the durable POA, which gives you – as his agent – the broadest latitude to finalize his affairs."

The lawyer focused on Lawrence. "Although it's not strictly by the book, I feel no reluctance about dating your signature to match the day your nephew signed." He moved his focus to Gwen. "If you'll show me your picture ID, ma'am, you can sign as the witness and then I'll notarize this document."

Though Gwen felt a bit uneasy about this less-than-legal plan, she suspected Lawrence was the only Tucker who'd bother to settle Hank's affairs, including debts.

The process moved along quickly, completed when the lawyer squeezed his Notary Public stamp on the document.

He pushed the POA toward Lawrence. "There you go,

Mr. Tucker. Again, my condolences for your family's loss."

"Thank you," Lawrence repeated, getting to his feet, then turning back. "Is there a fee for your service?"

The lawyer waved away the question. "Hank Payne paid for the POA creation when he came to see me. I'm surprised he never followed up with you."

Lawrence didn't offer that Hank had been in jail for the past few months nor that he'd died after being stabbed.

The lawyer snapped his fingers, startling Gwen. "Wait a second. Your nephew also asked me to draw up a simple will, but he never returned to finalize the details. If you can stay for a while longer, I'll locate his file folder with his initial input."

"We'll wait right here," Lawrence agreed.

The lawyer wandered out to the retired secretary's domain, repositioning storage boxes and rustling assorted piles of paperwork.

After a few minutes, Gwen touched Lawrence's sleeve. "You stay here. He might accept female assistance."

She exited the lawyer's office and approached the man as he hefted a box onto the desk. "Can I help you search?"

"That's kind of you, Mrs. Andrews. Yes, please take a look in that box." He pointed, then returned to his rifling.

Bingo! She plucked Hank's folder midway through the tight collection of other clients.

Holding it up, she announced, "Here it is."

263

"Oh, good job," the lawyer said, reaching for the file.

He glanced over his glasses. "Let me know if you're searching for a job."

She laughed and followed him back into his office.

While Gwen and Lawrence looked on, the lawyer removed a bank statement dated months before, a hand-written list of meager belongings, including his motorcycle, plus a request to donate his clothes to a homeless shelter. The final document was a half-completed generic Last Will & Testament, the form unsigned.

Upending the empty folder, the lawyer announced, "That's it."

When Lawrence reached for the papers, the lawyer held them aloft. "Don't be insulted, but I need to compare the handwriting to the other documents."

"Why is that?" Lawrence asked.

"Because you could have written your nephew's note and helped him fill out his POA form, but these items," he indicated the latest finds, "haven't left my office."

After a few minutes of scrutiny, the lawyer sat erect. "All the penmanship appears to be written by the same person."

Lawrence picked up his notarized Power of Attorney. "Will my nephew's bank allow me to close his account with this POA?"

The lawyer didn't answer right away. "They should. That document grants you permission to access any of his accounts. Do you have a copy of the death certificate?"

Lawrence shook his head.

"In that case," the lawyer added, "don't mention your nephew's death. That POA should suffice."

Withdrawing his money clip, Lawrence removed several twenties and placed them on the desk. "For your legal advice, sir."

"Thank you." The lawyer pocketed the cash. "Good day and good luck."

As they passed the secretary's desk on their way out, Gwen reached over and snagged a business card. She figured it wouldn't hurt to have one.

Chapter Forty-Six

…mid-afternoon, Saturday

Hearing a knock, Ben waved Cole to open the parlor door.

An elderly woman entered, saying, "Good afternoon, officers. I'm Filly's sister Minnie."

Ben introduced himself and Cole then gestured toward the unpopular settee.

Making a face at the antique furniture, Minnie remained standing. "We've been threatening to replace that old thing but never get around to it." She leaned against the door jamb just like Filly had and crossed her arms, her curious eyes moving from Ben to Cole and back again.

Ben rose from the side chair. "In that case, please sit here. May I call you Minnie?"

"Please do." She eyed the side chair. "That's not much better but I accept your courtesy." She took a few steps and eased into his abandoned chair, wiggling several times as Ben had done, saying, "These both need replacing as well."

Making no comment on the comfort of the furniture, Ben sat on the antique settee and soon understood why both she and Filly had refused it. The old springs pushed against Ben's bottom. He could only hope they wouldn't puncture

266

the fabric and prick him. Returning his attention to Minnie, he found her regarding him with raised eyebrows.

"What do you need from me, Detective Snowcrest?"

After guiding her through the basic questions, he asked, "What time did you come downstairs after hearing the scuffle on Monday morning?"

"Oh, gosh, I don't recall hearing anything. My rooms are at the very back of the third floor, so I'm quite removed from noises down here. This is a huge house, you know."

Cole held out his sketch of the third floor. "Have I got your location in the right space?"

Minnie squinted at his floor plan. "Yes, young man, you noted my rooms correctly."

Squirming on the worrisome upholstery, Ben maintained his focus on Minnie. "Let's not belabor your timing last Monday. What time do you normally arrive in the kitchen?"

"It varies," Minnie replied, gesturing with her hand. "I wake up when the sun brightens my bedroom. On cloudy days, I sleep a little later. Each morning I come down the back stairs to help Filly prepare breakfast. She doesn't allow the family members to cook in their rooms."

"So when you arrived in the kitchen last Monday, you learned about Hank's stabbing?" Ben ventured.

"I can't say that's true, Detective. My sister wasn't waiting for me, so I assumed she was perhaps not feeling well and still sleeping. I set the coffee machine to brew and was checking the refrigerator when the rest of the family wandered in looking for breakfast. They were murmuring about hearing an ambulance, but I didn't understand what had happened until my niece Shirley walked in with this young man." Minnie indicated Cole. "Then a tall man introduced himself as the lead detective. He questioned us, then left. That's when I found out that my great nephew Hank had been stabbed and my sister had gone to the hospital with her unconscious husband."

Minnie leaned against the chair back. "I really have nothing more to tell you."

"One question and we'll be done," Ben said, watching her closely. "What was your relationship with Hank?"

Her posture straightening, Minnie eyed him. "I wouldn't call my rare interactions with him a relationship. After his poor mother died in that awful accident, he attended very few family gatherings. Not even Christmas."

Understanding that Minnie had no more to add, Ben extended his hand to help her rise from the chair. "Thank you for your time. I believe Shirley is waiting in the kitchen. Please ask her to join us."

Minnie wasted no time exiting the parlor.

As they waited for Shirley, Ben perused Cole's floor plans to get a better feel for the connections between rooms and floors. He pointed at the kitchen corner. "We need to verify the location of those back steps."

"I'll add them to the sketch as we're leaving."

When Ben tossed Cole a questioning look, the young officer lifted one stockinged foot. "Our boots are waiting at the kitchen door, so we have to exit that way."

Ben glanced down at his own bootless feet. "Oh, right."

One second later, Shirley barged through the parlor door. "I saved myself for last so I could find out if you still suspect me of Hank's stabbing. Just because I'm the one who called 9-1-1 doesn't make me guilty."

Ben opted not to retake the chair Minnie had just abandoned so remained standing as he said, "Calm down, Shirley, and have a seat."

Seemingly unaware of the settee's reputation, Shirley plopped down then just as quickly hopped back up, rubbing her backside. "OMG, why didn't you warn me?"

Ben shrugged. "I thought you knew about it."

Shaking her head, Shirley raised her voice. "I haven't sat there since I was a teenager. Now I remember why." She took up a position at the door, echoing Filly's stance.

"To answer your question, Shirley, we're still investigating. We won't come to any conclusions until we're finished chasing all the clues."

Her eyes widened. "So you still consider me a suspect just because that Rossini cop did?"

"You're here to answer my questions. Not the other way around," Ben advised her.

Shirley deflated. "All right, let's get this over with."

***

After Shirley answered each question, adding unsolicited details, she rushed from the parlor.

Ben glanced at Cole. "I don't know about you, but Rossini didn't have enough evidence to suspect her."

"I tend to agree," Cole responded.

Ben nodded, satisfied that the wannabe detective agreed. "Let's bring everything back to the station and analyze what we've gathered."

Picking up the notes and floor plan sketches, they prepared to head out.

As Cole closed the parlor door behind them, a familiar bristly voice called over, "Officers, come over here."

Ben glanced toward the hospital bed to find Norman Tucker sitting up, waving his arm for them to approach.

The old man barked, "I understand from my wife that you two are trying to determine who stabbed our grandson."

"That's correct," Ben confirmed.

"I want you to know that if this damned broken leg hadn't stopped me, I might have prevented the violence."

"I have no doubt you would have, Mr. Tucker," Ben soothed, needing more details from Norman.

"Damn it all," Norman sputtered. "I was facing the other way when I heard my bedside drawer slide open. I figured someone was looking to steal my wallet, and I moved too

270

fast. Damn cast got tangled in the sheets and down I went. Couldn't have stopped my fall if I'd wanted to."

Ben interrupted. "I've been told that you have no memory of the incident beyond your tumble to the floor. Have any details surfaced since you came home?"

Norman shook his head. "Damn it, no. Don't you think I would have told someone and cleared up this mystery? But I promise you, Detective, that if any images show me who attacked my grandson, I'll call you right away."

Ben retrieved a business card and held it out. "Let's hope that happens, Mr. Tucker."

Chapter Forty-Seven
...mid-afternoon, Saturday

As Lawrence turned into the Tucker driveway, Gwen spotted a police SUV stopping further along at the North Street traffic light. When it continued north, Gwen had no idea if it was Cole and Ben returning to the police station. With no police vehicle parked at the Victorian, she assumed they'd at least left after finishing their interviews.

Following Lawrence into the kitchen, she wondered how he'd reveal their success at Hank's bank. The easy transaction had required nothing beyond Lawrence's POA and his driver's license.

"Welcome back, Lawrence," Filly called from the long kitchen table where she sat across from Minnie.

Filly Tucker's greeting had concentrated on her son. Minnie gave Gwen a wave and a grin. Opting not to take it personally – after all, Gwen wasn't a member of the family – she decided Filly was simply anxious to resolve the hubbub surrounding her grandson's burial expenses.

"Was your search a success or a bust?" Filly asked.

After removing his mud-and-snow-covered boots, Lawrence walked over to his mother and kissed her cheek.

"I have to say that Gwen was a perfect partner in crime. I'm glad Shirley suggested that she go with me."

Gwen winced at his use of the term *'partner in crime'*. Filly, Minnie, and Lawrence himself had no idea of Gwen's reason for inserting herself into the Tucker family.

Filly slid an impenetrable look in Gwen's direction, not quite making eye contact. "Thank you, Gwen."

Lawrence stretched backwards to glance into the dining room. "Any of the others still here?"

His mother answered, "Not down here. After Snowcrest and the young officer left, a few escaped to their rooms. The others went out to run errands. Do you want me to call down the ones who are upstairs?"

Lawrence shook his head. "Please don't. I'm not interested in another family squabble. I'll explain what Gwen and I found and let you deal with the rest of them."

"Thanks a lot, son," Filly groaned. "But that's probably the best way to reveal whatever you uncovered."

Minnie said, "I was just about to make tea, Gwen. Would you like a cup?"

"Tea sounds perfect," Gwen answered. "Thanks."

"None for me," Lawrence chimed in. "I'll grab a beer."

He strolled to their fridge, grabbed a beer, then removed the cap as he settled across from his mother. Reaching into his deep jacket pocket, he pulled out the oversized envelope and slapped it on the wide table.

Gwen chose the chair closest to the door.

Minnie placed a cup of tea in front of her.

Filly tapped Lawrence's envelope. "Okay, son. Show us what you brought back from your hunt."

At the sound of a leg cast thumping across the adjacent dining room floor, Lawrence paused.

His father leaned against the archway, breathing heavily.

"I heard your voices and decided to join you." He pointed one crutch tip toward the strange envelope. "That the result of your search for Hank's money?"

"It is, Dad," Lawrence answered. "Let's get you situated and then I'll explain to all of you."

Filly settled her husband at the far end of the table, pulling an extra chair close enough to support his leg cast.

Lawrence unclasped the envelope but didn't remove anything. "First, Gwen and I located Hank's apartment."

Gwen had expected curiosity about how they'd found the address and gained entrance, but neither Filly, Norman, nor Minnie asked for that detail.

And so Lawrence didn't mention that he'd stayed in touch with Hank over the years and possessed a spare key.

Lawrence began. "The landlord showed up and asked us why we were there. When I explained that Hank had died, the man told us to clean out the apartment. Gwen and I checked the bottoms of the dresser drawers and found this Power of Attorney." He pulled out the single document and pointed. "Gwen noticed it lacked my signature."

Filly nodded at Gwen, then refocused on Lawrence.

Holding out his hand, Norman snapped, "Let me see that document you found."

Lawrence passed over the POA.

"This says you have complete authority to access his accounts and handle anything else if he's unable." Norman brought the piece of paper closer to his eyes. "It's signed by you and witnessed by Gwen." He stared down the length of the table at her as if she were the only one with any knowledge. "Why are both your signatures backdated to match Hank's?"

"I'm about to tell you," Lawrence countered, reaching over and retaking possession of the POA.

Gwen sensed that easy-going Lawrence resented his father's question, implying that this was not the first time he'd been placed on the proverbial carpet.

She watched as Lawrence squared his shoulders, then sat quietly to listen.

He shared how they located the lawyer's office and the lawyer's willingness to backdate their signatures.

Filly leaned across the table. "Hank never told you that he intended to give you his Power of Attorney?"

"He never said a word," Lawrence confirmed.

Norman repositioned his leg cast. "I imagine Hank was back in jail before he had the chance."

Lawrence pulled out another document.

Gwen recognized Hank's Last Will & Testament.

"As we were leaving the lawyer's office, he remembered he'd begun a file for Hank. Gwen helped search his storage boxes and came upon the folder first."

Again, Filly nodded at Gwen but said nothing.

Minnie hadn't spoken since she'd served the tea.

Next came Hank's scrawled instructions for his will.

When Norman again wiggled his fingers, Lawrence dutifully passed over the will and the note.

Norman first scanned the note, then read the unfinished will. "Says here our grandson wants his clothes donated to a homeless shelter. Everything else to his Uncle Lawrence."

Before his father could express an objection, Lawrence jumped in. "And that's how the lawyer would have completed the will if Hank had returned to his office."

Norman eyed the big envelope. "Looks like there's more to show us."

Instead of answering, Lawrence pulled out Hank's bankbook.

Norman grabbed it, quickly flipping it open and running his finger down the multiple transactions.

"Oh, my God," Norman shouted. "Knowing our grandson's poor work history, he could have never saved this much. Where do you think this money came from?"

"Maybe pulled some robberies?" Lawrence suggested.

At that point, Gwen understood that the family was never told about the recent convenience store robbery.

"How much did Hank squirrel away?" Aunt Filly asked.

Lawrence allowed his father to retain the bank book. For his mother, he withdrew a fat bank envelope and dumped the contents in front of her. "Count it for yourself."

Without hesitation, Filly grabbed the paper money and made short work of separating the bills into piles of like denominations, her eyes growing bigger each time.

A thought occurred to Gwen. If Hank had this much money stashed away, why had he been mooching off his grandparents?

And if any of that cash came from the recent convenience store robbery, would the police confiscate and return to Phil and Wanda Gibbs? The date of deposit would be the key.

Chapter Forty-Eight

…mid-afternoon, Saturday

Ben and Cole sat across from Police Chief Mike Brown, providing a recap of the Hank Payne investigation. First, a review of Rossini's token interviews, then Ben and Cole's visit with the convenience store owners and the other police station, plus Gwen's input from her time with the family, ending with Minnie's visit for a private chat.

Ben leaned forward. "This morning, while I interviewed the other Tuckers, Gwen traveled with Lawrence to search for Hank Payne's belongings. The family is hoping they'll find cash to pay for his burial."

Mike tapped his desk blotter with a pencil "So we don't know yet what other clues Gwen might have uncovered?"

"Not yet. I'll meet with her later today."

"Well," Mike said, "at least you've eliminated the possibility of a second thief barging into the Tucker home."

For several moments, the three of them sat in silence until Cole filled the pregnant pause. "May I switch topics?"

"Of course," Mike said. "Is your new topic related to this case?"

"More a side bar," Cole answered.

"Go on," the chief said.

"Until we know the details Mrs. Andrews will share," Cole began, "I'd like Ben's opinion of the boot impressions she noticed in her backyard snow last weekend."

"Sounds like a good use of your time," the chief replied. "Why don't you take Ben to the conference room and share what you've gathered so far? And let me know if Gwen brings back any relevant discoveries."

"We certainly will," Ben promised.

Cole hopped to his feet. "Thanks, Chief. This way, Ben."

***

Their first stop was Cole's desk in the detective squad bullpen, where he retrieved his file for Gwen's safety check request plus three large envelopes from his in-box.

Two other detectives again waved a greeting to Ben, quickly turning back to their own investigations.

In the conference room, as Cole spread various photos across the large table, Ben rested his chin on his fisted hand. "How about this, Cole? Let's put Gwen's boot print mystery aside for the moment. Now that we've spoken to all the family members, let's put everything into sequence and see where it leads us. You toss out the first event."

Cole's altered body language implied the young officer was glad for this chance to express his developing skills. "Okay, let's begin at the beginning – Hank's unexpected arrival last Saturday night. He roared in on his motorcycle

279

and invited himself to stay with his grandparents. None of the Tuckers present for dinner were thrilled to see him."

When Cole paused, Ben nodded. "Good start."

"On Sunday morning," Cole continued, "Shirley sent Annabelle to fetch Gwen, thinking Gwen's calming demeanor would ease the family's angst about Hank's return. That's when Gwen met Hank."

"That's right," Ben agreed. "She called him scary."

Tapping the conference table, Cole moved forward in time. "Early Monday, Norman Tucker heard rummaging in his bedside table and decided someone was stealing his wallet. He rolled over to confront the person, got his cast tangled in the sheets, fell out of his bed, slammed his head on the hardwood floor, and was knocked unconscious."

Ben leaned on his forearms. "I'm questioning Norman's claim of no memories. Hard to say if he's holding back vital details. We might question him again."

Ben inserted the next event. "Assuming Hank was stealing Norman's wallet, the attacker came from behind and stabbed Hank in the back. Hank ran out the front door, lost his footing at the edge of the veranda, and flew down the steps, his head smacking the concrete before landing in the snow."

"That's where Shirley Knapp found him bleeding," Cole said, "and dialed 9-1-1."

"But we don't know how long he'd been bleeding in the

snow before she arrived," Ben countered, reaching for the note pad and scribbling another reminder.

"True. Her call to 9-1-1 is the sole reason Rossini suspected her of the stabbing. I arrived, along with the EMTs. After Hank was transported to the ER, I noticed the front door ajar a few inches and went inside. Mrs. Tucker was cradling her husband's head. That's when I called for a second ambulance."

Ben held up a finger. "Filly Tucker didn't mention how long she'd been sitting with Norman before you found her."

Another task added to the follow-up list.

"By the time Rossini arrived," Cole added, "both Hank and Norman had been transported to the emergency room, along with Filly Tucker, so he never questioned her."

Getting to his feet, Ben circled the conference table. "That's about the time Shirley asked Gwen to hurry to the Tucker home for moral support. Rossini asked her if she'd witnessed Shirley's arrival and ordered her to go home."

Still pacing, Ben stroked his white beard before returning to his chair. "I'm still amazed that the family living there claim they didn't hear the commotion downstairs."

"That struck me as odd, too," Cole said. "When a few woke up from hearing the sirens, they gathered in the guest room to gawk out the front window. None of them came downstairs until they smelled Minnie's coffee."

Silently digesting this odd behavior, Ben murmured,

"Giving each other an alibi depending on the timing."

A moment passed before Cole spoke up. "There's something I haven't mentioned."

"What's that?" Ben asked, curious to find out what the rookie officer had been holding back.

"Because Rossini didn't request the forensics team, I decided to check the kitchen door, the front door and a third door in the rear storage room for signs of a break-in."

Ben managed to control his irritation. "And you're just now telling me this?"

Cole's face turned beet red. "I'm sorry, Ben. With everything that's been going on, I forgot to mention it."

"Tell me again why Rossini didn't request the techs to collect evidence."

Seeming somewhat relieved, Cole replied, "He said that Hank Payne was only injured and not dead so it wasn't a crime scene."

"I suppose there's some logic there," Ben said. "What did your door inspection reveal?"

"No sign of forced entry on any of them." Cole reached for his sketches and added the third access point.

"Well, in the future," Ben instructed, "don't keep anything from the lead detective. Every piece of information is important to an investigation. Write up your inspection and add it to the case file."

Cole began to write a detailed explanation.

282

Chapter Forty-Nine
...late afternoon, Saturday

As he watched Cole's pencil record the results of the door exams, Ben mused out loud. "Have you given any more thought to Daryl Whitcomb's theory of two attackers?"

Cole looked up. "There's no evidence either way."

"When I was at the Victorian," Ben added, "Lawrence Tucker used his key to come in through the kitchen door. The family members who don't live in the Victorian must have a key as well. Your door inspection means that if there was an outside accomplice, a family member had to let him or her into the house."

Expecting no comment from Cole, Ben went on. "Mind you, without witnesses or solid evidence, we could be way off base. What's your takeaway from our interviews?"

Cole paused his writing. "None of them admitted anything that made me think they attacked Hank. Even Shirley Knapp's body language didn't hint she was lying."

Ben was quick to react. "Despite Rossini's conclusion, she's not automatically guilty because she called for help."

"That's true," Cole agreed. "It's too bad that Norman Tucker can't remember more details."

283

"Well, because we can't accuse a specific Tucker yet, let's hope Gwen adds substantial details after spending time with Lawrence today."

"How soon will she be back?"

"She'll text me when she walks in her door. Not much we can do until I meet with her."

Ben pushed aside the pad of follow-up notes. "Let's switch back to her backyard boot indentations. Show me what you've got." Despite his disappointment in Cole for holding back his doors inspection, Ben understood that every career includes a learning curve, and Rossini had not been a stellar mentor. Regardless, Ben wanted to delve into Gwen's back yard safety check.

Cole pulled snow imprint photos from Gwen's case file. "I shot these images with my cell phone more than a week ago. I hope to identify the boots' owner for Mrs. Andrews' peace of mind."

"How far did you get?"

"Not far. Rossini enlisted me to assist him with the Tucker-Payne case. Then you replaced Rossini and the chief teamed me up with you."

"So no progress on the boot prints?"

"A small window of time to compare after I dropped you at the Victorian the other day." Choosing one of the manila envelopes, Cole slid out professional-looking photos. "These are Annabelle's photos from the Victorian." He arranged them beneath his cell phone pics.

Without losing a beat, Cole opened the third envelope, adding a row of letter-sized boot soles. "I haven't had a chance to compare all three sets of photos."

"Let's do that now," Ben suggested, standing up to elevate his view of the pictures from above.

Several minutes later, they both concluded that none of the boot soles matched the ones in Gwen's back yard.

Ben glanced at Cole. "How about Hank's boots? Gwen said he stormed out of the Tucker kitchen after she turned him down for breakfast Sunday morning. Maybe he stalked her when she left."

Snapping his fingers, Cole shouted, "Great suggestion."

"His personal effects should have been returned to the Tuckers," Ben said. "Let's go back there now." Grabbing the notepad from the conference table, he held it up for Cole to see. "And we've got a few questions that need answers."

Cole arrived at his police SUV in the back lot and started the engine before Ben had settled in the passenger seat.

Buckling his safety belt, Ben said, "If Gwen is there with Lawrence, make believe you've never met her."

Chapter Fifty

…late afternoon, Saturday

Biding her time in the Tucker kitchen, Gwen half listened to the chatter about Hank's cash, waiting for the discussion to end. Now that she'd helped Lawrence locate Hank's belongings and settle his finances, their conflict about the funeral expenses didn't hold her attention.

But the Tucker battle had to be waged by them, irrelevant to Gwen's sleuthing assignment. During her hours with Lawrence, though he'd explained his years-long contact with his nephew, he hadn't mentioned Hank's stabbing once.

Gwen now understood Lawrence's lack of hostility toward Hank. She'd hoped he'd suggest which family members may have wanted to get rid of Hank but Lawrence had stopped short of expressing his opinion to Gwen.

Mentally, she drew a line through his name on Shirley's list of Tuckers, admitting that her time with Lawrence added no clues to her sleuthing on Shirley's behalf.

When Norman's fist banged on the table, Gwen jumped.

The old man waited for the cross-table discussions to subside. "That's a lot of cash. I can't imagine he saved this much from an occasional paycheck."

"I've come to the same conclusion, Dad, but I guess we'll never know where he got this money."

Again, it occurred to Gwen that the Tuckers were not aware of Hank's convenience store robbery, or that he'd been sought by law enforcement. After his death, that case was closed. Perhaps Ben hadn't deemed that detail relevant when he spoke with the family members.

Filly looked up from the piles of cash. "This money should be more than enough to pay for Hank's funeral."

Lawrence focused on his mother. "Do you have any idea how much the burial will cost?"

Her eyes glistening with unshed tears, Filly answered, "I've made inquiries. I'll request written quotes."

Gwen noted that this was the first time she'd witnessed emotions from anyone in the Tucker family.

Nodding his approval, Lawrence gathered the cash plus the legal documents and slid everything into his manila envelope. As if expecting resistance, he clutched it to his chest and stood up. "I'm heading out to deposit this cash in my bank account for safe keeping."

Baby screams from an upstairs bedroom bounced off the downstairs walls.

Filly jumped up and grabbed Minnie's hand. "Come on, Sis. Let's give Jessica a break from her teething daughter."

Looking back at Lawrence, she asked, "Are you coming for dinner tonight? I'm making pot roast."

Lawrence answered, "Sure, Mom. Tell Jessica I'll visit with her and Olivia when I get back."

When the two matrons disappeared up the back stairway, Lawrence paused beside Gwen. "Thanks for helping me today. You were a terrific sidekick."

"You're welcome." Gwen said nothing more.

"Can I give you a lift back to your place?"

"Thanks, Lawrence, but no. I'd rather walk home in the fresh air, but I need to use the bathroom before I go."

"Okay, if you're sure," he said. "Half bath is under the staircase. Maybe I'll see you around town someday."

He forced his feet into his boots and fastened his winter coat, quickly exiting by the kitchen door.

Norman Tucker reached noisily for his crutches. "Hey, Gwen. On your way to the half bath, could you help me into my hospital bed? I need a nap."

"I'd be glad to," she said, then walked beside him, soon arranging his unwieldy leg cast until he was comfortable.

***

After relieving herself, Gwen closed the half-bath door. Her stockinged feet made no sound on the hardwood floor as she circumvented Norman's bed, his snoring quiet.

As she passed into the dining room, she overheard two women speaking in urgent tones, her instincts on high alert.

Before she moved through the archway into the kitchen, Gwen paused to identify the voices.

Filly: "Did Gwen leave with Lawrence?"

Minnie: "I think so. You know, Sis, I've been wary of her since the day Shirley brought her to our family meeting. That's why I made the garden club connection. She invited me over to discuss flowers a little too quickly. Asked a few nosy questions while I was with her."

Filly: "Well, I think she's a threat, and I'd rather not have her in our home again. I regret offering an open invitation to visit anytime. She's been too willing to hang around our family, with or without Shirley by her side."

Minnie: "And look how conveniently she joined Lawrence's hunt for Hank's belongings."

Filly: "I'm afraid she'll figure out what I did."

Minnie: "Only if one of us tells her. And I don't plan to ever tattle on you, Sis."

Tattle on Filly? Gwen mentally inserted the unspoken words, the message loud and clear. Filly had stabbed Hank, and Minnie had seen her do it.

Gwen eased her cell from her pocket and quietly typed a text to Ben. *'Hurry to Victorian. Case solved.'* She tapped the send button and shrank further behind the archway to maintain her hiding place.

Chapter Fifty-One
…late afternoon, Saturday

Halfway to the Victorian, Ben read Gwen's text and shouted, "Step on it, Cole,"

"Why the sudden hurry?" Cole asked.

"Gwen's at the Tucker home and has solved the case. Her text says to hurry."

As the SUV lurched forward, Cole said, "Good thing the two of us are already headed over there."

"I'm texting that we're on our way."

Ben reached beneath his feet for the emergency light. When he rolled down his window, frigid air whipped into the interior, but he hardly noticed as he slapped the light onto the SUV's roof.

***

Gwen hadn't considered her cell's beep to announce Ben's reply. When it did, her heart raced.

The conversation in the kitchen halted.

Filly's voice: "Did you hear that?"

Minnie: "I sure did. I don't think we're alone."

Gwen whirled and ran through the dining room toward the stained-glass door, her stockinged feet slipping and sliding, slowing her progress. Still, she'd nearly reached the front door when two hands spun her around.

Filly's face was a bright red. "Just where do you think you're going, Ms. Gwen? Explain why you're spying on us and don't bother to lie.".

One sister on either side, they forced the resisting Gwen back to the kitchen, practically throwing her until she bumped into the table.

Gwen considered screaming in hopes someone else in the family would come to her rescue, but she didn't want to endanger any of them. Obviously Filly would go as far as she needed to in order to avoid the truth being revealed.

"How long were you hiding in the dining room?" Filly tilted her head in that direction.

Minnie's face came so close to Gwen's that she could detect the earlier herbal tea. "How much of our conversation did you hear, you little eavesdropper?"

When Gwen said nothing, Filly stalked to the counter and grabbed a knife from the wooden block. She let it dangle from her hand as she spoke. "I said explain yourself."

Gwen needed to distract the sisters, hoping that Ben was on his way. She hadn't had a chance to read his texted reply. Gwen tried a direct answer in an attempt to stall. "I heard enough to understand that you stabbed your grandson, Filly. Detective Rossini also suspected Shirley. Would you two have let her take the blame?"

"Well, no… no," Minnie sputtered.

Filly waved the knife. "But the police were getting nowhere with their inane questions. That Detective Snowcrest didn't act like he suspected me at all."

Gwen's brain whirled. What could she say? And where was Ben? She slid her foot a few inches toward the door.

"Hold on there, girly," Filly said. "You don't really think we're going to let you leave? You must think we're stupid."

Minnie touched her sister's sleeve. "Take it easy. You can't stab her in our kitchen. Too much blood to clean up. Let's devise a better plan."

The echo of Norman's tapping approach made them all look toward the kitchen archway.

He hobbled forward. "Let me have that, wife," he murmured as he reached for the knife in her hand. "Gwen heard your confession, but she's not the only one you need to worry about."

"Norman, what are you talking about?"

"I saw what you did, Filly."

She dropped into the nearest chair and gaped up at her husband. "But you said you didn't remember anything."

With the knife out of Filly's hand, Gwen couldn't stand by and say nothing. "All this time, Mr. Tucker, you knew who had stabbed your grandson?"

"That's right, Gwen. You can't possibly think I'd squeal on my devoted wife."

His demonic laugh worried her. She thought he'd come to her rescue, but maybe his intentions weren't so honorable.

Norman waved for Minnie to sit next to Filly and stared down at the two women. "We can surely come up with a smarter way to get rid of nosey Gwen here."

Panic overtook Gwen. If she told Norman that Ben was on his way, would he stop plotting her demise or would the three of them simply move faster to get rid of her?

***

Cole's SUV squealed into the Victorian's driveway.

Ben hopped from the passenger seat and rushed to the kitchen door, followed closely by the younger Cole. Finding it unlocked, they withdrew their pistols and burst in like every TV cop.

There was no one in the kitchen.

They raced through the downstairs rooms.

No Tuckers. No Gwen. Except for distant crying from a baby, the silence was deafening.

"Let's check outside," Ben yelled, doing an about face.

He and Cole headed for the back yard but saw no one. But they did see what appeared to be fresh footprints and drag marks. And then the sound of low voices made its way through the line of bushes.

Peeking through the branches, Ben signaled Cole to follow. Wincing at the scratches, they emerged into an overgrown pasture, spotting Gwen motionless in the snow.

Norman Tucker, balanced on his crutches, directed Filly and Minnie as they struggled to remove the concrete covering of what appeared to be an old well.

"Stop right there," Ben shouted, his gun trained on the Tucker threesome.

**

Gwen opened her eyes, taking a few moments to focus on a female EMT staring down at her. When she tried to sit up, the woman gently pushed on her shoulders.

"Don't struggle, Mrs. Andrews. You have a nasty cut on the back of your head. The bleeding has stopped."

Reaching around, Gwen felt the bulk of a bandage, wincing as she touched a very sore spot on her scalp.

Looking out the rear window of the ambulance, she saw three police sedans against the backdrop of the Victorian. Three patrolmen, each grasping one of the three Tuckers who'd threatened Gwen, led them toward the police cars.

As Norman hobbled past the ambulances' open door, he stared into the cavity and sneered at Gwen.

Behind him, the cuffed Filly and Minnie both turned their faces away from Gwen, their noses upturned.

And then Ben appeared, his expression relaxing when he saw she was looking back at him.

The EMT moved aside and waved him to sit at Gwen's side. "She's doing fine. Just a nasty cut on her head."

"Can I take her home or does she need an x-ray?"

"X-ray to be cautious. You can ride with us if you like."

"I'll do that," Ben said, settling in the companion seat. He leaned down and kissed Gwen's forehead. "You really scared me when I saw you lying in the snow back there." He indicated the row of bushes behind the Victorian.

"Oh, Minnie's forsythia," she murmured.

He placed a gentle finger against her lips. "Not now,. We'll talk later."

She relaxed against the pillow, her eyelids closing.

Chapter Fifty-Two

…early evening, Saturday

As Gwen approached her front steps, she gently shook off Ben and Cole's support, saying, "I appreciate your assistance but I'm not going to fall over."

Chuckling, the two men released their grip.

As Gwen turned her key in the lock and stepped over the threshold, she heaved a sigh of relief to return home after her horrendous experience at the Tucker Victorian.

Hearing a cat's cry, she kicked her boots toward the drip tray and walked gingerly toward the staircase, sweeping Amber into her arms and whispering into her pet's twitching ear, "I've never been more thrilled to hear you complain that you're hungry."

Ben came up beside her. "How is your head feeling? Can I fix you a cup of tea?"

"Nothing right now, thanks." She released the squirming cat. "I should tell you about my time with Lawrence and then what happened after we returned to the Victorian."

"You don't have to report the details right this second."

"But I need to," Gwen insisted. "Would you light a fire?"

"Of course," he said, lowering her onto the sofa.

He strolled to the fireplace, where he layered crinkled newspaper, kindling, and logs before striking a match.

The warmth of the flames swept into the chilly room.

Despite the instant coziness, Gwen pulled her feet beneath her and snagged the lap robe behind her head. She patted the adjacent cushion for Ben to join her.

"Ben?" Cole called as he approached. "Do you want me to go out to the SUV and bring in our notebooks?"

Ben shook his head. "Don't bother. Instead, record Gwen's statement on your cell phone, then have her words transcribed at the station to sign later."

Dutifully, Cole dropped into the comfortable chair beside the hearth and pulled his cell phone from his police parka pocket.

Gwen glanced at Parker's empty recliner. It reminded her that his spirit wouldn't appear to comfort her. Pushing her disappointment aside, she prepared to share the disturbing events that ended her time with the Tuckers.

Despite the warmth of the flames, she shivered at the flashback to her close call. Breathing in a lungful of air, she glanced at Ben, then Cole. "First, the harmless half of what happened today – my time with Lawrence as we searched for Hank's belongings."

Her apt listeners didn't interrupt as she detailed Lawrence's long-standing connection with Hank, the envelope and POA taped to the underside of the dresser drawer, the lawyer's file folder with unfinished will and bank book, plus closing out Hank's bank account. After sharing the final scene of Lawrence's discussion with Filly, Minnie, and Norman about the cash and Hank's funeral expenses, Gwen sat back and waited for a response.

Cole turned to Ben. "It doesn't sound like the Tuckers were aware of Hank's recent robbery."

Ben shrugged one shoulder. "It seemed irrelevant to our investigation into his assault, so I never mentioned it."

"I don't think Rossini knew either," Cole added.

"At least some of Hank's money could have come from his convenience store heist," Ben guessed.

"And maybe previous heists," Cole suggested,

"A distinct possibility," Ben agreed and turned sideways to face Gwen. "Who has possession of Hank's cash now?"

"Lawrence took it to his own bank for safekeeping."

Ben scrubbed at his beard. "I'll suggest that the police chief decides how to handle any reimbursement that might be due. The date and amount of Hank's most recent deposit will determine if there's a connection. One more question. Did Lawrence share his opinion about Hank's stabbing?"

Gwen shook her head. "He didn't even mention it."

"Too bad. He might have told you something that would have eliminated your later encounter with Filly, Minnie, and Norman, like drop you at home instead of the Victorian."

"But then," Gwen countered, "I wouldn't have been on

the premises to overhear Filly's confession."

"True enough," Ben conceded, "but seeing you lying in their backyard snow near that old well nearly gave me a heart attack." He reached over and gripped her hand.

"I'm so sorry, Ben."

"Not your fault."

Cole spoke up. "I'm glad we were halfway to the Victorian when you texted. Are you okay to tell us the rest of your story, Mrs. Andrews?"

"Yes, Cole. I want to get this off my mind so I can resume my boring winter lifestyle. Do you have enough battery life in your cell phone to continue recording?"

"I do," he answered. "Resume whenever you're ready."

"Okay, here is the scary part." A lump formed in her throat at the memory, but she didn't want to delay.

"After Lawrence headed out to his bank," Gwen began, "Norman asked me to help him to his bed on my way to the half bath beneath the staircase. When I headed back toward the kitchen, I overheard Filly tell Minnie that the police detective would never figure out what she'd done. I hid behind the dining room archway to text you. But I didn't think to silence my phone. When your reply dinged in, the sisters heard it and found me hiding."

Sitting forward, Cole said, "How chilling for you."

"It turned out to be more than chilling. They asked how much I'd overheard. Minnie told Filly I'd been too nosey ever since Shirley brought me over the first time. That's when Filly pulled a knife from the wooden block and waved it at me. When Norman hobbled into the kitchen, I assumed he came to save me from his wife's threat, but instead, he suggested they find a cleaner way to get rid of me. I have a dim memory of being dragged, but then nothing until I woke up in the ambulance."

Gwen glanced from Ben to Cole. "You need to fill in the rest for me."

Ben squeezed her hand again before getting to his feet, seemingly too anxious to remain seated. "I can only tell you what happened after we arrived at the Victorian. We searched the house but only heard Lawrence's granddaughter crying upstairs. Cole suggested we check outside, where we noticed footprints and drag marks in the snow. We followed them to a row of bushes behind the house, heard voices, and ducked through the broken branches. You were lying in the snow unconscious."

His voice cracking, Ben signaled Cole to continue.

"Norman, Filly, and Minnie were struggling to remove the cover of what looked like an old well," Cole reported. "When we ordered them to stop, they turned in opposite directions. Norman's cast tripped him so Ben and I easily caught the two women."

Ben regained his composure. "Cole called for an ambulance plus more squad cars to transport your attackers to the station. I was so relieved when you woke up with only a cut on your head."

"And you stayed with me in the emergency room until they allowed you and Cole to bring me back home," Gwen added. "I was so comforted to see your friendly faces."

Ben returned to the leather sofa and again grasped both of Gwen's hands and repeated, "You really scared me."

When the reality of how close she'd come to the end of her life at the bottom of a well, Gwen began to shake from the adrenalin rush. A tear tickled her cheek and she swiped at it, then threw her arms around Ben's neck, whispering, "Thank you. Thank you so much."

When Gwen yawned, her hand flew to her mouth. "Don't think I'm being rude, but I'm suddenly exhausted. I just want to close my eyes and take a nap."

"Totally understandable," Ben said. As she slid down to a napping position, he tucked the lap robe tighter around her. "Cole and I will take our recordings to the station. Your statement should be ready to sign in a few hours."

"Could you bring it tomorrow morning? I should be fully recovered and ready to review the details before signing."

"Your ER doctor said you shouldn't be alone," Ben reminder her. "I'd be glad to…"

The ding of Gwen's cell phone cut him off in mid-sentence. She held up a finger. "One second, Ben." Sitting up, she pushed the lap robe aside as she summarized the text.

"Jenna's being dropped off momentarily, so I won't be here by myself."

Ben's face fell. "That works. Text me in the morning when you're ready for a visitor."

From his chair, Cole interrupted. "I'll take you back to the station to retrieve your car, Ben."

Gwen said, "I'm forever grateful to you both for rescuing me." Finding a burst of energy, she tossed off the blanket and walked them through the foyer to open the front door.

As they exited, Jenna was coming up the walkway. "Hey, what are the two of you doing here this time of night?" Jenna looked from Cole to Ben to Gwen, her gaze resting on the bandage on Gwen's head. "What happened?"

Ben seemed hesitant to leave. "I'll let Gwen explain but Jenna, keep an eye on her tonight. If she starts to feel woozy, call an ambulance and then call me."

Jenna's eyes widened and she threw her arms around Gwen's waist as if preventing a fall.

Ben turned to go and Cole lifted a hand toward Jenna. "Can I call you tomorrow?"

"Sure," she said. "Right now, I need to hear what happened today."

After Ben and Cole drove off, Jenna guided Gwen inside locking the door before removing her boots.

"It's been one hell of a day, Jenna. Come and sit by the fire while I tell you."

Settling on the sofa, Jenna turned to Gwen, reaching toward the bandage on Gwen's head. "Does this hurt?"

Gwen moved the young woman's hand to her lap. "Only when I touch it."

After Gwen shared the day's events – without admitting she'd been snooping – she explained the ER doctor's instructions.

"Oh, my God, you could have disappeared down that well and we'd never have found you. I'm so relieved that Ben and Cole arrived in time. You need to be careful when you make new friends."

"You can say that again," Gwen said. "I hate to cut you short, but I'm exhausted."

"You go on up to bed. I'll check on you during the night."

Chapter Fifty-Three
…late evening, Saturday

Ascending the staircase, Gwen detoured to the sitting room and lowered herself onto one of many cushions below the bank of windows. Although the sun had set hours before, she peered through the nearest glass pane. Her gardens were barely visible in the dim quarter moon glow.

Amber hopped up and settled on the next cushion. As Gwen stroked her pet, her thoughts reverted to Parker. What would he think about her nearly fatal incident at the Tucker home only hours before?

Though she'd come to expect no response from his spirit, she whispered Parker's name.

Nothing happened. Was it time to abandon his promise to reconnect in the afterlife? Should she look forward to her future rather than back to her nearly perfect marriage?

Just what would her future look like without his sporadic, but recently non-existent, visitations?

Her eyes drooping, Gwen forced herself to her gable bedroom and collapsed without undressing, soon drifting into a deep sleep.

***

In the early hours of the morning, she bolted upright and stared into the shadows. After many long seconds, her vision adjusted, revealing she was in her own bedroom.

The dream that had jolted her awake surged into her memory with crystal clarity – Parker!

No surprise that he wore the same red polo shirt and black slacks of his first appearance several years before and each visitation since. But in her dream, he was not transparent like his visiting ghost. He was as solid as he'd been during their marriage.

Smiling at Gwen with his signature twinkle in his eye, he'd reached for her and kissed her cheek then hugged her tight – an embrace his spirit-self had always been denied.

First, Parker warned her that he suspected he was about to continue his journey into the next phase of the afterlife – whatever that might be – and sensed he would disappear any second. They managed a heartfelt conversation before he faded for the last time.

Unlike a normal dream about nonsensical bits and pieces that went poof upon waking, Gwen knew in her heart that his dream visit had been as real as anything else in her earthly life.

Certain that she'd recall his final loving words, she snuggled beneath the heavy comforter and promptly fell back to sleep.

Chapter Fifty-Four

…early morning, Sunday

When a tiny wet nose touched Gwen's cheek, she opened her eyes to stare into Amber's. The feline's quiet mew and a tap of her paw suggested that Gwen might be allowed a brief hug, though Amber had never been a willing lap cat.

Gwen pulled her arms from beneath the warmth of her bed covers and wrapped them around her pet, enjoying the soft fur and the weight of the small body atop hers.

Within seconds, the cat squirmed to be released and Gwen became aware that the assumed visit for a brief snuggle had been nothing more than a demand to be fed.

As Amber scampered off Gwen's bed, thoughts of Parker's dream-visit rushed forward.

Again, she questioned the reality of his appearance while she was sleeping. Had her own subconscious converted her wishful thinking into her all-too-real dream? Or had her disappointment with Parker's months-long absence encouraged his spirit to visit her?

His embrace. His final good-bye. His dream visit had to be a sure sign that Parker's parting moments with her had been much more a reality than imagination.

Every word of their conversation flooded back:

'Gwen, sweetheart, I'm coming to you one last time.'

'I'm so glad you're here, Parker, but why have you been ignoring me when I called your name the past few months?''

'I'm sorry, but I haven't heard you say my name until a little while ago. You fell asleep quickly so I'm appearing in your dreams.'

'And why do you say one last time?'

His shoulders shrugged. 'I can't explain the why of my experiences in the afterlife but I sense I'm about to advance to the next phase of my journey, whatever that may be. I can't promise that I'll be waiting for you to join me one day.'

Even in her dream, Gwen's shock had overwhelmed her.

'That just isn't fair, Parker. You've appeared to me for years since you died. That just isn't fair,' she repeated.

In the dream, she'd almost stomped her foot in protest.

He smiled at her then. 'Fair or not, sweetheart, I wish I understood, too. If I'm right that my journey will continue, there's something I want to say to you before I go.'

Fearing his next words, she said, 'Tell me, Parker.'

'You need to be free to enjoy your life among the living. If another man makes you happy, don't deny yourself human feelings and physical gratification.'

'I don't think I can abandon my devotion to you, Parker, and allow another man to take your place.'

"I was devoted to you, too, Gwen. Your big heart has room for more than one man. I wish you a joyful life.'

An instant later, her dream had ended. She bolted awake from the shock of Parker's wish for the rest of her life.

Now, hours later, the morning light began to brighten her bedroom, and Gwen knew she hadn't imagined Parker's message. She had no doubt he'd moved further into the afterlife and she might never see him again.

His hopes for the remainder of her life boggled her mind.

Rising from her bed, she glanced out her front window to the village green. As the sun's rays slanted across the snowy pathways, a single man walked his dog.

***

Distracted by Parker's final words, Gwen was only slightly aware of her morning routine. During her shower, she was careful not to get her bandage wet.

Dressed for the day, she stood at the top of the staircase and listened. Hearing no movement in the guest room, she assumed Jenna was still asleep.

Down in the kitchen, she set the coffee maker to brew. Only then did she remember she needed to text Ben that she was awake and ready to sign her statement about her experience with the Tuckers. She typed: *Coffee is brewing. Come over whenever you're ready.*

Unlocking the front door to retrieve the Sunday *Gazette,* Gwen was pleased to find it on her top step. Her paper girl had finally tossed it hard enough to land where it should have been all along.

Still preoccupied by her dream, Gwen was caught unaware when Ben called out, "Good morning."

He hurried around the back end of his Corvette parked at the curb. "How's your head feeling?"

She touched the bandage on the back of her skull. "I seem to have survived the night."

"Well, you look fine." Reaching her front steps, Ben glanced at the front page of the *Gazette* in her hands.

'Long-Time Residents Arrested'

Shivering, Gwen tucked it beneath her arm. "Let's go inside and read the article. It appears this story pre-empted the previous front-page news."

At the kitchen counter, they spread out the paper.

"Oh, look," Gwen said. "Shirley wrote this. This must be her last article before retiring."

'Filomena and Norman Tucker were arrested late yesterday afternoon, charged with the death of their grandson Hank Payne. The sister Winifred was also arrested as an accessory after the fact. An additional charge,

attempted murder of a police department investigator, was also added.

More details on page 3.'

"I'm glad she didn't state my name," Gwen murmured in quiet gratitude.

On page 3, Shirley's words sizzled off the page as she detailed the Tucker family's decades-long residency in Harbor Falls. Then a brief reveal of Hank's troubled childhood, resulting in his life of crime.

The police investigation came next, with quotes from both Ben and Cole that clues were chased until the guilty parties were uncovered and arrested.

The article ended with the schedule of arraignment on Monday morning.

The Tuckers' lawyer declared he'd pursue their release based on defense of the bedridden Norman Tucker.

Shirley promised readers that further updates would be provided when they became available.

"Defense?" Gwen asked.

"Yep," Ben confirmed. "During their questioning, Filly ignored her lawyer's advice to be quiet and blurted that Hank was stealing Norman's wallet and shoved him from the bed. She grabbed a kitchen knife and stabbed her grandson to stop his attack on her husband. She didn't think Hank would die as a result."

"How did Shirley know all these details?"

"After we officially questioned the Tuckers, the chief arranged a press conference with not only the *Gazette*, but papers from the surrounding towns. Afterwards, Shirley interviewed me and Cole for those quotes."

"It appears you asked her to omit my involvement?"

"When I reminded her, she confirmed that she'd never reveal your C.I. status connection to the police department."

"That's a good thing."

"Does that mean you plan to snoop again someday?" Ben asked with concern.

"Only if a friend is wrongly accused."

The coffee maker beeped and Gwen turned to pour two mugs for herself and Ben.

Jenna bounded down the staircase, glancing toward the kitchen. "Good morning, you two."

"Same to you," Gwen said, pouring a third mug.

Reaching for the steaming liquid, Jenna waved toward the newspaper. "Is that about Gwen's very horrible really awful day?" making a play on a popular book title.

Ben answered, "It is but not directly. Front page news about the Tucker family matriarchs that Cole and I arrested late yesterday."

Jenna leaned closer to read the article.

When the door chime echoed, Gwen said, "Company so early? I'll see who that is."

With only a slight dizziness when she hopped off the

stool, Gwen found her balance and opened the door.

As Cole stood on her top step, his expression was animated. "Morning, Gwen. I have research results for you."

"You do? Come in and show me what you found."

When Gwen led him to the kitchen, Ben looked up. "Hi, Cole. What have you got there?"

Cole held up a large paper sack, then placed it on an empty island stool. "The answer to Gwen's mysterious backyard boot impressions."

When he reached into the paper bag, Jenna sidled closer.

Before revealing what he'd brought, Cole explained, "Early this morning, I drove to the Victorian to retrieve Hank's boots."

Ben's eyebrows lifted. "Were the other members of the family in an uproar because of our arrests?"

"More in a daze," Cole supplied. "Lawrence was cooking breakfast with the help of his daughter. Daryl and Doris were filling coffee mugs. The other two couples who live upstairs stared at me. When I told them why I'd come, Daryl offered to bring down Hank's personal effects."

"While I waited for him, Baby Olivia flirted with me."

"Not surprising," Jenna wisecracked.

"Daryl did ask if I knew what would happen to Norman, Filly, and Minnie. I told him that's up to the legal system."

Ben cleared his throat. "Show us what you brought."

Withdrawing first a file folder, which Cole opened to

expose photographs, he then lifted a pair of well-worn boots and flattened the paper bag to catch dirt as he placed the boots on the bag. "These were returned to the family. I compared the soles to Gwen's snow impressions."

As Cole spread out his photos on the counter, Ben turned the boots upside down to expose their pattern.

"Definitely a match," he declared, "though we don't know why he followed Gwen from the Victorian."

Gwen moved to stand on Cole's other side. "His reason doesn't matter." She patted Cole on his shoulder. "Thank you for solving my mystery. I can rest easy that my stalker won't return."

Blushing, Cole said, "Glad to help."

Then he turned to Jenna. "If you haven't eaten, can I treat you to breakfast at the Bayside Café?"

"Sure. I'll grab my coat and boots in the foyer."

"Have fun," Gwen called as they hurried away.

Within seconds of the front door closing, it opened again.

"Did you forget something, Jenna?" Gwen called.

"Not Jenna," Shirley said as she exited the foyer and made a beeline toward the kitchen, her arms filled with extra copies of the Sunday *Gazette,* her smile upside down.

She pointed at Gwen's copy on the counter. "Oh, I see you're reading my final byline. What did you think?"

"You captured the essence of the Tucker family," Ben said, patting Shirley on the back.

313

Gwen placed her hand on Shirley's shoulder. "How are you and the family handling the shock of what happened?"

"The reporter in me is a buffer between my emotions and the fact that my relatives could do such a thing, but it'll hit me at some point. I'm heading over to the Victorian when I leave you. Though I won't be bragging about my by-line. Seems a bit tacky."

"How did you snag the front page?" Gwen asked.

A grin brightened Shirley's previously sullen expression. "I convinced the new editor that a person from inside the family would write a more personal story. I added that his permission would be my perfect retirement gift."

In an unexpected show of affection, Shirley encircled Gwen and squeezed tight. then held her at arm's length. "I can't begin to thank you enough for exposing Hank's stabber and her witnesses. Do you think Aunt Filly, Uncle Norman, and Aunt Minnie would have let me go to jail?"

"Hard to predict," Ben piped up. "As you know, Filly's lawyer is planning to plea defense of her bedridden husband."

"But what about their last-minute brainstorm to keep Gwen quiet by tossing her down that old well? That's attempted murder."

"We can only wait and see how the legal system handles both crimes," Ben advised.

Gwen backed away from Shirley. "This is a sad situation,

but at least you don't need to worry about being wrongly blamed for ending Hank's troubled life."

"You're saying be thankful for small favors?"

Gwen chucked. "Not so small, but yes."

Chapter Fifty-Five

…mid-morning, Sunday

When Shirley exited through Gwen's front door, a whoosh of chilly air slid into the foyer. Shirley gripped the iron railings for support.

Gwen called down to her, "I expect you to entertain me with the exciting details of your first retirement destination."

Shirley raised her hand in goodbye. "You'll be the first."

Closing the door, Gwen retreated to the living room, where Ben poked at the dying fire.

She watched from the leather sofa.

He joined her and said, "I'm curious about something."

"What's that?" she asked, her heart fluttering at her possible but not guaranteed future with this interesting man.

Seemingly a bit nervous, he pushed himself to his feet and leaned his back against the mantle. "Okay, I hope you don't think me overly bold, but something is different about you. Do you think your head injury is effecting your personality and mannerisms?"

Other than a brief dizzy spell, Gwen was not concerned about her well-being and decided the time had come to reveal Parker's dream visit and his wish for her.

Sharing Parker's paranormal existence with Ben didn't worry her either. He'd met Parker's ghost one summer day, and she'd introduced them to each other. The two men – one spirit, the other flesh – had even embarked on a short conversation until Parker disappeared.

Ben was no longer a skeptic about the afterlife, so Gwen knew that when she told him about Parker's middle-of-the-night goodbye, Ben wouldn't think she'd lost her marbles.

When she approached him at the hearth, Ben's gray eyes filled with curiosity.

"You're a very intuitive man, Benjamin Snowcrest," she began. "That's why you are such a good detective. But what I'm about to tell you is much more personal."

She reached up and cupped his bearded face. Though she'd adopted a recent habit of stroking his relatively new white whiskers, this time she used both hands.

When Ben's posture stiffened, Gwen panicked. She'd always side-stepped intense physical contact between them. Was Ben no longer pursuing a deeper relationship? Was he about to reject her new openness – courtesy of Parker?

She lowered her hands from his cheeks and stepped back, daring to ask, "What's wrong?"

Ben blushed. "Well, you usually avoid touching. Don't get me wrong, I liked it."

Giving him a timid smile, she didn't step back.

This man who'd become such a good friend and crime-solving partner over the past few years needed to hear the reason for her change of attitude.

Without prelude, she blurted, "Parker came to me in my dreams last night."

She paused, gauging Ben's reaction.

One white eyebrow shot upward. "Go on."

"You know he hasn't appeared since Halloween."

Ben nodded, reached for her hand, and led her to the sofa. "Let's sit while you tell me about your dream."

Grateful for Ben's willingness to listen, she shared Parker's apology for not hearing her call his name for the past few months, and his sense that he would soon be moving on in his afterlife journey.

At this point, Gwen held back a deep sob. "He said I should put aside my devotion to him and open my heart to a new man so I could live a fulfilling life while I'm alive."

Without a word, Ben drew her into his arms.

Gwen relaxed within his embrace. Tears trickled down her cheeks. Tears of sorrow for her final loss of Parker mingled with tears of joy for Ben's acceptance of not only her dream, but of the future looming before them.

Ben whispered into her hair, "I've always understood your devotion to Parker. Not every widow enjoys the attention of her husband's ghost. I admit I've been frustrated that I couldn't share my own affection for you. Your Parker has given us a great gift."

Gazing up through the mezzanine to the rooftop skylights, Ben saluted. "Thank you, Parker."

They remained in their embrace until the last log in the hearth fell apart and sent glowing embers up the chimney.

Ben laughed. "That must be a signal that we should make some plans."

After dabbing the moisture on her face, Gwen stood up and reached for Ben's hand. "Let's begin with your father. Have you decided where to spread his ashes?"

"Yes. I know just the right spot. If I recall, you wished for something to chase away your January melancholy."

Gwen chuckled. "The Tucker investigation banished that wish for sure. I'm much more interested in what you have in mind."

Grinning, he said, "I don't remember eating any breakfast. Let's walk down to the harbor for an early lunch at The Wharf."

Chapter Fifty-Six

…early morning, Monday

The next morning, from the Corvette driver's seat, Ben said, "Buckle up, buttercup. The sun is out, the snow and ice are melting, and it's time to show you where I grew up."

Gwen stretched across the console and kissed his cheek. "I'm ready. Let's go."

"And after we put my dad to rest, we can shop for my second vehicle." He patted the Corvette's dashboard. "This baby needs some down time."

He eased the sports car around the village green.

A laugh escaped Gwen.

"What's so amusing,"

"Do you recall your challenge?"

His eyebrows scrunched. "What challenge was that?"

"The one about which of us would discover who stabbed Hank to prove or disprove Shirley's guilt?"

Warily, he risked a quick glance in her direction. "I seem to recall something along those lines."

Again, Gwen chuckled. "I hate to rub it in, but I win."

THE END

320